FINDING THEIR FOREVER

LINDA FAUSNET

For all my readers.
It's always exciting when people read the first book in a series, but it's really something special when they read book five. Heartfelt thanks to you for coming along for the whole ride.

My books contain steamy sex, bad words, and human beings of all sorts, include gay people. If you're not a fan of those things, you may want to stop reading now. If you're cool with that stuff, come take my hand and join me on this journey…

Published by Wannabe Pride 2019

Editing by Linda Hill

Cover Design by Chuck DeKett

FIRST EDITION.

Library of Congress Control Number: 2019904214

ISBN: 978-1-944043-37-7

❀ Created with Vellum

CHAPTER 1

I was working outside on 45th Street in midtown Manhattan, freezing my nuts off.

"Have I mentioned how much load-in sucks in January?" I asked my co-workers as we loaded all the lighting equipment, scenery, and props into the Al Hirschfeld Theater. The next show was scheduled to open there in early March.

"A few hundred times, honey," Audra Martin responded. The pretty African-American woman in her thirties was half my size, so I figured she must be feeling a lot colder than I was. She never complained, though.

"Sac up, Roman," Rex said.

"Shut up, old man," I said, and he chuckled. Rex's beard stubble had started going gray though he was only in his mid-fifties. He was hardly an old man, but he was at least twenty years my senior. Rex, Audra, and I had worked together at the Al Hirschfeld Theater on Broadway for more than ten years. Audra was the head carpenter, Rex was the head property master, and I was the head electrician. Due to strict union rules, absolutely nothing could be done inside the theater unless all three of us were present.

The show we were unloading for was a comedy called *Pirated*. It sounded like fun—I much preferred comedies to the heavy dramas. Our last successful show at the Al Hirschfeld Theater was *Kinky Boots*, a glitzy yet heart-warming story about the friendship between a drag queen and his straight-laced boss at a shoe factory. We all had a blast on that show, and after a long run, it was tough on all of us when it closed.

The production we did after *Kinky Boots* closed quickly. That was always hard, too. After months of long hours and grueling work to prepare, it was awful to have a show shut down after a few weeks. Rex, Audra, and I were employed by the theater, not the individual production, so we were only out of work until the next show moved in.

I reached into the load-in truck and pulled out two rolling carts with pipes attached, better known as meat racks. Grateful for a chance to get back into the warmth of the theater, I brought them inside. After more than an hour out on the street, I figured I'd better step inside for a few. Maybe I would even be able to feel my toes again. I dug my cell phone out of my back pocket to check the time. At almost 10am, it was time for a coffee break anyway. I needed to make sure the guys on my crew weren't freezing to death.

"All right, take five, guys and gals. Coffee in the usual place, and we got donuts, too."

I headed to the tiny break room in the far back of the theater, as did most of the others.

I raised a steaming hot paper cup of coffee to my lips, wishing I could crawl inside the cup to warm up.

"I wonder how rehearsals are going," Audra said as she poured herself a cup of coffee.

"Me too," I said. While the crew took care of all the prep work at the theater, the actors and singers and choreographers were rehearsing in a studio a few blocks away. Rehearsals usually went on for about four to six weeks, six days a week. "I wouldn't think they'd have to do too much rehearsing on this one, though. They've been doing the show off-Broadway for a while, and it sounds like most of the performers made the cut to move to Broadway."

"Yep, that's what I hear," Rex said. "At least one of the ladies got the ax. You know who they got replacing her, right?"

"Rosemary Sutton," I said. "That ought to be interesting."

"Always helps to have some star power on board," Audra said.

"I guess. If you can call her a star," I said. "You gotta wonder if she would have gotten the part if she wasn't Johnny Creel's fiancée."

"Ain't that the truth." Rex stroked his chin.

"You've heard her sing," Audra replied. "She sounds amazing."

I nodded, knowing I couldn't argue with that. Everybody had heard Rosemary sing when a video of her and her famous boyfriend performing a song together went viral. At the time, Rosemary was a wannabe theater performer, a total unknown. Then she fell in love with The Johnny Creel, a notorious playboy who ran through money and women like there was no tomorrow. As the story went, he totally changed his ways when he fell in love with Rosemary. He must have screwed up somehow, because the viral video showed him on bended knee, apologizing to her through song. Rosemary sang back, and the rest was history. Now, he owned a theater arts foundation for underprivileged kids in Brooklyn.

"I just hope she isn't a total snob," I said. As much as I wanted to believe the best about people, the jerks in the last show had left a bad taste in my mouth. The two leads were total dicks. Velma Sikes and Ernie Cladwell were both C-list celebrities who thought they were better than everybody else and had no problem saying so. God, that sucked.

Despite my misgivings about working with celebrities, star power was generally a good thing for a show, and I had no doubt that Rosemary's presence would bring in some of her fans. If she was a total bitch, she'd ruin the production experience for everyone. When a star was rude and nasty to my crew, there was very little I could do about it, and it made me insane.

"So do I," Rex said. "Gotta be better than Prince Dick and the She-Devil."

I chuckled. "That's true." Not only were Ernie and Velma mean to my hardworking crew, but they were so damn ungrateful. Hundreds of thousands of actors, playwrights, songwriters, and crew members would give anything in the world to have the privilege of working on Broadway, and only the teeniest, tiniest percentage of people actually got the chance to do it. I had no patience for people who didn't appreciate how lucky they were. The Creel family was so rich, they could buy Rosemary any role she wanted, so there was a good chance she would be stuck up and ungrateful. We'd all find out in a few weeks, I guess.

Rex inhaled two donuts, then swigged down the rest of his coffee. "Back to the grind."

"Think it got any warmer out?" I asked.

"Whew!" said Les, one of my lighting guys, as he walked into the break room. "Starting to snow out there."

I closed my eyes and groaned. When I opened them, I groaned again seeing the mess my guys had made. Coffee stirrers and napkins on the table. Donut crumbs everywhere.

"Dammit," I muttered as I started to clean up. I couldn't help myself. I was a bit of a perfectionist, and I couldn't stand leaving a mess. Job hazard, I guess. Head electrician was a super-detail-oriented job, and if I didn't make sure everything was perfect at all times, the show would look sloppy. Worse, people could get hurt if I wasn't careful.

"I ain't your mother," Les said.

"What?"

"It's what you usually say when you're cleaning up their mess. Thought I'd beat you to it."

Chuckling, I nodded as I wiped down the table.

It only got colder throughout the afternoon and early evening. The snow wasn't helping things. Even during load-in, I still tried to keep my appearance respectable. I kept a comb in my back pocket, and I had to fix my hair all day. I have thick, dark brown hair that looked black, especially when it was wet all day like today, and it looked unruly if I didn't keep after it with a comb.

By 6pm, we were all sick of the cold and more than ready to get the hell out of there.

"Got any exciting plans this weekend, Roman?" Rex asked between grunts as he and Mitchell, one of the prop crew members, carried a large piece of the pirate ship into the building.

"I sure do. I have a date with Therese Andrews," I said with an emphasis on the "Z" sound in her name. *Therezzzze* Andrews had been an obsession of mine for half my life.

"You *do*?" Mitchell asked, eyes wide.

"Not literally," I said with a laugh. "Oh God, I wish. Can you imagine?"

Grateful for a chance to finally take a break and warm up, I leaned against the wall and did just that. Imagined what it would be like to go out with Therese Andrews. She was a hugely famous movie star with ice-blue eyes, light brown hair, and dainty, feminine features. Oh, how I adored her.

"I meant she's got a new movie coming out this weekend.

Therese Andrews is perfection, and that's all there is to it," I said, trying not to sigh like a lovesick teenager.

"Got that right," Mitchell said. "*Damn.*"

"Eh," Rex said. "I don't get the hype."

"Well, of course *you* don't," I told him, making the other crew guys laugh. "She's like, I don't know, your equivalent of Chris Hemsworth."

Rex paused for a moment. "Okay. Now I get it."

"I've been totally obsessed with her since I was fifteen years old. That was when I first learned how to, you know, *explore* my body. Just me and a poster of eighteen-year-old Therese."

"Zat so?" Audra said as she walked in carrying some wooden boards for the ship.

I don't usually blush, but I felt my face get hot. "Uh, sorry, Audra."

She laughed and shook her head. Audra worked around the mostly male crew ten to twelve hours a day for months at a time, so there wasn't much she hadn't heard already. Still, I tried to behave myself around her.

"She is beautiful. Can't argue with that," Audra agreed. "She's a good actress, too. She does all that dramatic stuff, but I was surprised how funny she was when she hosted *Saturday Night Live*. Her new movie's a comedy, right?"

"Yeah. It's some kind of romantic comedy. PG-13." I rolled my eyes.

"Damn," Mitchell said again. "Then you won't get to see her naked."

"Exactly," I said, though I really did enjoy watching anything featuring Therese Andrews. Audra was right. She was hilarious on *SNL*, which only intensified my attraction to her. She also seemed highly intelligent when she did TV interviews. Funny, beautiful, and smart. She was the perfect woman.

"Will never forget her in *Roxy Rose*." Mitchell practically salivated as he spoke.

"That's for damn sure," I said, picturing Therese in her sultriest role to date. *Roxy Rose* was a suspense film, featuring the title character as a federal agent going undercover as a sex worker to bring down a human trafficking ring. Therese had done a nude scene for that film, and I had just about lost my mind. My whole life I'd been fantasizing about seeing her naked. It was like a dream come true.

"Those stilettos, man," Mitchell said.

"Tell me about it," I said. Thoughts of her wearing those Roxy Rose stilettos and nothing else while I pounded her hard had given me hours and hours of pleasure. In my mind, she always screamed out my name, pleading with me not to stop. I glanced over at Audra, who was now out of earshot. "I've spent a lotta showers with Roxy Rose."

The guys chuckled.

"Who hasn't?" Mitchell said.

"I haven't," Rex chimed in.

I was about to say something naughty about Rex in the shower with Chris Hemsworth, but Audra walked back over.

"Okay, guys, can we call it for the day?" I asked.

Rex, Audra, and I usually tried to release our respective crew members at roughly the same time, so nobody had to look like the bad guy.

"Yep, I'm good," Audra said. "Rexy?"

"I'm ready to roll out. Roman might gonna explode if we don't let him go see his girl soon."

"You know it. It's funny," I said to Mitchell. "We all go through celebrity crushes, I guess, and then you move on when you find somebody hotter, or whatever. Don't know what it is, but it's always been Therese Andrews for me."

"Well I hope you enjoy the movie, honey," Audra said.

"Gettin' good reviews, I hear. And you be sure to enjoy a good, long shower afterward."

Okay, so maybe she *hadn't* been out of earshot during our conversation. I felt my face get hot again.

Audra cackled as she walked away, and my guys just laughed and laughed.

CHAPTER 2

I hopped in a cab and headed straight for the movie
theater. My stomach rumbled, but I figured
popcorn would work for dinner.

The cab dropped me off at 84th street. By the time I got
my tickets and spent even more time in line at the conces-
sion stand, I was starving. I ordered a hot dog along with my
popcorn and a large Coke.

Settling back in my cozy reclining seat, I wolfed down my
dinner during the previews. Once the movie got started, I
wanted to give Therese Andrews my full attention.

Therese Andrews.

My body tingled with excitement, just thinking about her.
Crazy to think of the effect the woman still had on me after
all these years. Her last movie had come out way too long
ago, and I couldn't wait to see her lovely face up on the big
screen. I didn't know what it was about her, but seeing
Therese always made me feel like a nervous teenager again.

Finally, the previews ended and the lights in the theater
went down. I drew in a breath of anticipation.

The beginning of the movie featured Therese's character

as a little girl, which was a little boring. The kid they had playing her was cute, and she did bear a slight resemblance to Therese. The movie was called *Little Brat*, about a girl named Sophie, a bratty little sister who, growing up, annoyed the shit out of her older brother and all his friends. I knew from the movie's trailer that when Sophie gets older, her brother's best friend falls in love with her.

Though I was impatient for little Sophie to turn into Therese already, I couldn't help laughing at some of little Sophie's clever lines. The movie was entertaining enough, and I hoped it would end up being a big hit for Therese.

After a brief montage showing Sophie growing up, suddenly there she was.

Therese Andrews, in all her perfect beauty and charm, smiling at me from the huge screen. My heart thumped in my chest, and my palms actually began to sweat. Though I felt kinda stupid for having such a physical reaction to her, it was involuntary.

Damn. I was no different than those fangirls who'd gone all gooey over *Twilight* when it first came out. It was crazy and childish to react like this to a movie star.

Even so, I didn't want this feeling to end. I didn't care if I was still getting raging hard-ons for Therese when I was eighty years old. I craved the high I felt whenever I saw her or heard her voice.

As adult Sophie, the character was even more brazen and sassy than when she was a child. Therese had excellent comic timing, and she knew how to get laughs. I watched Claude, Sophie's brother's best friend, fight his growing attraction to the bratty girl he'd once hated.

I watched jealously as Claude finally gave in to his need for Sophie and kissed her passionately. Sophie had been in love with Claude since she was little, so she reveled in his touch. As I watched their lips meet onscreen, I indulged in the familiar fantasy that I was the one kissing Sophie. Kissing Roxy. Kissing any number of the women Therese Andrews had played onscreen.

Naturally, my favorite fantasy was kissing Therese Andrews herself. What it would feel like to be on her arm, the envy of men everywhere. Kissing her when we were out in public. Pleasuring her behind closed doors, when we were at home.

For ninety blissful minutes I stared at Therese on the screen. Though I admired her flawless physique and I dreamed of fucking her senseless, I wasn't just attracted to her beauty. She also had kind eyes and the sweetest smile that melted my heart. She was genuinely talented, too. Therese immersed herself completely in her roles. Her characters were always believable, no matter what role she played. From sensual, secret agent to the girl next door, Therese *became* her characters.

On the subway ride home from the movie theater, I sat in a kind of daze, lost in fantasies of Therese. I frequently fantasized about her, but the images were much stronger when I'd just seen her onscreen. I loved the way I felt after seeing one of her movies. It was like I craved that high.

Pathetic as it was, I was pretty sure I would go see the film again tomorrow.

The trip back to my apartment in Little Italy went quickly, which was good. I couldn't wait to get back to my place. Though it could get kind of lonely living by myself, there were distinct advantages. Like being able to jerk off all I wanted.

Then again, if I had a girlfriend to come home to, maybe I wouldn't have to abuse myself all the time.

Sometimes I worried that maybe I was a little too obsessed with Therese Andrews. It certainly made it nearly impossible for any real woman to live up to those standards.

Which was stupid of me, being hardly a Hollywood hunk myself. What right did I have to even imagine I could be with a woman like Therese?

It didn't matter. Imagine, I would. In my fantasies, Therese Andrews was mine.

* * *

THE WEATHER WAS SLIGHTLY WARMER on Monday morning, making the work a lot easier. Amazing what a few degrees will do. We got a lot of the heavier equipment inside the building, which meant I could start tackling the lighting setup rather than just hauling shit into the theater. As head electrician, I got the lighting plan from the lighting designer, and I was in charge of executing it. In early days of production, that meant I worked on arranging and implementing the cables, lights, power distribution and all that.

Plenty of work to do *inside* the Al Hirschfeld, which was fine by me. We all started preparing the set on the stage.

"Got a meeting with the production stage manager at 10am today," Rex said.

"Why?" I asked.

"No idea," Rex said, looking slightly worried. I was, too. It was unusual to have a meeting with the PSM at this stage in the game. The production stage manager, Harriet Hill, in this case, was the one who ran the whole show once we were live. The PSM calls every cue during the show, like changes in scenery and lighting and stuff. I wondered why she was here at the theater instead of over with the actors in rehearsal.

I hoped it wasn't bad news. A show rarely got cancelled before it even started, but it happened occasionally. Broadway was an exciting business to work in, but it was as unstable as all hell.

We all filed into the break room at 10am, grabbing

donuts and coffee along the way. I tried to ignore all the crumpled napkins and half-empty sugar packets I'd wind up cleaning up at the end of the meeting. Having a crew was like having kids sometimes. I'd die for them, but sometimes I wanted to kill them, too.

Harriet stood up from the table to address us. She was a short yet feisty gal with shortish jet-black hair and dark makeup. In her late thirties or so, she already had an impressive résumé of successful Broadway shows. I hadn't worked with her before, but she had a good track record. I felt good having her at the helm of *Pirated.* That was, if we still had a show.

"Okay, this will be a brief meeting," she said.

Uh-oh. Won't take long to tell us it's all over.

We'd lost funding. The cast all quit. The Al Hirschfeld Theater had been condemned. I hated to be such a pessimist, but I'd had the rug pulled out from under me many times on this job.

"Chill out, it's not bad news," Harriet said, cracking a smile in my direction. I heard several sighs of relief from around me, so I wasn't the only one freaking out.

"I just wanted to let you know of a pretty important casting change."

My brow furrowed. Other than Rosemary Sutton joining the cast, I had no idea who else was in the show now, so why would we need to know about a change? Until tech rehearsals started, we wouldn't even see the cast.

"One of the leads from the original off-Broadway show is pregnant, so she had to bow out. The actor replacing her happens to be a huge movie star. Great news, because of course that means advanced ticket sales will go up immediately once word gets out."

"That *is* great news," Audra said, grinning ear-to-ear. Like me, she'd been through a lot with this business. Any advantage you could get on ticket sales was a big deal. The odds of *Pirated* being a hit just went up exponentially, and we all knew it.

"Who's the celebrity?" Rex asked.

"Of course, this means we will need a lot of extra security," Harriet said. "Gonna have to tighten stage door rules, be really careful about who's allowed in, and all that."

"But who is it?" Mitchell asked.

"All the hassle will be worth it, of course," Harriet continued, a gleam of mischief in her eye. She was dragging out the mystery just to tease us. "In terms of advance buzz, presales, media interest—"

"*Who is it?*" a bunch of us, including me, yelled out.

Harriet laughed. "Okay, okay. Our little production managed to get … an actress who has never been on Broadway, but apparently has always wanted the chance. She also really wants to do comedy, so this is kind of perfect."

Groans all around. Harriet was clearly enjoying her moment.

She smiled and said, "It's Therese Andrews."

It took me several seconds to fully process what she'd said. I replayed her words in my head several times to make sure I'd really heard what I thought I'd heard.

It's Therese Andrews. It's Therese Andrews.

I felt all the color drain from my face.

"Ho!" Rex said, slapping his knee. Audra laughed and clapped her hands.

I stared at Harriet, then glanced at all the crew members, only to see they were all staring at *me*. Everyone in the room, except Harriet, was fully aware of my obsession with Therese Andrews.

Well, I didn't think anyone was aware of how obsessed I *actually* was with her. I'd never admit to them that I saw *Little Brat* three times this past weekend. Or that I had saved tons of magazine articles and pictures of her for the last fifteen years. All they knew was I learned how to jerk off because of her. Which was bad enough.

"You've got to be kidding," I managed to say when I finally remembered how to speak.

"I know," Harriet said, eyes shining with joy. "I don't know how we got this lucky, but this is a huge deal."

Oh, Harriet. You have NO idea ...

A million thoughts and emotions overloaded my system.

I was going to meet Therese Andrews.

I was going to work closely with her for months on end.

Therese Andrews would actually know my *name.*

I might even get to touch her.

My pulse pounded in my ears. My heart raced. My breath caught in my throat. And everyone was still staring at me. As casually as I could, I sipped my coffee and leaned against the wall. I must have succeeded in playing it cool, because people turned their attention back to Harriet.

But I couldn't hear what Harriet was saying, because I had too many questions she couldn't possibly answer.

What would it be like to meet Therese Andrews?

Could I be in the same room with her without making a complete fool of myself?

What was the real Therese Andrews really like?

I already knew an awful lot about her life from magazine articles and television interviews, but I had no idea what kind of person she was when off-camera. Would she be kind to my crew?

Oh God. What if she turned out to be a raging bitch diva in real life?

The longer I sat there, the more questions filled my head. The only thing I knew for sure was I'd get all the answers in a few short weeks. I was excited.

And terrified.

CHAPTER 3

*I*t was my first day of rehearsals for *Pirated.* Taking a deep breath and shakily clutching my water bottle, I entered the studio rehearsal space in downtown Manhattan. I was nervous, feeling out of my element. Movie sets had stopped scaring me long ago. This was a whole different ballgame. Not only had I never performed on Broadway before, but most of this cast had been with this production for a long time in the off-Broadway production. They'd be totally comfortable with their parts by now, whereas I was stepping in at pretty much the last minute. Most of the actors knew each other, and I was the odd one out.

Even so, now I would be the one in charge.

Okay, well maybe not in *charge*, but as an international movie star, everyone would cater to my needs. Not my idea, but that was how these things worked. As the most famous actor on set, I would set the tone of the production. Showrunners always made sure "The Star" was happy. I'd been on enough movie sets as a struggling actor to know what it felt like to be at the mercy of an arrogant, demanding leading man or lady. I'd worked on sets before where lesser-known actors were not even allowed to *speak* to the star, which is kind of sick, to my way of thinking.

My first order of business today was to ease everyone's fears, and let them know I wasn't a diva. I had a lot to learn about working on Broadway, and this show had done quite well off-Broadway before I showed up. I had every intention of making this production experience as pleasant and fun as possible. People, even other actors, were often overwhelmed when they first met me because of my fame. The sooner they found out how boring and ordinary I was in real life, the better.

Taking a seat in the corner of the studio, I glanced around the rehearsal space which featured a huge bank of windows and shiny hardwood floors suitable for dance rehearsal. The first few moments on any set always went one of two ways. Either people would flock around me and ask me a million questions, or they would be too afraid to approach me. It appeared to be the latter. Several people glanced nervously in my direction, but no one dared come near me. I couldn't blame them. They didn't know my "rules" yet.

I scanned the room, not knowing a single soul here. I did, however, recognize Rosemary Sutton from her famous viral videos. She, too, had joined the cast later in the project. That, combined with the fact that she was pretty famous in her own right, made me hope we might hit it off. I managed to catch her eye and smile. Rosemary smiled back, and after a few moments, she worked up the nerve to approach me.

She hesitated once she got close to me, so I gestured to the seat next to me, and she sat down.

"So," I said with a smile. "May I see the ring?" I figured that would be a good icebreaker. It seemed silly to introduce ourselves by name, since it was obvious we recognized one another already.

Rosemary laughed, and her green eyes lit up with happiness. She was clearly excited about getting married soon.

"Of course," she said, offering me her left hand.

I slipped my hand under hers as I admired her engagement ring. "Oh my gosh. It's lovely."

I would have said that no matter what it looked like, but it was quite dazzling, with a large, clear diamond in the center and lots of smaller diamonds surrounding it. Johnny Creel must have spent a fortune on it. As well he should, considering he was a billionaire.

"Nice to meet you, Rosemary," I said.

"You too, Therese. I mean, should I call you Therese? Or …" Rosemary asked uncertainly.

"No, actually. Therese Andrews is my stage name. You can call me Tessa."

"Tessa. That's a pretty name."

"Thanks. So! I hear that Johnny Creel is quite a character. I can't imagine a more romantic proposal than what he did for you."

It was a bit odd, knowing so much about a stranger's personal life the way I knew all about Rosemary's relationship with Johnny. I figured the proposal was a safe topic, since Rosemary and Johnny had intentionally released the proposal video to the media. The first famous video of their argument and making up in public had been taken by some stranger and released publicly without her permission. I knew firsthand how difficult it was having your personal life played out in public, so I was careful about what I said to Rosemary.

"Oh, it was so lovely. Having Johnny on one knee and all my friends there," Rosemary said. She teared up a little, laughing. "Still gets me emotional when I think about it."

I laughed too. It was heartwarming to see how much Rosemary obviously loved Johnny. You never knew when it came to celebrity relationships. Some of them were nothing more than publicity stunts.

Rosemary seemed hesitant, unsure of what to say next. She undoubtedly knew just as much about my personal life as I did about hers. Everyone in the room was likely familiar with the story of my messy love life. About me dating Ricky Scrivello, an actor as famous as I was. It seemed everyone in the world was aware that our two-year relationship had ended when he cheated on me with another, lesser-known actress. It was bad enough to have your heart broken, but facing the pain and humiliation publicly was a true nightmare. Random strangers, reporters, and fans had absolutely no problem asking hurtful, personal questions right to my face.

At least Rosemary's uncomfortable silence likely meant she didn't plan to ask me about Ricky.

I glanced around the room to see everyone was staring at me. It didn't bother me. I was used to it. Even so, I looked forward to getting to know everyone on a personal level. Soon enough, they would stop thinking of me as Therese Andrews, movie star, and realize I was just Tessa Gumm from Grand Rapids, Minnesota. There was absolutely nothing exciting about the real me, so anybody expecting Roxy Rose would be sorely disappointed.

One tall, muscular guy was eying me hesitantly. I could tell he wanted to come over to talk to me. Sometimes I wished I could just stand up and make an announcement, saying *I'm not one of those mean movie stars who thinks I'm better than you. Please come and sit with me. Talk to me. It's okay.*

Rosemary followed my gaze, then she smiled at the tall drink of water watching us. "That's Luke Rannells. I was friends with him even before this show. He's a huge fan of yours, and he's nervous about meeting you."

Luke Rannells. He played the part of Captain Samuel

Nockboots, the pirate who falls in love with my character in the show. He had light brown eyes, brown hair, and was quite easy on the eyes. It always helped when I found my leading man attractive. I just hoped he wasn't a jerk, since we'd be spending an awful lot of time working together.

I turned my head and deliberately looked right into Luke's eyes. From across the room, I saw his muscles tense. It was cute, but I didn't want to embarrass him.

"Well come on over and say hi," I called over to him. "Roxy Rose might pack a weapon in her pantyhose, but I promise you, I don't."

Luke laughed and walked over to us. He stood there, looking down at us for a moment. My goodness, he was tall.

"I am totally fangirling right now," Luke gushed, making me laugh. I liked when people confessed to feeling starstruck. Trying to play it cool never worked. I could always tell when a fan was nervous when approaching me, so I did my best to put them at ease.

"Can I just ask you one question?" Luke asked eagerly.

"Well, of course you can, darling," I said in a faux movie-star voice. I wanted people to know I didn't take myself too seriously.

"What was it like to be on *SNL*?"

"Oh, wow," I said, smiling at the memory of performing on *Saturday Night Live*. I gestured for Luke to sit down in a chair near Rosemary and me. "It was fun and scary and exciting. It was a lot of work, but it was an experience I'll never forget."

Luke leaned forward in his chair, intently listening to me. I got a good vibe from the guy. Yes. He was going to be fun to work with.

"I really can't imagine what it must be like to put on a show like that every week," I continued. "The cast and crew put in *crazy* hours. I'm sure I didn't have to work anywhere near as hard as the regulars, but even as a guest star it was exhausting. But wow, what an honor it was to get to do that. Had my adrenaline pumping for the whole ninety minutes, that's for sure."

"I bet," Luke said, shaking his head in wonder. It was probably his dream to be on *SNL*. I hoped he would get to do it someday. *Pirated* becoming a big hit certainly wouldn't hurt his chances.

His eyes suddenly opened wide. "God, I'm so sorry! I swear, I'm not usually this rude. I'm Luke Rannells, by the way."

I shook his hand and smiled. "Very nice to meet you."

The director walked to the center of the room and turned to address us. "Okay, everyone, let's get started here," he announced, clapping his hands. Zach Deluca was in his mid-forties with darkish blond hair and grayish eyes.

Luke, Rosemary, and I stood up and turned our attention to the director.

"First of all, let's give a warm welcome to our new cast member, Therese Andrews!" he said with a grin. Everyone applauded for me, and I smiled.

"Thanks so much. I'm very excited to be here. Therese Andrews is my stage name, so please call me Tessa." Everyone stared at me curiously as I spoke. "I've heard so many wonderful things about this show. You all have done an amazing job with *Pirated*, and you guys are the reason the show made it to Broadway."

The smiles of pride all around warmed my heart. The show was hilarious on paper, and I couldn't wait to see everyone perform their parts live.

"You all are the theater experts, and I hope you'll bear with me. I'm off book for the most part, but I am a Broadway virgin, so please be gentle!"

That got a laugh out of people, and I could see the relief

on their faces. This show was their baby, and they had probably been worried I might come in and start demanding they do everything my way.

"Okay, let's start with a scene that involves all six leads, so we can get comfortable working with each other," Zach said.

I let out a breath and felt my body relax. It was a relief not to have to do one of my solo songs right away. With all six of us in the scene, I wouldn't have to do any heavy lifting yet.

Zach walked us through the choreography of the kidnapping scene. *Pirated* was a comic musical about three pirates who kidnap three women for ransom. One by one, each pirate falls in love with one of the women. None of them want to admit to their fellow pirates that they've gone soft and want to give up their marauding ways to settle down. Luke's Captain Samuel falls in love with my character, Mary, who keeps trying to escape. Mary loves him, but she is fiercely independent and wants her freedom. In the end, my character gets fed up and demands that he quit hiding his love for her from the other pirates. She gives an awesome, fiery speech about how true love does not hide but should be shown for all the world to see. Mary vows that if Samuel won't be honest with the other men about his love for her and grant her freedom, she will never speak to him again, and will starve herself to death in order to escape his grasp. Oooh, that was going to be such a fun scene to do! I would get to rant and rave and storm around onstage.

After we walked through the choreography a few times, we performed the scene. Luke kidnapped me, an actor named Jacob Cariou kidnapped Rosemary's character, and an actor named Gilbert Vansill kidnapped an actress named Sarah Stritch. Gilbert and Sarah were a few years younger than me in real life, but they played older characters in the show and would eventually be made up to look like they were in their seventies or so. It was a cute subplot about finding love in old age.

The scene was great fun to do. Luke had to put his hands all over me, and I got to keep yelling at him and pushing him away. The women were victims early on, but they were feisty and funny. We fought the pirates every step of the way. I even got to punch Luke/Captain Samuel. I had stage-fighting experience, so I made it look realistic.

Rosemary's character's love interest was a funny pirate named One-Eyed Jack, who really still had two eyes but kept forgetting which eye was supposed to have the eye patch. Tall, well-built, with dark hair and expressive blue-gray eyes, Rosemary's onstage partner was as handsome as mine. Jacob played the part to hilarious perfection, but he seemed cold when he wasn't acting. Oddly enough, he seemed to really dislike Rosemary—he stared daggers at her between takes. Weird, because Rosemary was warm and kind to me, and I'd only heard good things about her in the gossip columns. I wondered what Jacob's problem was with her.

Next up, we practiced a scene with just Luke and me. It involved Mary's first escape attempt where she climbs up a huge rope ladder on the ship, to get away from Captain Samuel. The captain shakes the ladder, causing her to fall a good six feet, right into his arms. When Captain Samuel stares into Mary's eyes after catching her, that's when he first realizes he's in love with her.

Before we tried it, Zach said, "When we get to the Al Hirschfeld for tech rehearsal, we'll go over all the technical details of this part. It's not a hugely dangerous stunt, but you'll be tumbling down a good ways, so we gotta make sure the timing is always perfect."

"Don't worry. I promise I'll catch you," Luke said, making my stomach flutter when he looked at me. I found myself looking forward to falling into his arms.

"Okay, let's try it with just a short distance for now," Zach said. He led me over to a table, and he put a chair next to it. "Climb up here as you say your lines."

I narrowed my eyes at Captain Samuel. "Don't you touch me!" I screamed at him as I stepped up on the chair and onto the table.

"Not so fast! You can't get ... away ..." the captain said, getting distracted when he looked up my skirt as I climbed up. People laughed as they watched. Luke was incredibly funny, and I wished I could see his face at that moment. "... from me!" he eventually finished.

"Stop that!" I yelled as Mary when I saw Captain Samuel looking up my dress. "How dare—"

I glanced at the director and he nodded. I looked down at Luke, who was ready to catch me. Nervous, I allowed myself to drop from the table and into Luke's arms.

Luke gazed down at me with his eyes full of adoration and love for a full ten seconds before softly saying my character's name. "*Mary.*"

As he held me tenderly in his arms, I wondered what it would be like to have a man look at me like that in real life, instead of just onstage.

I also wondered if Luke was single, which was ridiculous since I had no real intention of dating him. He was just so *gorgeous.*

"Okay, nice job!" Zach said, breaking the mood.

Luke carefully set me back down on my feet and smiled at me, making my stomach flutter again.

He was cute, charming, funny, and talented. The whole package. My attraction to him was real, which would certainly make it easy to play his lover.

I was apprehensive at the mere idea of getting into another romantic relationship. Ricky Scrivello wasn't the only romantic disaster I'd endured. The guy I dated before

Ricky turned out to be a creepy fanboy. Derek had seemed normal at first, claiming he didn't care that I was a movie star, and that he was interested in the real me. The press made a big deal out of the fact that I was dating a non-celebrity. The tabloids loved it, and for a while, it was rather good publicity for me. People said it showed I was down-to-earth. Then, when it turned out Derek couldn't separate me from Therese Andrews or Roxy Rose, I broke up with him. Naturally, the gossip rags wanted a reason for our breakup and didn't stop until they found one. The paparazzi managed to dig up evidence that Derek had been cheating on me. Without their interference, I might never have known he'd been unfaithful. Public knowledge of his affair just added humiliation to the layer of pain I'd already endured.

Therese Andrews could get a date with any guy. Men would kill to be seen in public with a movie star, and nothing got them hotter than the idea of sleeping with Roxy Rose. I shuddered whenever I thought about the last time I'd had sex with Derek. I'd dressed up in fishnet stockings and a lacy bra and panties, like Roxy Rose, in an effort to please him because I knew how much he loved me in that movie. When he suggested the role playing idea, I thought it might be fun and exciting to have sex in character, but when he called me Roxy during sex, it made me feel dirty. Violated. Maybe with the right guy it would have been okay, but it made me realize that Derek wasn't in love with me. He was in lust with my fictional characters. I lay there afterward, my eyes welling up with tears, feeling full of regret. He didn't even notice. I broke up with him soon after that.

Luke had admitted to being a fanboy, which was better than lying about it like Derek had.

Next up, we did the scene where Captain Samuel sings a love song about Mary, which she accidentally overhears.

Mary watches him quietly from a distance as he sings his heart out about finding the true love of his life.

Hearing Luke sing a beautiful ballad in his gorgeous, deep voice did little to quell my attraction to him. I briefly considered asking Rosemary if he was seeing anyone, but decided against it. She was good friends with him, and she might tell him I'd asked. It would be super awkward to work with him if he wasn't interested.

The director called a break, and we all grabbed some water bottles and sat down to rest for a few. Rosemary, Luke, and I took the same seats in the corner of the studio that we had earlier. Jacob glared at Rosemary as he sat alone across the room.

"How's Elyse doing?" Rosemary asked Luke, looking worried.

"Better. She's feeling a lot better, thank God," Luke responded.

Elyse. Sister, maybe? Hopefully?

"She's not in so much pain anymore," Luke continued. He smiled over at me. "My girlfriend. She's recovering from major surgery."

"Oh, that's too bad," I said, hoping the disappointment on my face would be taken as sympathy for her plight.

Oh well. Since Luke was a fan of mine, it would have been a bad idea to date him anyway.

"She had a hysterectomy," he said.

I gasped, my sadness at Luke's unavailability turning to genuine sympathy now. "Oh my gosh. Is she about your age? My God, she's so young for that!"

I held my breath, not wanting to ask personal questions but hoping Luke would elaborate. I hoped to God Elyse didn't have uterine cancer or something.

"Yeah, she's about my age. It's tough recovering from such major surgery, but it's for the best. She was in a lot of pain before, from endometriosis, so hopefully this will help in the long run."

I must have looked horrified, because Luke smiled at me.

"It's okay. We weren't planning on having kids, so it's not as tragic for us as it might have been for a lot of other couples."

"Oh, that's good," I said, relieved.

"I feel so bad I haven't gone to see her since I saw her in the hospital," Rosemary said.

"She understands, believe me. She knows how wiped out I am at the end of the day in rehearsals."

We were scheduled to rehearse six days a week, so it didn't leave time for much else.

"Maybe I can come visit her on Sunday?" Rosemary asked.

"I'm sure she'd love it," Luke said. "She's been miserable not being able to go to work. Elyse is not one to sit around."

"No, she sure isn't," Rosemary agreed.

Luke explained a little about Elyse's job. Apparently, she was a bigwig over at Wicket Pro in the Manhattan office. His light brown eyes flashed and his voice got louder and more enthusiastic when he spoke about her. Luke was in love, that was for sure.

I found myself wanting to visit Elyse, too. My heart ached for her. I tended to assume every other woman was as insecure as I was. Here she was, laid up after surgery, probably barely able to move, let alone have sex with her boyfriend, and now he was working alongside a famous movie star all day. As jealous as I was of Elyse that she had a great guy like Luke, I wished there was some way I could reassure her she had nothing to worry about. She was probably picturing Luke hanging out with Therese Andrews when he was really with plain old Tessa Gumm. I wished I could tell her Luke was here worrying about her and talking about her while he was with me.

I smiled at Luke as he spoke about Elyse. I kept thinking about the way he had looked at me while he was holding me, or Mary, in his arms. Oh well. It was a silly thought anyway. Men only looked at you like that when they were acting. I knew that better than anybody.

It was for the best. After all, we were soon going to be doing eight shows a week on Broadway. Who had time to date?

Still. It would be nice to have somebody to come home to after doing all those shows.

More people gathered around me while we took our break, as some of the actors in more minor roles got up the nerve to talk to me. I enjoyed chatting with them, but I couldn't help wondering how I could still feel alone when surrounded by so many people.

CHAPTER 4

*R*osemary invited me to spend the afternoon with her at her place in Chelsea the day before we started tech rehearsals at the Al Hirschfeld Theater. Well, she invited me to go out to lunch with her, but I talked her into staying home instead. Rosemary was used to being recognized by a lot of people, but she wasn't anywhere near as famous as I was yet. I didn't think she quite understood how crazy things got when I stepped out in public, and I didn't want to subject her to that. Besides, I wanted the chance to talk with her privately. We'd become pretty close over the last few weeks, and it was wonderful to have a friend to trust.

We sat in her comfy yet highly fashionable living room, me on a fluffy chair and her on the couch, sipping wine and chatting. The lovely apartment she shared with Johnny had a nice view of the city. Between the delicious wine and the wonderful company, I was more relaxed than I'd been in a long time.

"I'm so excited to start tech rehearsal tomorrow," Rosemary said, her pretty, green eyes shining with happiness. "I've been to the Al Hirschfeld Theater lots of times to see shows, and it's so beautiful. I can't believe I get to work there and be up onstage!"

"And in a starring role this time," I added, relishing her enthusiasm. Rosemary had been on Broadway once before as a member of the ensemble cast of the revival of *Hairspray*. I'd never met anyone with such a deep and abiding passion for musical theater, and it was a joy to see her excitement. She'd worked hard to get to this point, and nobody deserved a big break more than she did.

"Yes. Can you believe it?" she asked. "Then again, look who I'm talking to. You've been in starring roles lots of times."

"Not on Broadway. I'm excited too, but kind of nervous. There's a lot riding on this, you know? Luke and Sarah and Gilbert and everybody, they've put so much of their heart and soul into the show. One of the reasons I was brought onto the project was to sell advance tickets. They're hoping the show will start selling out immediately if my movie fans show up."

"Oh, I'm sure they will, Tessa. No doubt about that," Rosemary said, swirling the wine in her glass.

I nodded, knowing it was true. Many fans would travel to New York for the chance to see me in person, live and onstage.

"Yes. Even so, there are a lot of people rooting for me to fail."

"Really? What makes you say that?"

"Lots of people don't think I belong on Broadway. They think I should just stick to acting in movies. There's all kinds of talk about how I won't be a good enough singer, how I won't be able to handle the grueling schedule. I try to avoid all that negative news, but it's hard when it's everywhere," I told her. "So yes, people will show up to the theater to see me because I'm a household name, but if I suck, the show will fail, and it will be my fault. I'd be letting everybody down. All the cast and crew, and everybody who works so hard on the show."

"Don't put so much pressure on yourself," Rosemary said, her face filled with compassion. "There are tons of factors that go into whether or not a show becomes a success. You shouldn't feel like you have to carry all the weight. And believe me, I understand exactly how you feel. A lot of people think I don't belong on Broadway, either."

"Really?" I asked, genuinely astonished. "You're a natural. You're one of those people who was born to be a Broadway star. Not only are you incredibly talented, but you're so passionate about theater. I can't think of anybody who belongs on the Great White Way more than you do."

"You're so sweet," she said. "It's ... Well, it's because of Johnny. People think I use my connections to get roles. I guess I can't blame people for thinking that. I mean, Johnny came from a billionaire family, and everybody knows the Creels paid for me to go to NYU."

I nodded. It was common knowledge that the famous bank attorney Walter Creel had paid for Rosemary to get her theater degree at NYU. People loved the rags-to-riches story of how Rosemary had grown up dirt poor, but then she'd met The Johnny Creel, notorious playboy and heir to the Creel fortune, who came along and "saved" her. From what I'd read in the entertainment news, Rosemary insisted on getting into the college on her own merit and, of course, it was up to her to do the hard work at getting her degree. While she was still in school, she'd landed that role on Broadway, stirring up all kinds of rumors about how she got the part. I'd seen first-hand how talented Rosemary was and how hard she worked, so I had no doubt she had earned that role honestly. From my perspective, Johnny was a hot mess before Rosemary came along. It was more like she saved *him*.

"Sometimes …" Rosemary began, and then paused for a moment.

"What?" I asked gently.

Her eyes held a deep sadness when she looked over at me. "I worry they might be right. I mean, do you ever really know why you get a part? Maybe I was put in the show to sell more tickets because people know who I am, too. People are obsessed with Johnny. Always have been. And then I became famous because of him."

"Because people heard your beautiful singing voice and saw your incredible stage presence when that first video went viral." It was true. Rosemary had shown incredible strength and power, both in her Broadway-worthy vocals and her willingness to stand up to The Johnny Creel in a way nobody else ever had.

Rosemary offered me a weak smile and shrugged her shoulders. "You took over the part of Mary because the other actress got pregnant. For my character, Elizabeth, the girl who had the part before me got fired."

I nodded with sympathy, both for the actress who lost her job and for Rosemary. "It happens. Not everyone stays in the show when it gets transferred to Broadway."

"I know, but what if they got rid of her to make room for a so-called bigger name? Yes, I get recognized on the street all the time, but it's because of Johnny. It's certainly not because I've been on Broadway as a no-name character in the ensemble."

"Let me tell you something, Rosemary," I said in a firm voice as I set my wineglass on the coffee table. "I've seen an awful lot of nepotism in my career. After all, Hollywood is all about who you know. Knowing the right person can definitely get you an audition. It might buy you a chance. But it doesn't get you the role."

Rosemary gazed at me hopefully, wanting to believe my words.

"It's true. If you're a big star, people have to humor you when you say 'You gotta let my cousin audition, he's great,' and they will let him audition. But he won't get the role if he's not good enough. Broadway is a business, just like Hollywood. Rosemary, I swear to you, you would *not* have gotten the role of Elizabeth in *Pirated* if you weren't perfect for it."

"I hope so," she said.

"It's like you said, there are an awful lot of factors that go into making a show a success. There will be fans who will come to the show just to see me and you, and that's something to feel good about. It helps the show overall, which is good for everyone. The show itself is amazing. Funny, well-written, with great songs. We also happen to have a terrific cast."

"We really do," she said with a smile. "Gilbert and Sarah are so funny as the old couple, and you and Luke are a riot. You play so well off each other."

"And then there's Jacob …" I said.

Unsurprisingly, Rosemary's face fell at the mention of Jacob Cariou.

"Yeah. There's him."

"What is that guy's problem?" I asked.

"He hates me," Rosemary said sadly. "And I can honestly say I have no idea why."

"That's so weird."

"I know. Jacob's been with the show since the start, and Luke's good friends with him. I don't know what he has against me. He's pretty nice to everyone else." Rosemary sighed. "Maybe he was friends with Emily. The one who originated the role of Elizabeth."

"Maybe. But that's no reason to act like a complete jerk.

It's unprofessional. Do you want me to talk to him? Or talk to the director about him? The showrunners definitely want to keep me happy. I don't make many demands, but I'm happy to when it's warranted. And it certainly is in this case. I could have him fired. Seriously. Granted, that would be a last resort, but it's doable for sure. He's got an understudy, after all."

"No, no. That's okay. I pride myself on being a professional, and I don't want anyone to fight my battles for me. Everybody thinks Johnny fights all my battles anyway."

"I understand," I said, feeling slightly disappointed that I wouldn't get to kick Jacob's ass on her behalf. Rosemary was one of the kindest, most genuine people I knew. She deserved so much better than Jacob as her co-star. "It must be tough to pretend to be all lovey-dovey over him onstage. Yuck. I'm lucky. Luke is hunky and adorable."

"Yes, he sure is," Rosemary said with a fond smile.

"Wanna switch parts?"

"No!"

I laughed and then sipped my wine. The front door opened, and I heard a man singing as he walked in. I vaguely recognized the tune as a John Denver song. The two of us giggled as we listened to Johnny sing.

"He really does have a nice singing voice," I said, and Rosemary nodded.

Johnny walked into the living room and did a double take when he saw me. It was cute, and I laughed.

"Well, if it isn't Therese Andrews."

"And *The* Johnny Creel," I said, getting up from the couch to greet him. I offered my hand and he shook it. There was such warmth in his gray eyes. Not a trace of the hard-partying playboy I used to hear about in the news. He wasn't even married yet, but he already looked like a family man.

"Nice to meet you," he said. "You go by Tessa, I hear?"

"That's right."

Rosemary stood up and walked over to us. Johnny gave her a quick kiss, then wrapped his arm around her.

"There's my leading lady," he said with a smile. They were such a happy couple. I could feel the love between them. I thought of all those gossipy stories about how Rosemary was only marrying Johnny for his money. If any of those naysayers spent five minutes with the two of them, they would see how real their love was. Funny how people seemed to forget Rosemary fell in love with him during the time when Johnny was flat broke. After his father was suspected of illegal business activity, all the family's assets were frozen indefinitely. Rosemary had helped Johnny get back on his feet, even though he'd treated her terribly when he was her boss. She loved him for who he was and was there for him when he could offer her nothing but love in return. That was all she needed.

Rosemary was a dear friend, and I was genuinely happy for her, but I felt a twinge of jealousy. No man had ever loved the real me. All the guys I dated simply wanted to be with a celebrity. Even Ricky, a celebrity in his own right, loved being part of a celebrity couple.

"So, I hear things are going really well with the show," Johnny said.

"Yes, I think so," I said. "It'll be fun to finally start working in the actual theater."

"That's good. Rosemary has high hopes for the show. Came home the first day and told me she was surprised you had a good voice."

I laughed and then cocked an eyebrow at Rosemary.

"Johnny," Rosemary admonished, blushing a little.

"I don't mean it in a bad way. Everybody knows what a great actress you are, but who knew you could sing? Rosemary said you have a really pretty voice, and you're gonna blow everybody away once you get up on that stage."

"Thanks," I said. "I hope you're right."

"And you're gonna knock 'em dead, too, princess," Johnny said, squeezing Rosemary. She gazed up at him and smiled.

"He's a keeper, Rosemary. You're lucky to have him," I said, feeling the ache of jealousy again. How I hated that feeling. Why couldn't I just be happy for her? I couldn't help it. Seeing the two of them together reminded me of how lonely I was.

"Well, I'll let you two girls chat," he said. "Need more wine?"

"Don't think so. We're on our second bottle," I said.

"Okay," Johnny said with a boyish grin. "See you guys later."

He left the room, and Rosemary and I flopped back down in our seats.

"Well, he's completely adorable," I said with a smile.

Rosemary laughed. "He is."

She looked at me contemplatively for a moment.

"So," she began carefully. "Is there anyone special in your life?"

Rosemary probably knew I envied her happiness, and for once, it didn't make me feel like a lonely loser. It felt like she cared about me.

I thought before responding. "Not at the moment. It's like I'm scared to try anymore. It's horrible having my breakups all over the press. That mess with Ricky Scrivello was awful. A lot of people seemed glad that it happened. Like they were happy that Miss Perfect Movie Star isn't so perfect after all. Believe me, I never thought I was perfect. People learn quickly I don't have much in common with Roxy Rose, or even Therese Andrews. I'm just … me. There's really nothing special about me once you strip away the acting roles."

"Tessa! Is that really what you think?" Rosemary asked.

"Yes. I always felt that way. Like people will be disappointed when they get to know the real me. Having Ricky cheat on me confirmed my worst fears about myself. That I'm boring. I wasn't enough to keep him interested. And everybody in the world knew it. It was so painful having that drama splayed out all over the headlines."

"I can't imagine," Rosemary said. She looked sad, and then her expression hardened. "But you shouldn't blame yourself. He's the one who cheated, and that says a lot more about him than it does about you. Good guys don't cheat. If he wasn't happy in the relationship for whatever reason, he should have said so."

"I suppose," I said with a weary sigh. I had loved Ricky, and his unfaithfulness had cut me deeply. Though I missed being in a relationship, the thought of going through that again made it hard to trust a man. "The guy I dated before him wasn't much better. He turned out to be nothing more than a fanboy. He claimed he didn't care that I was a movie star, but it eventually became clear that he had me confused with my fictional characters."

Reflexively, I wrapped my arms around myself, as if that could protect me from the awful Roxy Rose memory.

"It's hard to imagine ever finding a good guy anymore. It's nearly impossible to tell if a guy is really interested in me, or if he's just a fanboy looking to have sex with a celebrity." I laughed a tad bitterly. "Too bad Luke's taken. Is it, you know, serious with his girlfriend?"

Not that I would ever go after another woman's man. I just wondered if there was any hope Luke could be single any time soon.

"Yeah. He and Elyse are perfect for each other," Rosemary informed me as gently as possible.

"Don't tell him I asked you that."

"Of course not," she said. "He's a great guy. Can't blame you for trying."

"Yep," I sighed again. "My choices for men pretty much come down to actors or fanboys. I don't mean to sound arrogant, but I'd have to go to Siberia or something to find somebody who's never heard of me."

"You're probably right."

"*Blech.* Listen to me. I sound so pathetic. I swear, I'm not one of those women who feels like she's nothing without a man in her life. It would just be nice to have someone to come home to, that's all."

"I understand."

"It's been really nice having you to talk to, Rosemary. Not just today. Every day. On our breaks and everything."

Rosemary smiled and nodded. "I feel the same way."

I lifted my wine glass and offered a toast. "Here's to surviving tech rehearsal."

She squealed excitedly and clinked my glass.

I was truly thrilled about working in theater, and incredibly grateful to have found such a warm and wonderful friend to share the experience with.

CHAPTER 5

*T*oday was the day. It was the first week of February, which meant it was time to start tech rehearsals for *Pirated*.

And Therese Andrews would be on set in an hour.

Rex had been busting my balls for weeks over my obsession with her, and I was genuinely worried about what he might say. He was a good guy overall, and he always had my back, but he was having way too much fun with this Therese Andrews thing. I was nervous enough as it was, and the last thing I needed was him humiliating me in front of her. Odds were, I could embarrass myself just fine without his help.

Despite having weeks to think it over, I still had absolutely no idea what I was going to say to her. Would I be able to keep up a poker face in front of her, after drooling over her in private for so many years? My body always had such a strong physical reaction to watching her onscreen or seeing her picture in magazines or on the entertainment news. What would happen when I saw her live and in person?

Good Christ, what if I got hard and she noticed?

I drew in a deep breath and tried to get my shit under

control. Yes, she was a movie star, but she was still a human being. I couldn't help thinking of her as a *goddess*.

"Guess who's here?" Rex said in his familiar, obnoxious teasing tone.

My breath caught in my throat. I wasn't ready. She wasn't supposed to be here for another hour. Not that I would be any more ready then. I swallowed hard and walked on shaky legs over to the stage area.

A woman stood on the stage. A woman with long red hair. Rosemary Sutton.

I let out my breath, glaring at Rex. He chuckled and went back to whatever he was doing. *Asshole.*

Rosemary was even prettier in person. Upon closer inspection, I saw she was crying.

I walked tentatively toward her.

"Hey, are you okay?" I asked.

She turned around. Her eyes were filled with tears, but she smiled. Laughing, she wiped her eyes with her wrist.

"Oh, yeah. I'm fine. I always get emotional when I'm in any theater, but this is *Broadway*." Her voice hitched a bit when she said that last word.

Okay. That's cool. At least she gets how lucky she is to be here.

She took another moment to take in her surroundings. I watched as Rosemary gazed out at the 1400-plus empty seats, and then she lifted her eyes to take in the ornate ceiling. Sometimes I forgot how beautiful this place was until I saw it through a newcomer's eyes.

Finally, she turned back to me. She offered her hand and said, "I'm Rosemary Sutton."

More points for her. She was super famous, but she didn't assume everybody knew who she was. She also looked me in the eye when she shook my hand.

"Roman Pinza," I said. "I'm the head electrician here."

"Very nice to meet you. I look forward to working with you."

"You too," I said, already feeling relieved that Rosemary Sutton seemed nice. Though she wasn't as famous as Therese Andrews, she still had plenty of clout. She could make all our lives miserable during the production if she wanted to, but she seemed humble and kind. I had a good feeling about her.

"That's Rex Heard. He's the head property master," I told Rosemary, and she walked over to greet him. I watched her look Rex in the eye, too. Some actors, not many, thank goodness, never bothered to learn the crew member's names during the run of the show.

Audra ventured over to where we were standing. "And I'm Audra Martin. I'm the head carpenter." She laughed and held up her dirty hands. "I'm a mess right now, so I'm gonna just say how do you do, instead of shaking your hand."

Audra bowed slightly, and Rosemary laughed. "Nice to meet you, Audra."

A few other crew members stepped forward and introduced themselves, and Rosemary spent a few minutes chatting with them. Once people started wandering off to get back to work, she walked back to the center of the stage and looked around in wonder.

"Go on. Try it out," I said with a grin. "Sing something."

Her eyes lit up. "Really?"

"Sure, why not? You showed up early and got the stage to yourself right now. I say go for it."

She squealed with excitement, and I laughed. I'd seen hundreds of actors come and go on this stage, but it was always fun to watch the ones who were especially passionate about Broadway. It was like watching someone's lifelong dream come true right before my eyes.

Rosemary sang a few lines from a song I didn't know, but I figured it was one from the show. The lyrics sounded familiar from the script, and it was a song her character would sing to her pirate lover. The sound of her beautiful voice, echoing off the walls in the theater, gave me chills. Of course, I'd known from her viral videos that she had a pretty voice. But it was something else to hear her sing live. My stomach tingled with excitement when I heard her sing. Rosemary sounded so good, it gave me hope that this show might be a hit.

"That sounded great, Rosemary. Really beautiful."

She graced me with another lovely smile. "Thanks, Roman."

Okay, mega points for Rosemary. She even remembered my name. What a sweetheart she was. Meeting her had given me a few minutes to calm myself, and had taken my mind off being equal parts excited and terrified to meet Therese Andrews.

As I got back to my job, my nerves started to take over again. My hands shook as I worked with a bank of incandescent lamps. That was not good. Somehow, I had to get my shit together, or I'd be a complete blithering idiot in front of the woman of my lifelong dreams.

"You're doing that wrong," came a stern male voice from right behind me. I turned around to see a tall, muscular guy with light brown eyes and brown hair.

"What?" I asked incredulously. Who the hell was this guy, and where did he get off telling me how to do my job?

He chuckled and clapped me on the back. "I'm just messin' with ya, man. I used to be head of maintenance at a high rise in Manhattan. I understand *some* of what you're doing here, but this is way more complicated than the stuff I did." He curiously inspected my electrical work for a few more seconds, then offered me his hand. "Luke Rannells. Nice to meet ya."

"Ah, you're one of the pirates, right?" I asked, shaking his hand.

"Arrrrr, yes I am," he said, making me laugh.

"Roman Pinza. Head electrician."

"Nice," Luke said, seeming impressed.

"Want to have a look around?"

"Yeah, I'd love that. Can I see the lighting board?" he asked.

"Sure."

He followed me over and studied the equipment located near the front of the stage.

"So, is Rosemary your leading lady?" I asked.

Luke glanced out at Rosemary, who was still standing on the stage. He smiled in her direction. "Nope. That would have been cool, though. She's a good friend of mine. At least I get to work with her, though. Therese Andrews is my girl in the show, which ain't too shabby."

That was an understatement if I'd ever heard one.

Luke and I talked shop for a few minutes, and I was rather impressed with his technical knowledge. Like me, he liked to figure out how technical things worked. He seemed to appreciate all the hard work me and my crew put in for the show, which was cool. Between him and Rosemary, I figured this production would be a lot more fun to work on than the last one.

"You ever been on Broadway before?" I asked him.

Luke grinned widely. "Nope. I can't believe I'm actually standing here. I feel like I could cry."

I got the feeling he was only half-joking. As he looked around the stage in wonder, I could see how being here affected him.

"Join the club," I said, nodding my head toward Rosemary.

Luke laughed. "Oh yeah. She can't even talk about Broadway without tearing up, God love her."

"Okay, so I gotta ask you. What's it like working with Therese Andrews?" I'd built up a bit of a rapport with Luke, so I thought it might be okay to ask some of the questions that had been burning in my brain for weeks.

Luke turned around and grinned at me. "She's a peach, man."

I let out a breath of relief. "Really? I'm such a huge fan. You have no idea. I was worried she might turn out to be, you know, a diva or something."

"Nah, dude. She's Suzy Cream Cheese. She's really nice, she's even prettier in person, and I get to kiss her *every single day*."

"Lucky bastard."

Luke chuckled and nodded. "You know it."

Out of the corner of my eye, I saw someone walk onto the stage. Strangely enough, I knew it was Therese before I saw her. Her overwhelming presence awed me.

Slowly, I turned my head. Therese Andrews. Live and in person, right before my eyes.

I froze.

My God, she was beautiful. She had longish light brown hair that flowed just past her shoulders and those *eyes* ... those bright and clear-blue eyes that seemed to stare directly into my soul from the movie screen ... shone brightly as she looked around the stage. I was dimly aware of everyone stopping to gawk at her. She was dressed comfortably in blue jeans and a white blouse that was unbuttoned a good ways down. I swallowed hard as I took in her impressive cleavage. Fortunately, I was too awed by her presence to get hard.

I held my breath, faced with the very real possibility that I wouldn't be able to speak in her presence.

Luke clapped me on the back, which helped smack some sense back into me.

He lowered his voice so Therese wouldn't hear. "Don't be

nervous, man. Really. She's cool. Very sweet and very approachable."

"Thanks," I managed to say in a small voice. Though it helped to know she was easy to talk to, it was alarming that Luke could see how freaked out I was. How could I possibly hide that from her?

I had to play it cool.

I didn't know where to begin, or how to approach her, so I didn't. I simply went about my work, or pretended to, messing with lighting arrangements near the stage that didn't need to be messed with. Therese and Rosemary stood on the stage together, gushing over being in the theater. They sounded like excited schoolgirls, and it was freakin' adorable. I couldn't even pretend to concentrate, knowing any moment now I was going to meet Therese Andrews.

Hi. I'm Roman Pinza, the head electrician.

That was all I had to say. I practiced it over and over in my head, knowing they might be the most important words of my entire life.

I looked up from my work, and she happened to glance my way. She smiled. My heart pounded in my chest, and I felt like I might faint. Swoon, like a woman in an old-timey romance novel. I offered her a weak smile.

Get it together, man!

Forcing myself to straighten up and act like a man, I walked across the stage to introduce myself. None of the other crew members had said a word to her since she walked in, so I hoped to make a good impression by being the first to approach her. I swallowed hard. *Hi. I'm Roman Pinza, the head electrician.* I figured once I got those first words out of the way, I'd be fine.

"Roman here is *obsessed* with you," Rex said, appearing out of absolutely nowhere, clapping me on the back, and wearing a shit-eating grin. "Has been since he was fifteen years old."

I closed my eyes and let out my breath.

Dear God. Please strike me dead right now. I beg you. Amen.

I couldn't keep my eyes closed forever, so I finally opened them only to find Therese glaring at Rex.

"Don't worry," Therese Andrews said in that lilting, feminine voice I had adored all my life. "We all have *friends* like him in our lives."

With that, she gazed at me with those bluer-than-the-ocean-eyes. Her face was filled with empathy as she was clearly not enjoying my humiliation. Oh, how I loved her for that.

"Very nice to meet you. Richard was it?"

"Roman," I said, relieved that my voice came out sounding deep and manly instead of squeaky, as I'd feared.

"Roman," she repeated. My knees went weak when she said my name. "Very nice to meet you."

Therese offered me her hand, and I shook it firmly.

I'm touching Therese Andrews.

For one terrifying moment, I was afraid I'd said the words aloud.

She smiled warmly at me, and I got the distinct impression she was deliberately ignoring Rex as punishment for embarrassing me.

"And what do you do here?" Therese asked.

"I'm the head electrician." I'd remembered my name *and* my occupation. I was damn proud of myself.

"Impressive," she said with a smile.

I literally pushed Rex out of the way as I gestured toward Les.

"And that's Les, one of my lighting guys."

Therese giggled when I shoved Rex, and my heart soared. I was still embarrassed that he'd outed me as an obsessive fan, but he hadn't managed to make me look like a total idiot. His plan had pretty much backfired—Therese was annoyed at him for being mean and was sympathetic toward me.

Therese smiled warmly at Les and shook his hand. Feeling a tad more confident, I introduced her to a bunch of my other guys. She couldn't have been more gracious. She looked each person in the eye and repeated his or her name.

I gestured toward Audra, who stepped forward and held out her hand as I introduced her. "This is Audra Martin, the head carpenter."

"So nice to meet you, Audra," Therese said. She turned and glanced at the stage. "You all have done such a great job. The pirate ship looks *awesome!*"

Audra grinned happily. "Thanks, Ms. Andrews."

"My friends and family call me Tessa, so that's what I'd like you all to call me," she said to the small crowd of crew members that had gathered.

Of course. Tessa Carol Gumm. Her real name. I couldn't believe she wanted us to be so informal with her. Luke wasn't kidding when he'd said how sweet and approachable she was. *Wow.*

The director, Zach, clapped his hands. "Okay, everybody. Let's gather 'round and get to know each other real quick before we launch into rehearsal here."

Zach was a cool guy. I didn't know him well, but we'd worked together on a small theater project some years ago, and I recalled he was a good director. He'd be on set during tech rehearsals, and then Harriet Hill would take over stage direction once the show actually started running.

"Allow me to introduce our pirates. Luke Rannells as Captain Samuel," Zach said.

Luke stepped forward and graced us with an exaggerated bow, making us laugh.

"Jacob Cariou as One-Eyed Jack."

We offered polite applause as Jacob stepped forward and

nodded. He looked sad. Or mad. I couldn't really tell, but there was a huge difference in his demeanor versus Luke's congenial manner.

"And Gilbert Vansill as Captain Graybeard."

Gilbert, a handsome guy in his twenties with reddish-brown hair stepped forward. He was, by far, the youngest guy in the cast, so it would be interesting to see what he looked like in old-man makeup.

"And now, our leading ladies," Zach said. A flutter of excitement rippled through me. I had made a concentrated effort not to stare at Tessa for the last few minutes, which was no easy feat. When she stepped forward, I'd be allowed to look at her again. I was so goddamn paranoid about staring at her, lest that asshole, Rex, call me out on it in front of her.

Damn you, Rex.

"Therese Andrews, better known as Tessa, as Mary."

Tessa stepped forward gracefully and nodded to us. I drew in a deep breath as if literally breathing in her beauty. It was *surreal* having her standing right in front of me. I agreed with Luke—she was prettier in person. I hadn't thought it was possible. We all clapped loud and long for her.

"Rosemary Sutton as Elizabeth."

I forced myself to look away from Tessa and focus on Rosemary, not that she was exactly hard on the eyes, either. It made me smile to see her eyes glisten with emotion over just being here. Luke chuckled and wrapped his arm around her when she walked back to him after taking her bow.

"And Sarah Stritch as Eleanor," Zach said, introducing the young girl with dark hair and a pretty smile who would be playing a little old lady.

"We have an absolutely top-notch crew here at the Al Hirschfeld, who have already put in a ton of hard work over the last few weeks," Zach said, starting a round of applause. I risked a glance at Tessa. She was smiling at some of the crew members as she clapped for us.

"Their goal is to make this a safe and efficient production, so if you have any questions, don't hesitate to ask. I know there's a lot of names to learn at first, but you'll get there. I do want to introduce our main department heads. Over there, we've got Rex Heard; he's our property master."

Rex nodded his head and I glowered at him. He was still my buddy, and I'd forgive him. Eventually.

"Audra Martin, our head carpenter." Audra nodded and smiled. "And Roman Pinza, our head electrician."

I nodded too, scanning the cast members as casually as I could. When my gaze landed on Tessa, she smiled at me. I gave her what I hoped was a manly, non-goofy smile in return.

As much as I would have loved to stand there and stare at Tessa all day, I had a job to do. It was time to start running through the light cues, and everything else. I took my job seriously, and I couldn't afford to be distracted by Tessa, even if she *was* the most beautiful woman in the world.

We started our first complete run-through of the show, which usually took about three times as long as the actual show. On this first day, the goal was to get all the way through it once, figuring out all the minute details along the way.

Luke, Jacob, and Gilbert were hilarious as the three pirates. They had a great rapport, and it was fun to watch their characters as they evolved through the show, starting out as tough guys, going around kidnapping women for ransom, as pirates tend to do. But when they kidnap Mary, Elizabeth, and Eleanor, each pirate falls in love and starts to go soft, all the while still pretending to be tough.

The lighting cues all went smoothly, but I had a tough time concentrating whenever I had to light Tessa. She was so damn beautiful, and under the lights, she looked like an angel.

I did my best to focus on my work, but I stopped in my tracks when she started to sing. Her delicate, feminine voice was the loveliest sound I'd ever heard in my life. In all my years of adoring Therese Andrews, I'd never heard her sing. I didn't know she *could* sing. Nobody did. Online news outlets went nuts when they'd heard she would be in a Broadway musical. Everybody was shocked.

I stood there, staring in awe as I watched her. I didn't care who saw me gawking, or if Rex made fun of me for it. My God, this woman really did have it all. She was *perfect*.

During the next scene Tessa could not keep a straight face, no matter how hard she tried. Luke's character, Captain Samuel, has just kidnapped her and he sees how beautiful she is. Every time Samuel talks to her, he keeps trailing off, forgetting what he's about to say as he gawks at her.

He was behaving exactly the way I feared I would in front of Tessa. It was hilarious. We had to keep stopping the scene because Tessa kept laughing.

"I'm sorry. I'm sorry!" she said, still giggling. "It's crazy after rehearsing this for weeks, this part is still so damned funny! Okay, okay. I'll be good now. I promise."

The cast and crew laughed with her, and it lifted all our spirits. Tessa was the star—if she thought it was funny when she messed up, maybe it wouldn't be so bad if we messed up, too. Not that we were lazy or careless in our work, but at least we wouldn't be screamed at by the stars like we were on the last show. Everybody was so chill on this set. I loved it.

"Okay, this time, I'm not gonna look at you, Luke," Tessa said. "I can't."

"Okay," Luke said with a chuckle. I could tell he loved making his leading lady laugh so hard. Who could blame him?

During the next take of the scene, Tessa looked past Luke and to the left. That way, from the audience perspective, she was still looking at Captain Samuel.

"Okay, great job," Zach said, looking relieved we'd finally made it through the scene. "Let's work on the rope ladder scene now. We need to be very careful to make sure nobody gets hurt."

Making sure "nobody gets hurt" referred directly to Tessa in this scene. She was to drop several feet from the ladder and into Luke's arms, so the timing had to be perfect. The moment he catches her, Captain Samuel and Mary first realize they're in love.

"First up, let's just practice the fall. This will help you get used to it, and you'll learn to trust that Rannells here will catch you," Zach said with a smile.

"I trust him," Tessa said. "It's just this will be a lot different than jumping off the table at the studio."

"I know," Zach said kindly. "Okay, go ahead and climb up. Get a good grip and go slow. We'll pick up the tempo later. Just get comfortable with the ladder for now."

Tessa grabbed hold of the ladder and started climbing up.

"Can I look up her skirt yet?" Luke asked, getting a laugh from all of us. Captain Samuel was supposed to try to look up Mary's skirt as she climbed up the ladder.

"Look all you want," Tessa said with a giggle as she climbed. "I'm wearing jeans."

"Go up just a little ways more," Zach said as he and Luke watched Tessa carefully in case she fell before her cue. Wow. She was *really* high up there. Luke damn well better catch her. It was nerve-wracking enough for me to watch. I saw stunts like this all the time, but it was scarier because it was Tessa.

"Okay, grip the ladder really tight," Zach instructed.

Tessa nodded, white-knuckling the rope ladder. She looked scared, and my heart ached for her.

"I'm gonna shake the ladder, just a bit, so you can start to get used to it. Ready?"

"Yup," Tessa said like a trouper.

I swallowed hard as Zach shook the ladder gently and Tessa held on tight. I was grateful that Zach wasn't forcing her to go through the stunt at a normal pace right away.

"Now look down at us," Zach said. Tessa turned to look at Luke and Zach waiting below. "I want you to jump on three. Normally, you won't be looking down at Luke. That's the hard part. You're gonna have to fall off the ladder backward, and Luke will catch you. Right now, to get you comfortable with the height and all, you can watch exactly where you're going."

"Okay, got it," Tessa said.

"Luke, get ready."

Luke nodded, the stress of keeping Tessa safe making him look as nervous as she did. It was a lot of pressure on him for sure. We would never forgive him if he broke our star by dropping her.

"Ready," Luke said in a strong, confident voice. Then he added softly, "It's okay, Tessa."

"Let go *on* the count of three," Zach instructed. "One … two … *three.*"

We all held our breath as Tessa let go of the ladder and dropped several feet through the air. Luke caught her easily, and everyone let out a sigh of relief. Then we applauded. He carefully set her back on her feet.

"Great job," Zach said with a grin. "It will get easier every time. I promise."

They ran through it a bunch more times to make sure Tessa and Luke were comfortable with the stunt. The last few times, they practiced having Tessa drop without looking behind her. She performed the stunt like a champ. I was so proud of her.

"Okay. Now let's run through the full scene with dialogue and everything," Zach instructed.

Tessa and Luke took their places.

"Get away from me, you scoundrel!" Tessa/Mary yelled at Luke/Captain Samuel. At this point in the show, Samuel has kidnapped Mary, and the two are hot for each other and trying to deny it to themselves.

We all watched nervously as Tessa climbed the rope ladder much faster now, as she was supposed to be trying to escape. Samuel follows her, first taking a few healthy glances at her ass as she climbs. That got a good laugh from us.

The captain mutters a few pirate curses, then begins shaking the ladder to get her to fall. Tessa screamed when she fell, as the script called for, but it still startled me. As he'd done throughout the rehearsal, Luke expertly caught her.

He held her in his arms and gazed down at her. "Mary," he said softly, like a man in love.

Lucky bastard. I wished I could stare at her that long without her thinking I was creepy.

Mary gazed up at him, too, for a moment. Then she said quietly, "Put me down."

Still staring, Captain Samuel didn't move.

"I said, put me down!" Mary shouted. Samuel's eyes went wide with alarm.

"Yes, Ma'am!" he said, quickly setting her back on her feet.

The crew chuckled, even though we were familiar with the script.

Mary and Samuel continue their back-and-forth banter for the rest of the scene. The dialogue was sharp and funny, and Luke and Tessa did a great job of bringing their characters to life. The captain constantly waffles between being tender with Mary because he's in love, and trying to be tough when he remembers he is supposed to be in charge of his kidnapping victim.

The scene ended with a passionate kiss. *Lucky bastard*, I thought for the millionth time. He and Tessa were just acting, but they had undeniable chemistry together.

I wondered if there was something going on between them in real life. Therese Andrews had certainly dated her share of costars over the years, so it was certainly a possibility. If Luke was sleeping with Tessa, I didn't want to know about it. The idea of anyone else sleeping with her was painful. I remember actively avoiding news articles that were focused on her relationship with Ricky Scrivello. It just hurt too much to read about it. Imagining Ricky having sex with her was torture for me.

I'd spent a lifetime fantasizing about having sex with her myself, but I knew it could never happen in real life. Although I was closer to her now than I'd thought I'd ever get, she might as well still be three thousand miles away in Los Angeles. She dated her costars because they were hot and sexy actors with dynamic personalities like Luke. I was a boring, anal-retentive neat freak, and a blue-collar electrician. I had absolutely nothing to offer a woman like her.

We moved on to scenes between Jacob and Rosemary, which made it much easier for me to concentrate on my work. The sparring scenes between One-Eyed Jack and Elizabeth were every bit as clever as the ones between Mary and Samuel, but in between scenes, it was a completely different story. Jacob was downright cold to Rosemary, and I couldn't figure out why. She seemed so nice. Everyone else on the set seemed to love her. Whatever the problem was between those two, I'd already pretty much made up my mind that it was Jacob's fault.

The rest of the rehearsal went well, but we were all exhausted by the time it was over. I refused to talk to Rex for the rest of the day. I was still pissed off at him. Though I doubted I could have hidden my adoration for Tessa completely, I might have been able to put up a halfway decent front. But no. Rex had to rat me out, and now she knew I had a thing for her.

Oh well. It was too late to make a better first impression, but with any luck, I would get to work with her for a long time.

I hoped and prayed *Pirated* would have a lengthy and successful run.

CHAPTER 6

After a long day of rehearsal, I got to my house in Manhattan feeling exhausted but happy. I could hardly believe I'd be performing on Broadway in a few short weeks.

I collapsed onto my big, fluffy couch and flipped on the television, needing to decompress a bit before going to sleep. I found an old rerun of *Friends*, which was perfect. Half-watching the show, I reflected on today's rehearsal. Rehearsing *Pirated* for a new audience had been fun. Even though the crew knew the script, as they needed to for the lighting and scenery cues and all that, this was the first time they'd seen the show performed live. They'd laughed in all the right spots, which energized me with confidence.

Everyone on the crew was very kind to me, but that was no surprise. When you're famous, everybody is nice to you. At least to your face. They have to be. Trouble was, you never knew if anybody actually liked you when you were famous, or if they were just trying to protect their job or advance their career by sucking up to you.

Even so, this set felt a lot different than the last few

movies I'd worked on. In a good way. Rosemary and Luke were wonderful to work with, and I had high hopes of remaining friends with them once the show closed or, if the show ran long enough, until one or more of us decided it was time to move on.

I smiled just thinking about Rosemary. Having her in my life made me feel less lonely. She understood what it was like to live in the public eye. The pressures. The fake friendships. The feeling you're nowhere near as wonderful as everybody says you are.

Glancing around my huge, empty house, I found myself wishing I had someone to share it with. Not just anybody. Somebody who I cared about and who cared about me. Maybe if we were a few years younger, Rosemary and I could have been roommates or something. I didn't necessarily need a romantic partner in my life, but somebody to share downtime when I wasn't working would be wonderful.

Knowing it would likely be a mistake, I reached for the phone to call my mother. I was excited about *Pirated*, and I wanted someone to share it with.

"Hey, Mom," I said when she answered the phone.

"Tessa, honey. How are you?" she said, and I felt better about calling. I had seen her several weeks ago at Christmas, but I hadn't talked to her since. I should be better about calling her in between visits.

"I'm doing pretty well. We started tech rehearsal for the show today, and it was so exciting to be in the actual theater."

"That's wonderful, dear. Wouldn't it be something if you won a Tony for this?"

My stomach tightened. No matter what I was working on, my mother was always looking for the next thing for me to do, to win, to be recognized for. Making it to Broadway wasn't enough.

"I guess. Right now, I'm just trying to enjoy the moment, you know? It's exciting to be working on Broadway."

"Of course it is, dear." The way she said "dear" sounded condescending. Only my mother would act like being in a Broadway show was no big deal.

Patsy Gumm was the ultimate stage mother. She'd pushed me into acting at a very young age, loving the attention it brought her. Lucky for me, I loved acting and had a genuine passion for it. I supposed I should be grateful for her help in launching my career, but I knew it had nothing to do with me personally. Mom wanted to be famous. She'd majored in theater and tried her hand at acting, but she soon found it was too much work, so she quit. Instead, she married rich. She'd wanted to raise a whole bunch of kids in the hopes of making them all famous, but nature had other plans. I was an only child, which meant all the pressure was on me to succeed.

"The show is really funny, and we have a great cast. I have a feeling it might run for a while," I said.

"Wouldn't that be something? If you could originate a role on Broadway in a show that stood the test of time, like *Chicago* or *A Chorus Line?*"

My stomach clenched again. Leave it to Mom to expect *Pirated* to measure up to some of the longest running shows on Broadway. It was a wonder I didn't have an ulcer from all the pressure she'd put on me all these years.

"Even if the show did run for years, you want to make sure you don't stay on too long," she continued.

"What do you mean?"

"You should stay long enough to cement the role as your own, so everybody knows Therese Andrews originated the role. But then you need to leave so you can go back to doing movies. That's where you really belong."

Translation: movies were much more glamorous than the

Broadway stage. Movie premieres were a much bigger deal than Broadway ones, and it was better to be a movie star than a Broadway star. Mom had been one of those wannabe actors who only cared about stardom, whereas I relished the craft of acting. I loved the process of developing and becoming a character, and the chance to act and sing on a Broadway stage thrilled me. Sure, fewer people would see the show in the theater than when I released a movie, but I didn't care.

I sighed. Instead of sharing my passion, my mother had taken some of the wind out of my sails. I still felt like I had no one to share my feelings with. Well, that wasn't entirely true. The cast of *Pirated* was amazing, and Luke and Rosemary were just as giddy as I was. Probably more so, since they hadn't had half the acting opportunities I'd had. Still, at the end of the day, Rosemary went home to Johnny and Luke went home to Elyse. They had someone to share their day with.

"We'll just see how it goes, Mom. Way too early to decide how long I want to stay. The choice might not be up to me. The show could close in a few weeks for all I know."

My chest hurt just imagining that possibility. I loved the show, and I wanted so badly for it to succeed. Not to mention the fact that, if it closed, a lot of people would be out of work.

"Well, let's hope that doesn't happen," Mom said. "A flop won't look good on your record."

Okay. Enough. Time to disentangle myself from this conversation. I never should have called. It was much better to be lonely than to talk to my hypercritical mother.

"Well, I better get some rest. I got an early call time tomorrow."

"Yes, be sure to get some rest. Otherwise you'll get ugly circles under your eyes."

My eyes suddenly welled up with tears. I didn't know why that last comment hurt so much, but it really stung. Just once, I wished my mother would show concern for me and not just for my career. I wanted her to tell me to get some rest because I needed it. I wanted to hear she was concerned for my health. This attitude from my mother was nothing new, so I wasn't sure why it hurt so much right now. I guess I was already feeling vulnerable.

"Okay." I tried not to let my voice shake. "Goodnight," I said, eager to hang up before she could say anything else to hurt me.

"And keep an eye on your figure. You've put on a few pounds."

I hung up the phone, pretending I hadn't heard her. When I closed my eyes, tears began to fall. Now I felt lonely *and* degraded.

"No," I said out loud as I wiped my tears with the back of my hand. "I'm not letting her do this to me."

Today had been a great day, and I was proud of the work we were doing on the show. Making it to Broadway was a very big deal, far more than my mother was able to do in her own career, and I wasn't about to let anybody take that away from me.

As I brushed my teeth and washed my face before bed, I reflected on today's tech rehearsal. How much fun it had been. The laughs we got. I was tired, but still motivated to go back tomorrow. No more calls to Mom. Instead, I'd focus on Rosemary and Luke. My real friends. Who knew? Maybe I would make even more friends with some of the new crew members I'd met today. No matter how long the show ran or how successful—or not—it might be, I was going to have a great time and revel in every moment.

I crawled into bed, feeling exhausted, still alone, but excited about the future.

* * *

IT FELT good going back to rehearsal the next day. I loved the people and the warm feeling I enjoyed while working on this set, which made me determined to stay with the show as long as I pleased, no matter what my mother said.

Sipping from my water bottle, I took in the sights and sounds around me. The place smelled of fresh wood and paint. It was similar but not exactly the same as the way a movie set smelled. It was just as hectic as a movie set, though, with crew members scurrying around doing last-minute checks on lighting and props before we got started.

"Good morning, Audra," I said to the head carpenter lady.

"Good morning," Audra responded with a smile.

I greeted a few more crew members by name, then I glanced over to see the head electrician guy.

Oh, no.

I couldn't remember his name. Dammit. Of all people for me to forget. That guy Rex—of course I could remember *his* name—had said the electrician had been obsessed with me since he was fifteen years old. No doubt he was exaggerating, but the guy was clearly a fan of mine. He'd tried to hide it yesterday, but I could tell he'd been incredibly nervous when he talked to me. His hands had visibly shaken. I always tried to take special care of fans who were nervous around me. When they approached me on the street, stuttering and stammering, they'd probably kick themselves for a long time if they felt like they'd made a fool of themselves in front of me. I always pretended not to notice their nervousness, and try to make the encounter as pleasant as possible.

Since he was obviously a fan, I was sure it would mean a lot to him if I remembered his name. I felt *awful.* I glanced around, hoping to find Rosemary or Luke, to see if they knew his name. I didn't see them on set yet, and the electrician was doing that staring-but-trying-not-to-stare thing. Ignoring him would probably be more hurtful than forgetting his name, so I walked over to him.

"I am so, so sorry. I know you're the head electrician here, but I am completely blanking on your name," I admitted.

I could see the apprehension in his dark brown eyes as he smiled at me. His nervousness was endearing. He was tall with thick, dark brown-black hair, and he was quite handsome. I was flattered that he was jittery around me, though it was only due to my fame.

"It's okay. It's Roman. Roman Pinza."

"Roman," I repeated. "Okay, I promise I won't forget again."

"It's okay," he repeated. I got the feeling he wanted to say more, but he wasn't sure what to say. To save him from any awkwardness, I just smiled at him and walked away. After we got to know each other better, he'd probably be more comfortable with me and we could have an actual conversation. Roman was still starstruck, but he'd get over it once he realized I was not the same Therese Andrews from the big screen. I was just *me*.

Rehearsal went a little faster today, which made it more fun. I looked forward to running straight through the whole show without stopping, though. Falling off the ladder was still a little scary, but I trusted Luke completely. There were a lot worse things than falling into his arms every day. I didn't mind kissing him, either. It was the most physical contact I'd had with a man since I'd broken up with Ricky, so I would take what I could get.

After surviving the fall off the ladder once again, I stood off to the side, sipping from my water bottle as I watched the next scene with Jacob and Rosemary. In it, Elizabeth teaches One-Eyed Jack how to read by introducing him to poetry. First, Jack struggles with the words and then becomes dreamy-eyed as he reads the mushy parts to Elizabeth. Like Captain Samuel, One-Eyed Jack pretends to be tough around his pirate buddies but turns soft when he's with the woman he loves. Jack is hilarious as he gets more and more pumped up and passionate the more he reads to Elizabeth. When they finish with the lesson, Jack closes the poetry book and leaves Elizabeth alone for the night. Elizabeth then walks to the center of the stage to sing about loving him, and how confusing it is to fall for a man who kidnapped her.

When Rosemary finished, Zach gave her notes about her acting choices and told her, kindly yet firmly, that she was still a little pitchy in spots and she would need to work on that. Rosemary listened intently and nodded. She was always such a pro, and she took direction well. Until Jacob audibly scoffed. Rosemary swallowed hard, and I could see tears in her eyes. She remained outwardly stoic, but it was clear that Jacob was making her a nervous wreck. I despised him for that. Luke and I supported each other in our scenes, like you were supposed to. Jacob was a complete jerk.

"I'm gonna kick that guy's ass one of these days," Roman muttered as he watched the scene.

"Get in line," I agreed. He whirled around, eyes wide. Clearly, he hadn't realized I was standing right next to him. "I can't stand the way he treats her."

"Me neither," Roman agreed. He was still shaky around me, but right now, his anger at Jacob took precedence. "What's his problem? Rosemary is so nice to everybody, and she's doin' a great job."

I shook my head, glaring in Jacob's direction. "I have no idea, but he's treated her like this the whole way through rehearsals. I don't know how she can stand it. I offered to step in and help, but she won't let me. With her connection to the Creel family, she doesn't even need my help. She could get him fired any time she wanted, but she won't go that route."

Roman shook his head. "Gotta admire her for that, I guess. Lotta other people would've pulled strings to get him outta here."

"True," I said. I planned to give Rosemary a big hug as soon as she was done with the scene. And I would try my best not to give Jacob a well-deserved punch in the face.

"Gettin' harder and harder not to knock that guy out," Roman said.

I laughed. "I was just thinking the same thing."

Roman looked into my eyes and smiled, and I was glad of it. I didn't want anybody feeling awkward around me.

Rosemary ran through the song again, getting praise from Zach this time.

"'Bout damn time you got it right," Jacob said, loud enough for everyone to hear.

"Take it easy, Jacob," Zach warned.

I drew in a deep, slow breath, trying to quell my renewed urge to deck Jacob. Roman's steely-eyed glare made it clear he was as mad as I was. If anyone punched Jacob out, it should be Roman. He was big and muscular, and could do a lot more damage than my tiny fists.

Rosemary walked toward me, but before I could give her a hug, Luke intervened.

"Can I talk to you for a sec?" Luke asked, looking concerned.

"Sure," Rosemary said.

"It'll just take a minute," Luke said, lowering his voice. I wondered if I should walk away to give them some space, but he started speaking again before I could go.

"Look, I know Jacob's been giving you a really hard time," Luke began.

"You could say that," Rosemary said wearily.

"It sucks, because I've known him a long time, and he's actually not a bad guy."

Rosemary and I exchanged wary looks.

"I know, I know," Luke said grimly. "Look, I've been debating back and forth on whether to tell you this. I'm still not sure if this will make you feel worse, or if it will help you understand why he's being such a jerk."

Rosemary and I looked at Luke intently, waiting for him to finish.

"The girl who used to play Elizabeth in the off-Broadway version of the show—Emily ... Well, she's Jacob's wife."

Rosemary gasped and covered her mouth with her hand.

"Oh my God," she said, her face going pale.

"Look, I want you to know this in no way excuses Jacob's behavior, and I've told him as much. I consider him a friend, but I said in no uncertain terms that carrying on like this is bullshit. It's unprofessional, and it's cruel," Luke said, his jaw set in anger.

"Oh, I feel awful," Rosemary said sadly.

"I know you do, sweetie, but you shouldn't," Luke said. "The only reason I'm telling you this is so you'll understand that Jacob's hurt and he's angry, but it has absolutely nothing to do with you personally."

Rosemary sighed heavily. Luke put his arm around her and squeezed her tightly. I felt so bad for Rosemary.

"I'm sure everybody here thinks I got the part because I'm famous for marrying into the Creel family," Rosemary said with a hitch in her voice that broke my heart. In the background, I heard the crew chuckling at the scene Gilbert and Sarah were performing, but I was focused on comforting Rosemary.

"I'm sure some people did think that, Rosemary," I told her honestly. "At first. But now that everyone's seen how well you do in the role, they can see you're perfect for it."

"Not so perfect today," she said, glancing over at the director.

"You think Emily didn't get direction?" Luke asked. "'Cause she did. All the time. Just like we all do."

"I guess," Rosemary said quietly. She gazed out across the stage. "Sometimes I wonder if I've really earned the right to be here."

"Of course you have!" Luke exclaimed.

"Tell me honestly," Rosemary implored us both. "Do you think I got this part because of who I am? Because of who Johnny is?"

For one terrible moment, neither Luke nor I answered. Rosemary's eyes filled with fresh tears.

"You listen to me," I said firmly. "The truth of the matter is, we might never know how you got the part. You think I got this part because I'm a better singer than other actresses who might have auditioned for Mary? *Highly* doubtful. I'm here because I'm already a famous name."

"Because you worked your way up," Rosemary said. "You didn't have any show biz connections when you started out."

"No, I didn't. Even so, I'm here because I'm famous for acting, and now I'm gonna have to work twice as hard as a singer to prove that I belong here. Otherwise, the reviews will be brutal. And that scares the hell out of me."

Rosemary nodded with empathy, but I wasn't trying to make her sorrow all about me.

"My point is, regardless of how I got here, all I can do is get out there onstage and give it everything I've got. And that's what you've got to do. Take a deep breath and never forget how lucky you are to be here, regardless of how you got here. Respect the Broadway stage, and do your best to respect your fellow actors, even when they're complete jerks."

Rosemary laughed and nodded.

"Put your heart and soul into the character, and give the best performance you know how to give. In the end, that's all that matters."

"Hear, hear," Roman said, having overheard our whole conversation. He smiled at me, and then turned to smile at Rosemary. "Not gonna lie. I thought you got the part just 'cause you're a famous name. Then I heard you sing, and I kinda forgot all about that stuff. You're doin' great, Rosemary."

"Thank you," she said, wiping her tears. "All of you."

First she hugged Luke, and then me. Then she turned to Roman, whom she didn't know all that well. He chuckled and held out his arms. She gave him a hug, too.

I let out a happy sigh. Forget Jacob. Aside from him, we had the greatest cast and crew I'd ever worked with in my entire career.

CHAPTER 7

*T*essa forgot my name yesterday. It didn't even bother me that much since she was so apologetic about it, and I got extra attention from her.

God, she was such a wonderful woman.

The more I got to know the real person behind the celebrity, the more I liked her. I was glad to see she was as pissed off at Jacob as I was, and she was sweet to talk to Rosemary about it the way she did. They seemed to be close friends, and it made me happy that they had each other to share the theater experience with.

In a futile attempt to quit obsessing over Tessa, I studied the lighting board to make sure everything was in working order. We'd had a few glitches yesterday, but it seemed fine now.

"Good morning!"

My heart jumped in my chest at the sound of Tessa's voice, and it thumped harder when I glanced up and saw her. Sometimes I wondered if I would ever be calm around her. I watched as she greeted Luke, Rex, Mitchell, Les, Rosemary, and Audra each by name. Her face fell when she got to me.

"Oh my God," she said, shaking her head.

It took me a moment to figure out what was wrong. Then I laughed.

"You forgot my name again, didn't you?"

"What is wrong with me?" she asked, her blue eyes wide. "I know exactly who you are. Head electrician. Does a great job with the lighting. The guy with the pretty, dark brown eyes."

I started to hope she would never remember my name if this was how she'd handle it every day.

She thinks I have pretty eyes.

"I know it begins with an 'R,'" Tessa said, wincing and looking genuinely upset with herself.

"Yeah. It's Roman."

Tessa grabbed my shoulders and stared deeply into my eyes. "Roman, Roman, Roman. I got it. I *promise*. I mean it this time!"

I gazed into her eyes for a few blissful seconds before she let go of me.

To no one in particular, Tessa said, "I'm going to go grab an orange from the break room before we get started. I didn't have time to eat before I came. Be right back!"

After she rushed off, I stood there in a daze.

Tessa touched me.

"You all right there, buddy?" Luke asked, chuckling at my expression.

"Yeah. Just a little lightheaded," I said, not bothering to hide how much Tessa's touch had affected me.

"You got it *bad* for her, man," Les said, shaking his head and smirking. Rex and Audra both laughed when they saw my expression.

Luke grinned at me. "Did I mention that I get to kiss her every single—"

"Yeah, yeah, yeah," I said, waving him off.

"She is a wonderful woman," Rosemary said with a smile. "You've got good taste."

I couldn't hide my feelings for Tessa so I'd pretty much quit trying. The cast and crew teased me about it, but it didn't bother me for the most part. It was all in good fun. I just hoped they wouldn't ever do it with Tessa around. She had to know by now I had a silly crush on her, but I'd be humiliated if the guys teased me about it in front of her. I still hadn't fully forgiven Rex for doing that to me when I first met her.

I was still a bit dazed as I went about my work. I was enthralled with having Tessa around every day. A tingle of excitement went through my body every time I heard that familiar voice I'd heard so many times in the movies and on television. It was hard to wrap my mind around the fact that I could talk to her. And now she had actually *touched* me.

When she arrived the next day, in a bold move, I pointed at her and said, "Tesla, right?"

She laughed and said, "Close enough, Roman, Roman, Roman."

From that day forward, she called me Roman, Roman, Roman. I loved it.

Tech rehearsals were going well, and the show was really coming together. We could run straight through the whole shebang several times a day now, which was important since we opened in two weeks. The cast all wore their costumes now. Luke looked annoyingly dashing in his pirate outfit, with the dark black makeup around his eyes and his shirt hanging open for most of the show. I liked the guy, but I was resentful every time he got to hold Tessa and kiss her. Tessa looked like a goddess in all the old-timey dresses they had her wear. She was especially alluring in this blue, fairly low-cut sweeping gown that brought out her eyes, not to mention her cleavage.

Though things were running well overall, Tessa had a particularly rough time one day in rehearsal. About a week from opening night, Tessa seemed unusually stressed. She was a veteran performer and no stranger to pressure. Sure, Broadway was the big time, but she'd been in high-profile Hollywood movies for years. I would have expected people like Luke, who hadn't hit the big time, to be the ones cracking under pressure.

She showed up late that day and seemed behind all day. My heart ached for her as I watched her struggle through one particular scene. She tended to forget her lines when she was overly stressed. The scene involved most of the cast, which made it especially hard on her to keep messing up.

"I'm sorry," she said in a soft voice after making her third mistake. I heard the catch in her voice, and I knew she was fighting tears.

"It's okay," Zach said, obviously worried about Tessa messing up so much this far into rehearsal. But he kept his mouth shut rather than pile more stress onto her. "We'll keep going until we get it right."

Tessa nodded, taking a deep breath. My stomach clenched. I couldn't bear the thought of watching her mess up the scene again. I knew her well enough by now to know she was inwardly torturing herself. She needed a few minutes to re-center herself. I'd seen her do it before, and it usually worked.

Pulling Zach aside, I said, "Hey, why don't we just take a quick break."

He met my gaze for a moment, knowing I was biased toward her and trying to protect her, but I also happened to be right. Zach nodded.

"Okay, let's take a breather for a few minutes," Zach said.

Tessa let out an audible sigh of relief. She went right over to a small table just off the stage and picked up her script.

Biting her lip, she flipped through the pages to find the right scene. I found myself wishing I could go over and talk to her. Comfort her. Rub her shoulders and tell her it would all be okay. That was ridiculous, of course. She barely knew me, even though I felt like I knew her so well. Yeah. Going over there and rubbing her shoulders would result in more stress for her and probably a well-deserved sexual harassment complaint for me. Still, I wished *somebody* would go over and talk to her.

Rosemary and Luke both sent worried glances in her direction, but they clearly felt it best to leave her alone. Audra stood by, watching Tessa sadly.

"She puts so much pressure on herself," Audra said, verbalizing what we were all thinking. Rosemary and Luke nodded.

"She wants this show to succeed so much," Rosemary said. "She keeps saying she thinks she was brought in, at least in part, to sell tickets. She says if she screws up, it could bring the whole show down with her. I keep telling her it's an ensemble show, and we're all in this together."

"She'll be okay," Luke said.

Luke didn't sound too convincing, which was unnerving. Tessa left the stage area for a few minutes. When she came back, her eyes were red. All I could do was watch her suffer. I wanted to help her, but it wasn't my place. I was just an obsessive fan to her, and anything I said to her might sound insincere.

"I don't know what to do," I said quietly, mostly to myself. Rosemary offered me a sad smile.

Tessa walked over to me. Well, okay, she walked toward Rosemary, but I was grateful to be standing in the right place at the right time.

"I'm sorry," she said to Rosemary and Luke. "I promise I'll get it together."

"Sweetie, don't be sorry," Rosemary said. To my immense relief, she engulfed Tessa in the hug she so desperately needed. Tessa let out a deep breath as Rosemary squeezed her tight.

"I feel so bad," Tessa said when she finally let go. She glanced over at Zach who was pacing the floor. "Anybody else would have gotten yelled at by the director. I get a pass because of who I am."

"The director doesn't have to yell at you," I said, unable to keep quiet a moment longer. Seeing her in pain was killing me. "You're beating yourself up plenty all by yourself."

Tessa's pretty, blue eyes brightened a bit as she looked at me. I could see how badly she needed reassurance.

"You're doing fine, Tessa. Really. You know the part cold. You just need to quit being so damn hard on yourself."

"We open next week. What if I screw up on opening night?"

It hurt to see the fear in her eyes, but I knew she had nothing to be afraid of.

"You won't," I said loudly and firmly. My ability to be so bold in front of her surprised me, but I wasn't talking to Therese Andrews anymore. This was Tessa. A kindhearted and wonderful woman who was crazy talented but some-times needed reminding of it. "You know what you're doing. You get out on that stage and you *are* Mary. The lady who keeps Captain Samuel in line and doesn't take shit from anybody."

Tears glistened in her eyes, but she laughed.

"I've seen a lot of shows come through here," I continued. "Everybody messes up, Tessa. *Everybody.*"

"Even this close to opening?"

"Yes," I told her honestly. It didn't happen a lot, but it did happen. "I wish you would give yourself a break. At least you don't blame other people when you screw up.

Know what Velma Sikes would do when she flubbed a scene?"

Tessa shook her head as she listened intently to me. This was the longest conversation I'd ever had with her. I loved talking with her, and I was grateful that my pep talk seemed to be helping a bit.

"She would yell at us when she screwed up. One time she screamed at one of my guys for being in her sight line."

"Oh, that's awful," Tessa said sadly. She was a much bigger star than Velma, and she would never do a thing like that.

"Yeah," I said, my fists clenching involuntarily at the memory. Velma's behavior, calling him out in front of the whole cast and crew, had scared and embarrassed the guy—one who was new on the job, too. "But she was the star, so there was nothing I could do about it, you know?"

"Yes, I know," Tessa said softly. She understood the privilege she enjoyed as a star, and yet I'd never seen her exploit it. It wasn't in her nature.

"Just take a few minutes to regroup, and you're gonna be just fine," I said. For once, I wasn't a nervous wreck talking to her. She was vulnerable right now, and all I cared about was making her feel better.

She nodded. "I guess so. I'm tired. I'm just so tired, that's all. I had to be dressed and out of the house at 4am," Tessa said.

"Oh my gosh, that's right!" Rosemary exclaimed. "You had that *Good Morning America* interview this morning. I have it set up to record at home. How did it go?"

"Good, I think," Tessa responded. "Pretty good. I also had that radio interview yesterday, plus I did some pre-recorded segments for a few local New York City news stations. Got more late-night interview shows coming up, too."

"Tessa, I hope you know how much we all appreciate the publicity you're doing for the show," Rosemary said.

"Hell yeah, we do," Luke said with a grin. "It's gonna be a huge help when we open. Even so, we don't want you burning out. Get some rest when we finish up today, okay?"

Tessa smiled weakly and nodded. People often thought that big stars had it made. That their lives were easy. Much as I hated to admit it, there were plenty of times I'd thought that, too. Tessa was the biggest star I'd ever worked with, and she was also one of the most hardworking actresses I'd met. Sure, she got special privileges, like not being yelled at by the director and not getting in trouble when she was late, but she also bore the brunt of the pressure when it came to the show. Luke, at least for now, was an unknown. If he messed up, it wouldn't be a big deal. If Therese Andrews messed up her lines on opening night?

I shuddered to think about it. My God, the entertainment news would go nuts with the headlines. It would be bad for the show, too, and Tessa damn well knew it. Thank God we had such a supportive cast and crew for *Pirated*. We would all help Tessa, and make sure she never felt alone. Together, we would make this show great.

"I will get some rest, Luke. Thank you," Tessa said, hugging him. I felt a bit left out—both Rosemary and Luke got hugs from Tessa.

Tessa glanced over at Rosemary and said, "I don't know what I would do if Jacob was my scene partner. I don't know how you do it."

"No choice, I guess," Rosemary said with a sigh.

"Okay, I just need to review my lines for a quick minute, and then I'll be ready to go," Tessa said.

We all stepped away to give her some space. Rosemary and Luke walked away, but I stuck nearby to keep an eye on Tessa. And a good thing I did. She began searching on tables and chairs around the set, and it soon became obvious she'd misplaced her script again. Tessa frequently misplaced her things, which I found endearing. She was forever losing her water bottle. She left it everywhere, and it had become a running joke. She was careless about where she left her sweater in between scenes and had trouble finding her coat at the end of the day. Tessa was also frequently late. Not super late. Just a few minutes here and there, and she was always apologetic about it. She wasn't a diva star who got off on the power of keeping everyone waiting. She just had trouble getting it together on time.

Our talk had calmed her down, but I could see her stress level rising again. I had to do something. I started looking all over for her script, both because I wanted to help and I wanted to be a hero when I found it for her.

After a few moments of frantic searching on both our parts—though I doubted she knew it was a joint effort—the damn thing was nowhere to be found. Then I suddenly got an idea.

"Hey, Rosemary."

"Yeah?" she said, looking a bit startled to see me rushing up to her. I gestured over to Tessa, who was still hunting around the stage area, lifting up papers and junk to look underneath. "She can't find her script. Could you go check the ladies' room?"

"Oh, sure," Rosemary said, putting down her water bottle. "Definitely."

She ran off to look. My anxiety grew as I watched Tessa look everywhere for the script, and Zach continued to pace the floor. He probably wouldn't call everybody back until Tessa signaled she was ready, but he was clearly getting impatient.

Rosemary emerged, script in hand, just a few seconds later.

"Oh, thank God," I said.

"Here," she said with a knowing smile. "You should give it to her."

"Thanks. Thanks, you are the *best*."

She laughed as I darted away.

"Tessa," I said, holding up the script. "Looking for this?"

"Oh, thank God," Tessa said, blue eyes shining. "Thank you so much. Where was it?"

I hesitated for a moment. "Well, it was in the ladies' room. I mean, I didn't … I wouldn't … Rosemary found it."

"Oh, good. Thank you, thank you, thank you!" With that, she gave me a quick hug before turning away to study the script.

I watched Tessa as discreetly as I could as brow furrowing, lips moving, she reviewed several pages. Then she closed the script, closed her eyes, and took in a few deep breaths. She did that a lot, I'd noticed. I wondered if it was how she got herself in character.

Tessa nodded at the director, and Zach called everybody back to set. To my—and probably everybody else's—immense relief, the rest of the scene went fine.

Next up was my favorite scene in the show—the part where Mary finally has enough of Samuel's waffling back and forth between being a tender lover and a ruthless pirate. She's sick of being held captive and tired of Samuel hiding his affection for her from everybody else. Basically, this was the scene where Mary is done with his bullshit, and she tells him so.

"Enough!" Tessa as Mary roared when Captain Samuel kept sputtering and making excuses about why he couldn't tell the others that he was in love with her. Eyes blazing, she told him off but good. "True love does not hide! True love is not ashamed! It announces itself, loudly and boldly. Love is to be celebrated and shared, not hidden."

Tessa's hands shook with rage and her eyes filled with

tears. This scene always gave me chills. Fully committed to it, she gave it all the passion and emotion she had. Unlike in a movie theater, a live theater audience couldn't really see her tears, but it didn't matter. They would be able to feel her pain and rage and love and despair. She truly was an incredible actress.

"You, sir," she raged on, poking Luke hard in the chest with her finger and nearly knocking him down. "Will not hide me any longer. I see now you made your choice long ago. You chose your men. Your marauding pirate ways. So, I shall leave you to it. Gather your ransom from my father, and then we never shall meet again. Until then, bring me no food or water, for I'd rather die than live in captivity any longer. You cannot gather ransom for a dead woman, so you'd best be quick about it. One way or another, this ends *now.*"

Mary stares defiantly at Samuel, and he gazes back at her with a lovesick look of despair. Just as Mary turns to storm away from him, the other two pirates walk in. Elizabeth and Eleanor also enter to see what all the shouting is about.

Samuel looks at One-Eyed Jack and Captain Graybeard and says in a whiny voice, "I don't wanna be a pirate anymore!"

I remembered the huge laugh Luke had gotten the first time he delivered that line in rehearsal. After nearly two hours of storming around the stage and acting like a ruthless pirate, it was funny to hear him sound like a petulant child.

Samuel turns to Mary and places his hand over his heart. She watches him, cautious hopefulness on her face. He turns back to his fellow pirates.

"I love her. I love her, I love her, I love her, okay?" Samuel shouts. "I love Mary. I hate being a pirate. I want to run away with her and start a family and be happy."

Samuel folds his arms haughtily, waiting for the

inevitable reaction from Jack and Graybeard. They stare at him, literally slack-jawed.

That, too, had gotten huge laughs from us before we'd seen the show a million times.

Samuel finally gets tired of waiting for them to speak. Waving them off, he crosses the stage to Mary.

He takes her hands tenderly in his. Gazing into her eyes, he says, "I love you, Mary. And I want the whole world to know it."

"Oh, Samuel," Mary cries, wrapping her arms around him. They embrace for a moment and then, still hugging, they turn to look at the other pirates.

One-Eyed Jack and Graybeard finally close their mouths after all this time, and One-Eyed Jack crosses the stage to Elizabeth. He takes her hands in his just as Samuel did with Mary.

"And I love Elizabeth. I want to be with her, too."

Samuel and Mary look at the couple, astonished.

"All right!" Samuel says with a grin, eagerly fist-bumping Jack.

From what I understood, Luke had ad-libbed that part as a joke early in rehearsal. It cracked everybody up, so they decided to keep it in the show.

Samuel and Jack turn to look over at Graybeard. The audience knows Graybeard is in love with Eleanor, but the pirates don't know yet. Just as the other pirates did, he makes his way over to see Eleanor, but he's an old guy so it takes forever. Jack and Samuel watch Captain Graybeard slowly hobble over. Jack lets out an audible sigh, and Samuel taps his foot impatiently. Eventually, he shakily takes Eleanor's hands.

"What's going on?" Samuel exclaims in shock.

His voice and expression were so damn funny, as Samuel should have realized what was going on the second the old man started walking over. He certainly had plenty of time to figure it out.

Then, as a perfect capper for the scene, saucy old Graybeard dips Eleanor and plants a huge kiss on her lips. The show ends with the pirates being domesticated and everybody living happily ever after.

We all clapped and cheered loudly, something we had stopped doing weeks ago in rehearsal. It seemed like everybody knew that Tessa and the rest of the cast needed a little encouragement today.

After the applause died down, Tessa looked around, meeting as many eyes as possible.

"Thank you all so much for your patience and your support."

We applauded once more, and it felt good to see her smile again.

* * *

AFTER BRUSHING my teeth and putting on some pajama bottoms, I lay in bed staring at the ceiling. I lived in a tiny apartment in a noisy neighborhood in Little Italy. Trying to tune out the old couple next door arguing in Italian, I thought about the day's events. Even though I was exhausted from the rigors of tech rehearsal, I found it hard to sleep. My mind was spinning like crazy, and I couldn't stop it. As much as I'd tried to deny the truth to myself over the past few weeks, I knew exactly what my problem was.

I was in love with Tessa.

Not the immature, adolescent kind of devotion I'd had for Therese Andrews since I was fifteen years old. This felt completely different. I was in love with the real woman, not the fictional movie star I'd admired from afar all these years. I used to spend hours fantasizing about having sex with her, jerking off and imagining I was pounding her as she screamed my name in ecstasy.

Okay, maybe I still did that. A lot. But more and more I found myself fantasizing about simply being with her. Talking with her. Laughing with her. Comforting her, like I had today. Helping her understand she was doing great, and she should stop being so damn hard on herself.

It felt strange and right at the same time. Being obsessed with an untouchable movie star who I'd never expected to meet was one thing, but loving Tessa was a new and incredible feeling. I'd learned so much about her over these last few weeks. She wasn't completely put together all the time like she was in the movies. Though she was very professional, she sometimes still forgot her lines and messed up the blocking of a scene. Then there was the way she kept losing her water bottle, her script, her coat. One time, she showed up with two different shoes. That gave me a chuckle, though of course I never mentioned her mistake. The shoes were the identical style, but one was brown and one was black. I was probably the only one obsessed with her enough to notice. She made mistakes like that all the time.

In other words, Tessa was human.

There was no question I had idealized her my whole life. Therese Andrews was perfect in my fantasies. Stunningly beautiful, strong and brave with the ability to fend off bad guys, and sensual with the ability to gratify my every sexual need. I understood now there was a difference between Therese Andrews the movie star and Tessa Gumm the person.

Sure, Tessa was messy and disorganized, but she was also hardworking and talented. She was passionate about her work and gave the role of Mary everything she had. Perhaps most importantly, Tessa was kind and compassionate. She was the type of person who cared about everybody and tried to make sure everybody was happy. That was why she didn't think it was funny when Rex tried to embarrass me when we first met. She was forever complimenting people on their work and not just the performers. Tessa took time to talk with the carpenters to tell them how much she adored the set, and she told wardrobe how beautiful she thought all the costumes were. And yes, she even complimented me and my guys on the lighting. Lighting was one of those things that was critical for every performance and yet rarely got any recognition. Tessa was the only performer who had ever mentioned it, as far as I could recall.

Now that I really knew her, it was easy to forget she was *Therese Andrews*, international movie star. To me, she was only Tessa. The talented woman with the warm, inviting smile. The charmingly absent-minded girl who was forever losing her things. The tenderhearted person who lifted others up when they were down and was always ready with a kind word and a gentle hug.

Yes.

I loved her.

I loved her so much.

And there was absolutely nothing I could do about it.

Even though I saw her as sweet Tessa, she was still Therese Andrews. Maybe in fairytales the grungy stable boy wound up with the princess, but this was real life. Ordinary electricians—even ones who worked on Broadway—did not wind up with gorgeous movie stars. She could have any man she wanted, and it was highly doubtful she would ever want me.

As much as I loved the feeling of euphoria whenever I was near Tessa, deep down I felt mostly despair. "Out of my league" did not even begin to describe the situation. She would never see me as the right man for her, even though I had this weird gut feeling she truly was the one for me. I'd never believed there was such a thing as having one true love, a soulmate, until now.

To Tessa, I was still just another fan who was hot and heavy over sexy Therese Andrews. That wasn't the case anymore, but she had no way of knowing it.

Closing my eyes, I pictured Tessa's pretty smile and warm, bright blue eyes. Captain Samuel's words to Mary echoed in my mind as I finally drifted off to sleep.

I love her, I love her, I love her.

CHAPTER 8

Today had been a good one for Tessa. I could tell she was well rested, and she nailed the show straight through. The lighting, on the other hand, was another story.

Technical problems had plagued us all day. There was nothing worse than having to hold up the show on my end, but shit happened, and it couldn't be helped. As stressful as it had been, being near Tessa made me feel better.

As we finally wrapped for the day, I took time to look at her. I'd made a conscientious effort not to stare at her all day, so I figured I'd earned a moment of indulgence. I watched her gather up her belongings, brushing her pretty hair out of her face as she did. I imagined what it would feel like to brush the hair out of her face before I kissed her.

"Jeez, Roman. Give her a break. Quit staring," Rex said, snapping me out of my fantasy. The guy didn't know the meaning of the phrase "indoor voice." He was always so damn loud.

Tessa glanced up briefly at Rex's words. Her eyes met

mine. Bless her kind heart, she turned away quickly, pretending not to have heard.

Heat rushed to my face, both from embarrassment at being called out for staring, and with fury at Rex. I'd never be able to convince Tessa that I was more than a goofy, starstruck fan if Rex kept saying shit like that in front of her.

Slowly, I turned my head to glare at him. If looks could kill, the guy would have been dead and buried. To my surprise, Rex winced and actually seemed remorseful.

"I said that too loud, didn't I?" he said quietly, proving he did have an indoor voice after all. It was too little, too late, though. The damage had been done. Helpless, I watched Tessa walk off the stage to go home. There was nothing I could do to salvage the situation. With a heavy feeling in my heart, I feared she'd never see me as a real man. Just another lovesick fanboy—one of millions of admirers who didn't stand a chance of being with her.

"Sorry, man. I swear I didn't do it on purpose," Rex insisted.

"She already thinks I'm just a crazy fan, you know," I snapped.

Rex had no response to that because he knew it was true. What he didn't know was how badly I was hurting over it. That it was so much more than just feeling stupid and pathetic in front of a famous movie star. Times like this, I almost wished I had never met Tessa in person. Suffering from hopeless, unrequited love was so much worse than harmlessly admiring her from afar.

Les jogged up to me with an apologetic look on his face. "Lycian spotlights are out again."

"Goddammit," I muttered. Those things had been giving me trouble all day. "All right. I'm on it. Thanks."

Rosemary and Luke stood nearby chatting. They stopped talking for a moment to look at me with sympathy. Their pity might have been because of the lighting troubles I was dealing with, or because I'd been humiliated in front of Tessa yet again. I was pretty sure they chalked me up as a fan with a crush on Tessa, too, but they didn't get pleasure out of my discomfort. Sure, they joked about it with me in private, but never when she was around. They did just the opposite, always trying to make me look good in front of her. Like when Rosemary insisted that I be the one to give Tessa her script back.

"Anything we can do to help?" Luke asked, gazing over at the lights that had been misbehaving all day.

"We don't mind sticking around if there's something we can do," Rosemary said.

I grinned at the two of them. "You guys are a hell of a lot different than the last lead actors we had. They wouldn't be caught dead offering assistance to *the help*." I grimaced when I said it, and Luke and Rosemary laughed. "Nah, it's all good. I appreciate the offer, though. Pretty sure I know what the issue is and it shouldn't take long to fix."

"Okay, well a bunch of us are headed over to Squip's to have a few drinks if you want to join us." Rosemary said.

"Ah, I'll see. Maybe. Been kind of a long day, so I might just head on home," I said.

"Come on, man. I'll grab Audra and we'll all go," Rex said. "Lemme buy you a drink."

Wow. He really *was* sorry. Rex was usually a cheap bastard.

"Fine," I said gruffly. I figured I deserved a drink or two after the day I'd had.

"Cool," Rex said, clapping me on the back. It was impossible to stay mad at him. He plucked my nerves sometimes, but he was a good guy. He was like the annoying big brother I'd never had.

It didn't take too long to fix the lights, so I was able to

head over to the bar not too long after the cast did. Luke and Rosemary were sitting at a table near the back. Squip's was a fairly upscale bar with a relatively cozy atmosphere. The place always had at least a dozen craft beers on tap and served a mix of bar appetizers and fancier dinner entrees. There were a few larger tables in the back, which enabled us all to sit together.

"You made it!" Rex said, hoisting his beer glass. He'd left at the same time I did. Leave it to him to get there ahead of me anyway.

"Yeah, yeah, I made it. Now buy me a beer," I said as I plopped into a chair. Rex signaled our server and held up two fingers, and she quickly brought out two more beers. Rex was only halfway finished his first glass, but I guess he wanted a spare one at the ready.

Audra walked into the bar, and I waved her over. She grinned and jogged over to our table.

"God, what a long day," I said after taking a healthy gulp.

"Got that right," Audra said as she slid into a seat next to Rex. She'd had to make a ton of repairs on the set, too. Seemed like nothing had worked right today. Oh, well. Better now than on opening night.

We all bitched about tech rehearsal for a while, and it felt good to commiserate. Wasn't long before the beer kicked in, and I felt pleasantly lightheaded. Drinking a couple of strong microbrews on an empty stomach was just what the doctor ordered.

"You still hate me?" Rex asked, after there was a brief lull in the conversation.

"What'd you do now, Rexy?" Audra asked.

"Called me out for staring at Tessa right in front of her face, that's what," I griped, getting mad all over again.

"Rex, for God's sake, give him a break," Audra said, punching him on the shoulder.

"I was only kiddin' around," Rex said.

My face got hot when I remembered Tessa's quizzical look when she'd heard Rex's comment. God, she must have thought I was pathetic, staring at her like a lovesick teenager. She'd probably never know that my feelings for her were so much more. My anger flared when I remembered how hard I'd worked all day *not* to stare at her, and then the second I did look at her, Rex called me out in front of the whole cast and crew.

"Just knock it off. At least when she's around, okay?" I snapped angrily. "This is hard enough as it is."

"What is?" Rosemary asked.

"Nothing. Forget it," I said glumly, staring blankly at my nearly empty beer.

"You don't have to tell us what's on your mind, Roman," Rosemary said with a sympathetic smile. "But if you do, whatever you say stays here."

Luke nodded, his expression serious for once.

Our server brought us a fresh round of drinks, which gave me a few more seconds to consider whether or not I wanted to spill my guts. I was sorely tempted to unburden myself because I was tired of feeling lonely and helpless. I hadn't known Luke and Rosemary for long, but I could trust them. But it wasn't them I was worried about.

I took a swig of my beer and glared at Rex. "How do I know you won't tell her everything I say? And loud enough for everybody on the damn set to hear?"

Rex seemed genuinely guilty and contrite. Deep down, I knew he hadn't meant to embarrass me in front of Tessa *again*.

"I won't do you like that. You know that. I was just bustin' your balls before. I'll be cool. I promise," Rex said.

I gazed around the table and saw nothing but supportive faces.

"With Tessa, it's not just some stupid celebrity crush. I mean, that's how it started out, but now that I know her, it's so much more than that."

Rosemary nodded and smiled encouragingly. She didn't seem surprised by my confession.

"I really care about her. And I mean the real *her*. She's not just my fantasy movie star crush. Not anymore. She's sweet and kind and, you know, she's this amazing woman."

I stopped short of confessing that I was in love with Tessa. I wasn't *that* drunk, and people would think I was crazy. After all, I'd only known the woman for a few weeks. Still, I wanted people to understand that my feelings for her were real, and teasing me about it in front of Tessa was killing me.

"It just sucks because I finally found this incredible woman I really want to be with, but it's impossible. It's completely hopeless. I have to find a way to accept that and move on with my life." I took another huge gulp of my beer, refusing to look at anyone.

"Why do you think it's hopeless?" Luke asked.

"Are you kidding?" I asked. "Out of my league is putting it mildly. It's like saying I want to date a princess. Tessa is an internationally famous movie star. What in the hell would she want with me? That's the fucked-up thing—"

I glanced at Rosemary apologetically. "Sorry."

She laughed and shrugged. "I live with Johnny Creel. He drops f-bombs on a daily basis."

I grinned at her. "I believe it. I just mean … the messed up thing is I don't *care* that she's a movie star. I really don't. That's not why I'm into her. It used to be. I admit I used to think of her as this perfect goddess from the movies, but I don't anymore. The real Tessa is messy and imperfect and really sweet and nice, and I'm absolutely crazy about her."

Maybe I was tipsier than I'd thought. I was babbling and

should probably shut up, but I couldn't help it. Being around Tessa every day and not being able to tell her how I felt was like having my hands tied behind my back.

"I'm sorry, man," Rex said, his voice filled with regret. "I really didn't know."

"I know you didn't," I said gruffly. "Everybody, especially Tessa, thinks I'm a crazy, obsessed fan."

"I'm sure she doesn't think that," Rosemary said kindly. I got the feeling she was only saying that to be nice. She was good friends with Tessa, and I was half-tempted to ask if Tessa had ever said anything about me. I quickly decided I didn't want to know.

"The whole thing is just nuts. I feel better to finally be able to talk about it, but like I said, I need to figure out how to let it go. Let *her* go."

The deep sadness in my own voice surprised even me. I knew everyone heard it, because nobody spoke for a moment or two.

"You're a good guy, Roman. I don't think the idea of you two together is crazy at all," Rosemary finally said.

"Really?" I figured she was still just being nice, but I found myself clinging to any hope she could offer me.

Rosemary nodded thoughtfully. After another moment of silence, she said, "She's lonely sometimes. It's like because she's famous, she has people around her all the time, but not too many people are close to her."

"You are, though," I said.

"Yes." Rosemary smiled. "Tessa's a good friend of mine. And she could always use more."

I stared at Rosemary. I held my breath, waiting for her to say more. To give me more hope that maybe there was at least a minuscule chance Tessa and I could be together someday.

"You should know she's been badly hurt before," she warned.

"I know." Everybody knew about her awful breakup with Ricky Scrivello.

"No, not just Ricky. She's a bit wary of fans and of getting too close to them. She dated somebody once who couldn't really separate her from her characters, and she was pretty hurt by it."

My heart sank. I felt terrible that she'd been hurt, and I couldn't help wallowing in self-pity. How could I ever convince Tessa I wouldn't be like that other guy? That this time would be different?

"Even so, it's not hopeless. Really," Rosemary said, reaching across the table to squeeze my hand. "I'd have never guessed in a million years I would fall in love with Johnny Creel. I couldn't *stand* him when he was my boss."

That got a laugh from all of us. It was hard to imagine that now.

"But then I got to know him. The *real* Johnny. And I fell in love," she said with a beautiful smile that lit up her pretty face. "Let Tessa get to know the real you. And then see what happens."

I nodded, finally feeling a glimmer of hope.

CHAPTER 9

*R*osemary and I sat in a small room offstage, in between rehearsal scenes. It was fairly cramped backstage, but we'd found this room suited our purposes. Namely, we needed a place with enough space to sit and where we could still hear what was happening onstage, so we wouldn't miss our cues. The room had a few chairs pushed up against all the random stage props on the floor and on tables. This was the longest break we got during the show—first there was a scene with Luke singing about how much he loved my character, then there was a scene with the old couple. It was nice because it gave us a chance to catch our breath.

"Do you have any hand lotion?" I asked Rosemary. "My hands get so dry and cracked during the winter."

"Ugh, mine too. I hate that," Rosemary said, rummaging through her purse. "Here you go."

"Thanks. I had a bottle, but I lost it."

She laughed and nodded. "It's probably somewhere on set hanging out with your water bottle."

I laughed too. "Most likely. Thanks, that feels much better. I hate winter."

"So do I," Rosemary said. She took a drink from her water bottle. "I'm glad I have a minute to talk to you. There's a certain great guy I know who is very interested in you."

"Is that so?" I'd never say it to anyone—not even my closest friend, for fear of sounding like a snob—but it wasn't a big deal to find out a guy was hot for me. It happened all the time. Even then, what they were really interested in was Therese Andrews. Not me.

"Yup," Rosemary said with a smile. "It's not Luke."

"Oh, shut *up*. I know that." I punched her in the shoulder as we both giggled. I still thought Luke was sexy as hell, and I adored his sense of humor, but I'd long ago accepted that his heart belonged to somebody else. Luke talked about Elyse a lot, and it was actually very sweet. He'd told me she was recovering pretty well from her surgery and was back at work. Even though I was a tad jealous of Elyse, I was genuinely looking forward to meeting her at some point.

"Okay, so who is this great guy?"

"Roman Pinza," she said.

"Rosemary!"

"What?" Rosemary asked, her eyes wide.

"Oh, he's so sweet, but talk about a *fanboy*." Roman was a nice guy and quite handsome, but he was in lust with Therese Andrews. Like all the other men who pursued me, or at least fantasized about pursuing me.

"I know, I know. It's true he was definitely infatuated with the movie star part of you at first, but I get the feeling there's more to it than that," Rosemary said.

"I highly doubt it."

"I don't blame you for thinking that. He was starstruck around you when he first met you. We all tease him, and he's been a really good sport about it. But lately, I think it's more than just the fan stuff, you know?"

It was a nice thought in theory, but there was no way it was true. Roman acted like a nervous teenager around me. I tried to put him at ease, to make him more comfortable. He stared at me a lot, and I did my best to pretend not to notice. It was pretty obvious to me that he was still quite starstruck, which was a little surprising since he worked around celebrities all the time. I guess Therese Andrews had always been his favorite, his fantasy woman, and he still thought of me that way. It was nice, but it wouldn't last. It never did.

"He can barely speak to me, Rosemary. I know a fan when I see one."

"Yeah, but something in the way he looks at you makes me think it might be different this time," she said, her green eyes full of thoughtful concern. "I know it sounds strange, but I can't help but feel like you might be missing out on something great if you don't give him a chance."

"You're very kind to be looking out for me." I gave her a grateful smile. She knew how lonely I got sometimes, and she only wanted to help. But there was simply no way that Roman was the answer.

"Will you at least think about it? The ball's totally in your court. I don't think he'll ever make a move on you unless you encourage it."

"Why?"

"He says you're way out of his league. He said having a crush on you is like falling for royalty. Never gonna happen."

"Oh, it's not like that. Really. I appreciate you trying to help, but I can't bear the idea of dating a fan. Those guys, they have no idea what I'm really like. They're in lust with a fantasy. When they get to know the real me, they get disappointed and bored. Then they cheat on me with somebody they find more exciting."

94

I looked down at my hands, feeling tears form behind my eyes.

"Oh, Tessa," Rosemary said sadly.

Still looking down, I said, "As everybody knows, that fan guy cheated on me, too. Just like Ricky did. At this point, I don't know why I even want a man in my life, because I don't see how I could ever trust one again."

"I can't imagine," Rosemary said. "I'm so sorry. I didn't mean to dredge up all these painful memories for you."

I finally lifted my head and met her gaze. "I know you didn't. It's okay. In a way, it helps to talk about it."

"I'm glad."

"My biggest fear is I'll never be enough for anyone. There are thousands of men fawning all over me because I'm famous." I knew in my heart I could confide this to Rosemary, after all. She wouldn't judge. She always seemed to understand what I was trying to say. "They're all hot and heavy for Therese Andrews, but then when they get to know me, I'm not enough. I'll never be enough. How can I be? How can I compete with the woman who spends hours in the makeup chair? The one who has all these crazy special effects and lighting tricks to make me look sexy and exciting? I know I can't measure up to the fantasy. And having two men cheat on me only confirmed it."

I sighed heavily, picturing Roman's gentle, dark brown eyes. Maybe a few years ago I might have fallen for a guy like him, but the older and wiser girl in me knew better.

"Look, it's sweet that Roman has a crush on me. Best to leave it at that. Let him have his crush. He'll get over it once he gets to know the real me."

"Given everything you've been through, I understand exactly why you would think that. But I'm telling you, he doesn't look at you like you're a movie star. And he never talks about your fame. He talks about you. The real you."

"What does he say?"

"That you're sweet and kind. He seems to think it's cute you're so disorganized."

I laughed. "At least someone does. I feel bad about that. I really do. I hate messing things up, especially when it affects other people."

Rosemary gazed at me for a moment.

"What?"

"There's just something about Roman. Something real. I don't know how to explain it. The way he looks at you. The expression on his face when he talks about you. I think he really cares about you, Tessa."

"I guess it's possible," I said. I could hear the doubt in my voice, and I knew Rosemary heard it too.

"Think about it, okay?" Rosemary asked.

"I will. But no promises."

"Fair enough," she said with a smile.

I went back onstage and sang my heart out to Captain Samuel. During the song, I glanced around and saw Roman, but he wasn't looking at me. He was busy working on some complicated wiring thing. I was disappointed for a moment before I realized how ridiculous that was. I wasn't interested in him, and it was stupid of me to expect him to do nothing but pay attention to me all day. Roman had a job to do. An important one, at that. He must be very smart to have gotten the job of head electrician.

I walked past Roman later in the day, and he smiled at me. Perhaps he did seem a bit less nervous around me now. A few weeks ago, he would never have been brave enough to meet my eye and smile like that. He would look away, and he even blushed sometimes. On top of his new boldness, I saw a touch of tenderness in his gaze, so I could sort of see what Rosemary had talked about. He certainly didn't look at me like I was a piece of meat like a lot of my other male fans did. He made me feel valued. Noticed, and not just for my fame.

When I got to the theater the next morning, I went right up to Roman where he stood at the lighting board. I squeezed his shoulder briefly and said, "Good morning, Roman, Roman, Roman."

"Good morning," he responded with a handsome smile. Once again, he didn't shyly turn his gaze. He looked me in the eye when he spoke to me, and he still had that tender expression on his face.

As I walked away, I heard him let out a soft sigh, like it had made him happy that I'd touched him.

How adorable.

I couldn't deny that it felt good when Roman looked at me that way. I found myself noticing him a lot more. Watching him to see if he was watching me. Each time I caught him looking my way, a tingle of excitement went through me. I began to realize Rosemary might be on to something. There really was something different in Roman's gaze, and I wasn't at all sure what to make of it.

I felt a bit guilty about enjoying his attention. Sure, it was an ego boost that such an attractive man had a crush on me, but it couldn't be much fun for him. Rosemary told me he knew there was no future for us, so it wasn't fair to play with his emotions. I wanted to be kind to him, especially since he seemed to love any attention I gave him, but I had to be careful not to hurt him. Surely there was some wonderful woman out there for him, and I hoped he would find her someday. Once he did, he'd forget all about me.

The sudden pang of sadness I felt when picturing Roman with another woman caught me off guard. Why should it bother me if this wonderful, caring man had a girlfriend who returned his affections? Why wouldn't I want him to be happy with someone else?

How selfish I am. To want him to pine over me, even when it's painful.

Roman deserved so much better than me anyway.

Not only was I selfish, I was probably being stupid. Sure, there was a sweetness in the way Roman looked at me, but it was likely because he was a nice guy and fond of me as a friend. No doubt I was making way too much of the whole thing. Lots of fans gazed at me with affection. Plenty of them thought they had genuine feelings for me, but they were mistaken. The best thing I could do was be kind to Roman, but not foster his crush on me. Which meant I needed to quit obsessing over whether he was or wasn't looking at me.

These days, tech rehearsals were running smoothly. It was exciting to see how well a show came together when you have such a terrific cast and crew. The hours were grueling, though, and I looked forward to finally opening. We would perform only once on most days with a couple of matinees during the week. It would still involve a lot of work, but not as bad as rehearsing two or three times every day. *Pirated* would also feel fresh and exciting again once we started performing in front of new crowds every night.

Even as I decided to stop paying close attention to what Roman was doing, I happened to catch him watching me as I sat alone offstage when I wasn't in the scene.

I was taken aback by his expression. He looked at me almost like …

Like Luke looks at me as Captain Samuel. Like he loves me more than life itself.

My stomach tingled and my heart caught in my throat. It was just so unexpected, even though this was exactly what Rosemary had tried to tell me. I had managed to thoroughly convince myself that there was nothing to Roman's feelings for me, but it was hard to rationalize the intense look on his face. Roman seemed a bit startled when I caught him staring, so I smiled at him. He smiled back, his tense shoulders relaxing a little. I casually turned my head to watch Gilbert and Sarah perform their comical scene and kept my expression neutral. My mind spun as I tried to make sense of what I had seen in Roman's eyes.

No one had ever looked at me like that before. Not in real life. Only my leading men in movies and onstage had gazed lovingly at me when they were acting.

It wasn't an act with Roman, because he didn't know I would see him.

Men stared at me with desire all the time. When I walked down the street, when I met actors on a movie set for the first time, production staff when I did TV interviews—I always got the same looks from them. First, it was shock at meeting someone so famous. Then, it was like they ran through all the movie characters I'd played. From flirty girl-next-door types to sultry Roxy Rose. Next, I could almost see them replaying my sex scene from *Roxy Rose* in their head. Sometimes the attention was flattering, other times it felt creepy and gross. Like they were imagining me naked.

Not all fans were like that. There were the nervous, yet sweet type. I gave them a smile or a quick hello, and the smiles I so often got back warmed my heart.

Roman didn't seem like he was either type of fan. He had definitely been the "nervous yet sweet" fan in the beginning, but I was beginning to realize he was neither of those types. I shook my head as if to ward off that thought.

He's still just a fanboy. Don't get carried away. It's Therese he desires, not Tessa.

I could never measure up to the fantasy version of me that he had in his head. The fantasy, according to Rex, that Roman had had of me since he was fifteen years old.

Let him keep his fantasy. He could see me up onstage every night as Mary, dressed in gorgeous gowns and singing and performing. That was far more exciting than seeing me as Tessa at home. When the show's run ended, we would part ways forever, and he would get over whatever misplaced feelings he had—or *thought* he had—for me.

That way, I'd never have to worry if I could trust him, and he'd never have to be disappointed in me.

CHAPTER 10

*A*s we got closer to opening night, it seemed like Tessa was paying more attention to me. It could have been my imagination, or most likely wishful thinking, but she seemed to notice me. She spoke to me a bit more it seemed, but she talked to everybody, so it probably didn't mean anything.

My feelings for her grew stronger day by day, and I started to wonder if maybe a long and successful run of *Pirated* might not be such a great thing after all. Of course, I wanted everyone to succeed. We'd all worked so hard, and we counted on the show to earn a living. But working alongside Tessa for months and months might be too damn painful. What if she started dating somebody during that time? A woman like her couldn't possibly stay single for long. God knows I wanted her to be happy, but it would kill me to have to stand back and watch somebody else with her. It was hard enough watching her pretend to be in love with Luke every day. Thank God for his girlfriend. He talked about Elyse all the time and was obviously very much in love with her.

After work, I headed over to meet with Rosemary and Luke and the others at Squip's for drinks, as we did about once a week. Everybody had been cool about the whole Tessa thing since I'd confessed I had real feelings for her. Even Rex had behaved lately. It was nice to have people who would listen to me whine about my problems now and again, people who were on my side. I didn't think any of us believed a relationship between Tessa and me was possible, but it felt good to have people rooting for it anyway.

I pulled up a chair and sat down, grinning as I saw a beer already waiting for me.

"You guys are the best," I said, looking at Rosemary. It was a safe bet that she'd been the one thoughtful enough to order ahead for me. "Thanks!"

"Oh, you know me," Luke said with a proud grin. "I live to give."

"Thanks, *Rosemary*," I said, hoisting my glass to her. She giggled.

"You know, I actually asked Tessa if she wanted to join us tonight," Rosemary said after taking a sip of her wine.

"Yeah?" I said. Having her hang out with us would be a great way for her to get to know me a little without all the pressure of being alone together. Although, I would *love* to be alone with her, but she might not be crazy about the idea.

"She said she might come out with us sometime, but she was too tired right now," Rosemary said.

"Yeah, she did seem tired today." I'd noticed dark circles under her eyes. She'd also sat down a lot today, which meant she didn't have a ton of energy. The closer we got to opening night, the more publicity she'd been doing for the show. "Probably good she just went home. She works too damn hard. I mean, we all do, but she's so hard on herself."

There were nods from around the table.

"It's also tough for her to go out in public," Rosemary said.

"That, alone, takes a lot of energy because she gets recognized all the time. Makes it hard for her to relax."

I nodded. "I'm sure. People always think celebrities have it so easy because they're rich, but I'm sure it's really hard sometimes. Fans come up to them constantly, night and day, and if you don't greet them with a smile every time, then you're a bitch."

"Oh, I know," Luke said with a toss of his head. "It's tough on us big stars."

We laughed. Luke might be an unknown now, but who knew? Maybe he'd become somewhat famous after *Pirated* debuted, at least among theater fans. He was a cool guy. I hoped he'd go on to have a crazy, successful career.

"That's the thing with Tessa," Luke said, his smile fading. "She can't turn down a fan. Ever. She can't say no when they stop her on the street for a picture, even when she's half-dead from exhaustion."

"Yeah," I said quietly, knowing all too well how hard Tessa pushed herself.

"Do you know she tries to answer a lot of her fan mail herself?" Rosemary shook her head. "Or at least she signs a bunch of autographed photos every day for her assistant to send to as many fans as possible."

Tessa was so sweet. It was one of the many, many reasons I loved her.

I let out a sigh that was so deep, it was more like a groan.

"You okay there, sport?" Luke asked with a knowing grin.

I chuckled. "Yeah, yeah. I don't know. It's just this whole thing with Tessa is as hopeless as ever. I mean, the more I get to know her ..." I trailed off before I could admit too much.

"I know, Roman," Rosemary said gently.

"The more you know about her, the more she means to you. The more you care about her," Audra said softly. She was about my age, but sometimes she was like a mother hen to me. She looked out for me, and she kept Rex in check when he was being a dick. I was in her wedding a few years ago. She loved her husband with all her heart, and she was forever telling me she hoped I would find my dream woman someday.

"Exactly," I said, meeting her sympathetic gaze. I think we both knew I'd found my dream woman, but it wouldn't matter if Tessa never returned my feelings. "I know I need to just let the whole thing go, but I can't. I just can't."

Frustrated and tired of feeling sad all the time, I crumpled up a napkin in my fist. Looking up, I saw nothing but kind expressions. Kind, but a little sad, too.

They know it's hopeless, too. I can see it in their eyes.

As always, it felt good to unload on my poor, patient friends. I'd probably come to regret admitting the truth, but right now, I wanted to share how deep my pain really was.

Out of the corner of my eye, I saw our waitress walking toward the table to refresh our drinks. I didn't care about saying this in front of a stranger. If I didn't confess to my friends now, I never would.

"The problem is, I'm in love with Tessa. Like really, actually in love with her. And I have absolutely no idea what to do about it."

I'd hoped my friends would understand, but everyone at the table had such a look of shock, you'd think I'd just confessed to murder.

I turned my head, and to my utter horror, I realized it wasn't the server standing right next to me.

It was Tessa.

CHAPTER 11

Oh, dear God.

My brain could hardly process the words I was so clearly *not* meant to hear. Then Roman turned to see me, his dark brown eyes wide with horror. Our eyes locked, and there was no possible way I could pretend I hadn't heard him profess his love for me.

Do something! You can be as shocked as you want later, but you have to act now, or Roman will be utterly humiliated.

I switched on my actress face. Yes. I could do this.

Smiling at Roman, I squeezed his shoulder. "Oh Roman, Roman, Roman. You're in love with me like I've been in love with Harrison Ford since I was a little kid. It's all Hollywood magic and nothing more. Believe me, I'm no Roxy Rose in real life. Work with me for a few months, and you'll get over it real quick."

Roman was still frozen in place, clearly not sure what to do or say. As much as I wanted to run, I knew that would only make things worse. I had to stay and have at least one drink. Sit there and act like this was no big deal.

Oh God, how my heart hurt for him. Upon reflection, I

realized all the ways he looked out for me, protecting me, cheering me on when I needed encouragement. He was such a good man. I hated to think what must be going through his mind. His face was a deep red, and he hadn't looked so flustered since the first day we met.

Oh Roman, I'm so sorry.

My eyes darted to Rosemary—her eyes were wide and filled with compassion. Mortified for poor Roman.

Mercifully, our server showed up just then. The young girl gasped and did a double take. She stuttered and stammered for a moment, which I hoped would take some of the pressure and focus off Roman.

"Uhh … um … are you …?" she began.

"She is the one and only Ms. Therese Andrews. But you can refer to her as Your Royal Highness," Luke quipped.

Luke caught my eye, and the unspoken look between us confirmed that he, Rosemary, and I were all on the same page—that we would do everything possible to ease this awkward situation. I just hoped to God Rex would keep his damned mouth shut for once and not make this worse. So help me God, if he said one disparaging word about Roman, I would let him have it. I despised conflict and usually did my best to keep everyone happy, but I couldn't help feeling defensive for Roman. If Rex was mean to him, I'd shut him down quick.

"What can I get you, Miss Andrews?" the server asked.

I looked at Roman, determined to get him to look me in the eye and face me, to get it over with. I wanted to assure him everything was okay. Still red-faced, he wouldn't meet my gaze.

"Roman?" I asked, trying to sound as normal as possible. "Do you like what you're drinking?"

Roman swallowed and forced himself to look at me. "Uh. Yeah. Yeah, I guess so."

"Okay, I'll have the same thing as him," I told the server with a smile. "I can't stay long," I said, addressing the table. "In case you haven't noticed, I'm a total mess when I don't get enough sleep."

Things were still rather quiet and awkward. Nobody knew what to say.

Roman still looked down. I always felt bad when fans were nervous and said silly things around me because I knew they would be filled with regret later. This was so much worse because I knew Roman personally.

"So," I began, determined to keep the ball rolling and get through the next twenty minutes, or however long it would take for me to drink a beer once I got it. "Maybe I'm crazy, but I really think we have something amazing with this show, you know?"

I paused for a moment before continuing. Though I was talking to keep things light, I meant it. "I can't help but be excited about *Pirated*. I'm trying not to get ahead of myself, but it's hard not to get excited about all the possibilities. Like how incredible would it be if this musical went on to be one of the classics, you know what I mean? Like if we had a really long and successful run, and the show would get revived again and again over the years, and we'd all be remembered for being the cast members who originated these roles?"

My stomach tingled with excitement. I'd thought about these things a lot, and it was fun to share my passion with the others.

"I agree it's fun to think about," Rosemary said, her green eyes glittering. "And I know what you mean. You try not to get carried away with your hopes and dreams with the show, but it's hard sometimes."

"You know what I can't stop thinking about?" Luke asked. He sounded semi-serious, but you never knew what was going to come out of his mouth. "The Tony's. I know, I know.

It's crazy. But can you imagine if the show got nominated for a Tony Award?"

Luke's brown eyes lit up at the very idea. He shook his head with wonder.

"Oh, I've imagined it," I said with a giggle. "Believe me."

The server arrived with my beer and I thanked her. I was still eager to get out of there, but I had to play it casual for Roman's sake. Besides, it was nice to talk with my friends, and it had been a while since I'd had a beer. My diet was pretty strict, so indulging in a brew was rare.

"Oh, that is good," I said, relishing the first sip. "Good choice, Roman, Roman, Roman."

He smiled weakly. For a moment, it looked like he was going to say something, and then thought the better of it.

"We have such an amazing cast. And crew, for that matter," I said, making a point to look at Roman, and then at Audra and Rex. I was relieved to see that Rex wore a sympathetic expression. He and Roman seemed to be good friends, and I got the feeling Rex felt a little bad about embarrassing Roman in front of me so many times. Roman was an easy target tonight. It was the perfect opportunity for Rex to tease him mercilessly, but he didn't.

"You're right," Rosemary said. "We all work together so well. I mean, for the *most* part."

Everyone murmured in agreement. We all knew she was referring to Jacob and his bad attitude. He was the one rotten apple among us.

We chatted lightly for a little while, and I savored my beer. Finally, I figured enough time had passed that I could make a graceful exit. I quickly texted my driver to meet me out front.

"Well," I said with a sigh. "This has been fun, but I better call it a night. I'll just settle up and be on my way."

I glanced around for the server. Hopefully, she would

bring my check quickly.

"Oh, I'll get it. Don't worry about it," Rosemary said, shooting me a discreet glance. She knew I needed to get out of there.

"Perfect. Thanks! I'll get yours next time. Goodnight, everybody!"

They all offered me cheerful "Good nights," and I walked out of the place fighting the urge to run.

When I got outside, I peeked briefly back through the window in time to see Roman slam his head, face-first, down onto the table. I saw Luke laugh good-naturedly and squeeze his shoulder and Rosemary lean in to say something.

Oh, poor Roman.

At least his friends were there to cheer him up.

My driver, Ben, was double-parked on the street waiting for me. I quickly opened the side door and climbed into the back of my Lexus RX 350 SUV. Though I could have afforded to take a limo everywhere I went, I preferred something a bit more discreet. The gray SUV was luxurious and comfortable, but it didn't stand out and draw attention to itself like a limo would. The back windows were tinted to hide my identity and to give me some privacy.

"Hi, Ben. Home, please. Thanks."

"You got it." Ben was a cool guy in his twenties, with dark black skin and pretty, dark brown eyes. I'd contacted the NYU theater department when I first bought my house in New York, to see if they could set me up with a recent graduate for a driver. Ben was perfect. He was available most of the time when I needed him, yet he still had the freedom to go to auditions whenever he could. Like everyone who worked for me, he'd signed a non-disclosure agreement and couldn't reveal any details of my personal life to the press or anyone else. He was quiet and kind and, most importantly, trustworthy. Ben knew my habits and routines and was respectful of them. He knew I didn't talk much during rides, and he was cool with it. He also knew he could play whatever music he wanted while he drove with me, so long as it wasn't too loud. Though I'd hate to lose him as my driver, I hoped he would land a great acting gig soon. He deserved it.

Once settled in the backseat, I took out my phone to text Rosemary.

Oh my God , I wrote to her.

I know, came her quick response.

Oh, that poor man. Is he okay? What did he say after I left?

Well …

I bit my lip while I watched the dots squiggle as Rosemary typed a response.

He kinda said if he was lucky a lightning bolt would strike him dead.

I groaned. That poor guy wouldn't ever want to face me again.

Please tell him it's not a big deal! Tell him people say stuff like that all the time and it's okay.

I will. We'll take good care of him. I promise.

I sighed, hoping Roman wouldn't beat himself up too much over this.

The next day, I made sure to seek out Roman first thing in the morning. I didn't want him dreading the idea of running into me all day.

Roman literally winced when he saw me walk onto the stage area. Deliberately making eye contact with him, I smiled. He managed to smile back.

I went over to him and squeezed his shoulder, like I'd done once or twice before. "Good morning, Roman, Roman, Roman."

"Good morning, Tessa," he said, trying to avoid my gaze. He was still so embarrassed.

I was determined to act like nothing had happened, and I

hoped everyone else would do the same. Rosemary and Luke would never blab to the other cast or crew members, but I didn't know Audra and Rex well enough to know for sure what they would do. I doubted they would betray him by spreading gossip, though.

I watched Roman for a moment as he busied himself with work. I could tell he felt awkward and uncomfortable around me now, but I figured that would fade with time. We'd probably be working together for a long time, and yesterday's debacle would soon be forgotten.

I hoped.

I didn't see Roman too much throughout the day as we went through rehearsal. Everything was going well with the production, and it looked like we were more or less ready to go on soon for real.

This was the most exciting, yet scariest thing I'd done in a long time. I hadn't performed before a live audience since *SNL*, and that had been scary enough. Even so, I'd been a professional actress for years. I just hoped I could handle Broadway. I wasn't the only Broadway first-timer in the cast, but Luke was an off-Broadway veteran, and so were many of the others. They'd all worked hard on this show. I hoped I wouldn't let them down.

Today's show was going perfectly. We all hit our marks, and there were no technical glitches. That was, until we got to the ladder scene.

On cue, I ran onto the stage with Luke close on my heels. He grabbed my dress, but I managed to get away from him. Having no way to go but up, I started climbing the ladder to escape him. Luke took a few seconds to look up my skirt. I couldn't see him, but I looked forward to the laughs he would get from the audience when we went live.

"Mary! Get back here!" Luke hollered and then he began shaking the rope ladder to get me to fall.

As I grabbed the highest rung, my hand slipped and I began to fall before I was ready. To my horror, I realized I was falling on the opposite side of where I was supposed to land.

Where there was no one waiting to catch me.

I screamed as I plummeted to the ground. It wasn't the dainty, damsel-in-distress cry I usually let out. This was a scream of real terror, and anyone within earshot would know something had gone terribly wrong.

I didn't even remember landing. I must have blacked out for at least a few seconds when my body hit the ground. When I opened my eyes, I saw that Roman had gotten to my side even before Luke had.

Roman hunched over me, his eyes wide with terror.

"Tessa. *Tessa!*" Roman yelled.

Yes, I must have blacked out, because Roman was yelling my name as if trying to wake me up.

I was dimly aware of the hushed crowd that had gathered around me. Two pairs of brown eyes stared at me with concern. Luke's light brown eyes as he knelt beside me, and Roman's dark brown ones as he slipped an arm underneath my neck and back to shield me from the floor. I felt cloth underneath my body and realized I'd landed partially on the thin mattress where Jacob's character sat with Elizabeth. Thank God I hadn't landed directly on the hardwood floor.

Luke's eyes had the look of a man who was worried about his friend, but Roman's eyes … there was something so different in the way he looked at me.

My eyes locked on his, and I was struck by the strangest realization—more of a feeling than a thought.

He really does love me.

Time stopped for a moment as I stared into his eyes. Roman's gaze held a softness, a tenderness, mixed in with his fear. Like he was looking right into my soul. Past all the glitz and glamour of Hollywood, and straight through to the real me. Like he was looking at Tessa Gumm from Minnesota. And he was looking at her like he was in love with her. Like he was terrified of losing her.

Roman looked so terrorized, that I was desperate to set his mind at ease.

At first, I couldn't speak. I didn't think I was badly hurt. I could still feel my legs, and my back was starting to hurt, but I was more or less okay. But I struggled to get the words out.

"I—I'm oh—oh—okay. I just … got the … wind … knocked out of me," I finally managed to say.

Roman's face relaxed a bit. I started to sit up.

"Easy, easy," Roman said as he carefully helped me move to a sitting position. Rosemary rushed over with a bottle of water.

"Here, try some cold water," she said, her eyes full of worry. "Might help clear your head a little."

I nodded, weakly reaching for the bottle. Roman took hold of it and helped hold it to my lips. Our eyes locked again as I drank the water. The tenderness in his gaze made my eyes tear up. No one had ever looked at me with such concern before, and it felt good to know that somebody cared. He wasn't looking at me like he was afraid of what would happen to the production if the biggest "name" on the cast got injured. Roman just wanted me to be okay.

"Thanks," I said to Roman as I set the bottle of water down.

I started to try to get up, and Roman put his arm around my back and helped me to my feet. I was a little wobbly, but I took a few steps. I heard sighs of relief all around me.

"I'm all right," I assured everyone. I was grateful for Roman's hand on my back.

"Tessa," Luke said. "I am so, so sorry. I must have shaken the ladder too hard."

"No, Luke. This wasn't your fault," I assured him. "Not at all. It was mine. I put too much hand lotion on my hands before I climbed the ladder, and I just slipped. You didn't do anything wrong. It was all me."

"Are you okay?" Luke asked, his eyes filled with concern.

"Yes, I'll be fine. Really. All I need is a few minutes, and I'll be ready to do the stunt again."

"I don't think that's such a good idea," Roman said. "You need to take it easy for a while."

I smiled wearily at him. "I can't do that. We start previews in a few days. I have to make sure I get this right *now*."

Previews were kind of like soft opening nights. For the first few nights we went live, some of the major news and media outlets would come and see the show. TV critics, some talk show people, newspapers, and some bloggers. Then, after our official opening night next week, all the reviews would be released.

This was *not* the time for me to be screwing up. Tears prickled the corner of my eyes. What if something like this happened when we were live? It would ruin the show. And it would be all my fault.

"We have to run through the scene again. Now. Luke, you do exactly what you did before. It has to look real, like you're deliberately trying to get me to fall. Let's do it again."

Roman opened his mouth to protest, but the director beat him to it.

"No, no, no, no," Zach said. "First, we're gonna get you checked out and make sure you're all right. Second, we gotta fill out an accident report. Union rules."

Tears dripped from my eyes. I couldn't help it. How could I have been so stupid? So careless? The entire production would be held up because of me.

"I'm sorry," I managed to say as I wiped my eyes.

"Don't be sorry, Tess," Zach said. "Accidents happen. All

that matters is that you're okay."

I still felt horrible, and I found myself looking up at Roman because seeing him would bring me comfort. It did. He smiled sadly at me, and a warm feeling washed over me. Somehow, I felt safe with him around. He still cared about me, even though I'd done something totally stupid. I got the impression he wanted to hug me, but he didn't make a move.

"Tessa, it's okay," Luke said. He did give me a warm hug, and I was grateful. His embrace made my back hurt, but I didn't care. I needed a friend's touch. "Get checked out and take a break for a bit. It's all gonna be okay."

"Thanks, Luke," I said, then finally let go of him.

At Zach's insistence, I got checked out by a doctor who came to the set to see me. After that, I went to my dressing room to rest for a little while. I'd made it clear that I would not go home until we'd performed the ladder scene again. When we first practiced the stunt, I'd had to learn to trust that Luke would catch me. Now, I had to get him to trust *me*. That I would hold on and not fall down before he was ready. That I wouldn't act like a complete idiot again.

As I lay down, I closed my eyes and thought of Roman. After recovering from my initial shock from my accident, I realized how crazy it was that I'd thought, even for a moment, that he was really in love with me. The mere idea was insane. Roman had been a big fan of Therese Andrews since he was a teenager, and now that he knew me in person and had found out that I was a reasonably nice person, he had a silly crush on me. That was all. He was a nice guy who didn't want to see anyone get hurt.

Still …

I knew I would never forget the way he looked at me when he was holding me in his arms after I fell. I wrapped my arms around myself, reveling in the warmth and comfort I felt just thinking about his kind face.

CHAPTER 12

uck it.

When Tessa overheard me professing my love for her publicly like a fucking moron, I was so humiliated I thought I'd never be able to look her in the eye again. My plan was to avoid her as much as possible for the rest of the production's run. Keep my head down and focus on my job.

Then, she'd had that terrifying accident on set.

I knew I'd never forget the sound of her scream, the way she looked lying on the stage floor when she hit the ground. My God, she could have been paralyzed. She could have *died.*

Yeah. Fuck it. Life was too short for me to hide my feelings for Tessa. She already knew anyway, so what was the point? She'd never love me back, but I would learn to live with that. I only knew I was done trying to pretend I wasn't completely and utterly in love with her.

I kept a close eye on her when she returned to the set after her doctor's visit and after a nice, long rest. I needed to look out for her because she never looked out for herself. Tessa always worried about everybody else. Nobody could know for sure how badly she was hurt. Knowing her, she'd walk around the set in agony and not say a word about it.

Tessa seemed a bit tired when she got back to the stage area, but that was to be expected. I felt a flicker of shame and humiliation when I looked at her, but I pushed past it and walked right up to her.

"Are you okay?" I asked her.

Tessa graced me with the prettiest smile I'd ever seen. "Yes, I'm fine, Roman, Roman, Roman. Thanks for asking. I just need to get through this stunt again."

"Are you sure that's such a good idea?" I asked. "Are you still in a lot of pain?"

"Well, not a lot of pain. I'm pretty sore, but nothing I can't handle. Don't you worry about me."

"I can't help it. I *am* worried about you," I said. "I always worry about you."

"Oh Roman," Tessa said, putting a hand on my shoulder and looking me right in the eye. "You're so sweet. Thank you for looking out for me. I really appreciate it."

Her eyes lingered on my face for a moment, sending a thrill straight up my spine. God, I loved when she looked at me like that. I already felt less self-conscious about the whole thing. Tessa had that way about her. She made everybody feel comfortable around her.

Tessa walked up to Zach and said, "Okay, I want to run through the ladder scene three times, straight through."

"Tes—" Zach tried to argue.

She put her hand on his mouth to stop him. "Look, if we were earlier in the rehearsal, this wouldn't be such a big deal, but we don't have any time to play around. We need to make sure we get this right. Knowing Luke, he'll be afraid he's gonna hurt me, so I have to get him comfortable with shaking the ladder again. Come on. Let's do it."

Zach nodded, looking a bit surprised. Tessa was rarely

this direct about what she wanted, even though she was such a big star; she could have called the shots all day long if she'd wanted to. Zach looked reluctant to jump right back into the stunt, but he knew Tessa was right. There was no time to drag this out.

We all held our breath as Tessa and Luke ran through the scene they'd done perfectly dozens of times before. This time, it was as scary as the first time they'd practiced on a real stage. At least, it was for me. Luke shook the ladder as instructed, and Tessa tumbled down safely into his arms.

I let out my breath when Luke caught her, but my stomach clenched when I saw her wince. Her back must have been pretty bruised up. It was awful to watch Tessa go through the stunt three times, but we all knew there was no talking her out of it. As always, she put the needs of the production above her own.

"It hurts when I catch you, doesn't it?" Luke asked sadly when they finally finished the third run-through.

"A little." It was an understatement. "But I'll be fine. Don't worry. I promise not to wince when we're live. Besides, I'll probably be a hundred percent by then anyway," she said with a dismissive wave of her hand.

Luke didn't look any more convinced than I was. At least Tessa could rest for a few minutes because she wasn't in the next scene. I watched as she wandered around backstage, holding her back with her hand. I couldn't help but chuckle to myself when I saw her searching for something. That girl was forever losing her stuff. Tessa finally found the bottle of pain medication the doctor must have given her. She held the bottle in her hand, but she was still looking for something else.

Chuckling again, I spied her familiar pink water bottle under one of the prop tables off to the side. I grabbed it and quickly walked over to her.

"Looking for this?" I asked.

Tessa giggled when she saw it. "Yes. Thank you."

She took the water from me and swallowed two pain pills with it. Then, she gingerly eased herself into a chair, and I sat down in one across from her.

"How are you feeling?" I asked, figuring she probably wouldn't tell me the truth.

"Oh, I'm fine. The pain pills really help."

"You just took them two seconds ago."

Tessa smiled. "I'm okay. Really."

"Don't push yourself too hard, okay?"

"I won't," she said with a grateful smile. She seemed to feel better to know somebody cared. I loved talking to her instead of hiding from her.

As I watched Rosemary and Jacob perform their scene, I figured I should probably get up and go back to work, but I couldn't. I was so happy to be near Tessa. It was probably more wishful thinking, but it almost felt like she was glad to be near me, too.

Then again, maybe not. Probably not. Probably just felt good for her to finally sit down and rest a bit.

The scene between Rosemary and Jacob seemed to be going fine until Jacob angrily broke character in the middle of it.

"God, I hate the way you do this scene," Jacob grumbled at Rosemary.

Rosemary winced and backed away as if he'd struck her.

"What? What do you mean?" she asked.

"You keep pacing back and forth when you're talking. It'll block the view of the audience."

"It's part of her character," Zach said. "Elizabeth paces when she's nervous or upset."

"But, it's not part of the script," Jacob fired back.

"It's a character choice!" Tessa snapped angrily. She rarely got angry, but Rosemary was her friend, and we'd all had enough of Jacob's attitude already.

Rosemary shot Tessa a look of weary gratitude, and Tessa smiled at her with sympathy. Tessa turned to look at me, and we shared a look of disgust over Jacob's behavior.

"The real problem is you, Jacob," the director said. "You're supposed to be in love with her, and lately you've just been looking annoyed with her. When she paces, I think you should try to follow her around," Zach suggested.

"What?" Jacob asked with a grimace.

"Yeah, I think that actually might be funny," Luke offered, trying to defuse the situation a bit. He was friends with both of them, but he knew damn well Jacob was in the wrong for treating his leading lady so rudely.

"Just give it a try, Jacob," Zach said.

"It's a little late to make blocking changes!"

"You brought it up," Zach said with an edge in his voice. "Try it. When she starts pacing, follow behind her. Then when she turns around, act like you weren't trying to follow her. And maybe struggle with your eyepatch again."

Jacob sighed irritably. We all watched as Jacob and Rosemary ran through the scene again, and it turned out to be goddamn hilarious. Rosemary wrung her hands and paced nervously while Jacob followed close on her heels. When she spun around to face him, Jacob stopped short, his one eye open wide. He put his hands behind his back and gave a quick whistle, exaggeratedly pretending he hadn't been following her. Next time she stopped pacing, he fumbled with his patch, once again forgetting which eye it was supposed to cover. As mad as we all were at Jacob, we all laughed.

I saw a tiny glint of grudging amusement in Jacob's eyes. This small change would get him more laughs, and he damn well knew it.

"God, if he would quit being such an ass and work with Rosemary, everything would be fine," I grumbled.

"You got that right," Tessa agreed.

The director worked with Rosemary and Jacob for a few minutes, giving me more precious time with Tessa. I gazed over at her as she sipped her water and watched Zach give directions. It surprised me how comfortable I felt sitting here with her. When I first met her, I'd been so nervous and tongue-tied at meeting Therese Andrews, I thought I'd never be able to speak to her coherently. And then, after I'd gotten to know her, not to mention fallen in love with her, I'd made such a complete fool of myself that I'd figured I'd never be comfortable around her again. Yet, here I was sitting close to her, relishing every moment.

"So, are you ready for previews?" I asked her.

Tessa looked over at me and smiled, but she didn't answer right away. In fact, she took so long to respond that I thought she might not have heard my question.

"I'm scared," she said softly.

"Why?"

She paused again, and then said, "I'm excited, but I still feel out of my element. Everyone else here is a theater veteran. Even if some of them haven't been on Broadway, they do theater all the time. I guess it's just different than what I'm used to. In the movies, you can redo the scene over and over again until you get it right. In theater, you have one shot, especially in front of the critics."

I was going to say something supportive, but I got the feeling there was more she wanted to say. Tessa watched Rosemary and Jacob for a moment and then turned back to me.

"Falling off that ladder was such a nightmare," Tessa said, with fear in her pretty blue eyes.

"For all of us," I said, mentally reliving how scary it had been.

"Thank you for helping me, Roman. It was such a comfort to have you there with me after I fell."

"Glad I could help."

Tessa sighed sadly. "It wasn't just getting hurt that was scary. I've literally had nightmares about something like that happening during the show. Me screwing something up and ruining the show for everybody."

"Sounds to me like you're psyching yourself out." As always, she blamed herself for anything that went wrong. It was awful that she felt the ladder accident had been her fault.

"Yeah, I tend to do that sometimes. There are lots of people hoping for me to fail, and I'd hate to prove them right."

"Why would anybody want you to fail? Everybody loves you!" Too late, I realized what a stupid thing I'd said. It would undoubtedly remind her I had confessed to loving her. My face got hot, but I tried to ignore it.

"The cast and crew have all been wonderful," Tessa said. She never looked away, and my face got hotter. If she noticed I was blushing, she was doing a good job of pretending she didn't. "Nobody here wants me to fail. Like anybody famous, I have my share of haters who would love to see me fall flat on my face. I try to stay away from social media, but it's hard when it's everywhere."

My chest hurt when I saw the pain in her eyes. Was there anything more cowardly than those idiot online trolls who posted nasty comments about celebrities, without using their real names? People like that didn't understand that celebrities were real people with real feelings. I always said if you wouldn't say something right to someone's face, you shouldn't post it online.

"That sucks," I said, unable to think of anything more eloquent. "I get why that stresses you out."

"I'm also not used to performing live anymore. It's been so long since I've done any theater. Not since college. I guess I'm nervous about what will happen when I step out onstage for the first time with a full house." Tessa gazed apprehensively out at the empty seats.

"You did *Saturday Night Live* fairly recently, right?"

She nodded.

"What happened when you walked out onstage in front of the camera to do your live monologue?"

Tessa smiled.

"Ah, see?" I jabbed a finger at her. "You smiled. What happened when you walked out?"

Tessa laughed. It was such a pretty, light sound. I was happy and proud that I'd managed to make her laugh.

"As soon as I got started, I forgot to be nervous. I just dove in and did my monologue, and people laughed. The rest of the show was amazing. It was crazy and hectic and so much fun. It went by so fast, I was sad when it was over."

She smiled again at the memory.

"The same thing's gonna happen here. I guarantee it. When my stage light hits you," I said with a grin, "you'll forget to be worried. You're an incredible actress, Tessa, and you know what you're doing."

Tessa sat up in her chair, leaning toward me a little. I could see how much she wanted to believe what I was telling her.

"But this is *Broadway*. Acting and singing and performing live. I'm not used to all that."

"Yeah, but it's still the same craft. I know the singing part is kinda new to you, but you've got an incredible voice. You've probably done voice lessons, and you have a voice coach, right?" She nodded. "I can tell. You sound great, and

I'm not just saying that. I've worked on Broadway for years, and I know what I'm talking about. You're gonna surprise a lot of people, Tessa, because you're gonna blow them all away. Haters can hate all they want, 'cause they're gonna have another reason to be jealous. You're not just beautiful and a good actress, but you can sing, too, so they can just *suck it!*"

I hadn't meant to ramble on like that, but I wasn't sorry. I meant every word. I would have said it even if I wasn't in love with Tessa, because it happened to be the truth.

She fell silent for a moment. I glanced over at the stage, then back at her. "You got this, Tessa. You really do. This is what you know. Yeah, it's a different venue, but this is where you shine. When you're acting, you *become* the character so completely, no matter what the role. You *are* Mary when you're onstage."

"Roman!" Rex yelled. "Les needs you. I don't wanna say he broke something … but he broke something."

I stifled a groan.

"Sorry. I gotta go," I said as I stood. I wanted to pummel Les for tearing me away from Tessa.

"It's okay," she said.

I turned to her before I left, and said, "I believe in you, Tessa. It's time you started believing in yourself."

She looked up at me with those lovely blue eyes and said, "Thank you, Roman. For everything."

"Anytime," I said with a smile.

CHAPTER 13

The time had finally come. Tonight, we would step out onstage and perform live for the audience. Entertainment critics, bloggers, and regular people would be in the audience for this first of several nights of previews.

I'd known I would be nervous, but I hadn't expected to be this terrified.

Dressed and ready in a sweeping, medieval-type gown, I took a deep breath and tried to center myself before I walked onstage. I recalled Roman's sage words: *You're not just beautiful and a good actress, but you can sing, too, so they can just suck it!*

I bit my lip to stifle a giggle, and the queasiness in my stomach eased a bit. I thought about the other things he'd said—that this was my craft and it was what I knew, how I became my characters, how my fears would go away as soon as I got started.

I believe in you. It's time you started believing in yourself.

Roman's voice in my head sounded as clearly as if he were standing right beside me.

Deep in my heart, I knew he was right. It was time to show the world what I could do.

Look out Broadway. Here I come.

Drawing in a breath, I stepped out onto the stage.

* * *

STANDING AT THE LIGHTING BOARD, my breath caught in my throat as I watched Tessa step onstage. I'd caught sight of her a few minutes ago, and she'd looked terrified. She was a terrific actress, capable of fucking nailing this show, but she was also capable of psyching herself out completely. My stomach clenched when I thought of that day when she kept forgetting her lines. Worse than that, the awful ladder accident. Tessa would never, ever forgive herself if she wasn't perfect tonight.

"Just what do you think you're doing?" Tessa, as Mary, asked Captain Samuel angrily.

"Ah, um, I'm trying to, you know, kidnap you. For ransom. I'm a pirate. Kinda … what I do," Luke/Captain Samuel said, getting the show's first big laugh.

"Well, you're doing it quite poorly," Mary replied haughtily. My anxiety abated a bit when Tessa got her first laugh. I scrutinized her face—she seemed to be doing perfectly fine, no trace of the terror I'd seen in her earlier. Swallowing hard, I forced myself to focus on my lighting board. I was worried about her messing up, but I had an important job to do, too. After all, nobody paid much attention to the lights until something went wrong.

As I looked down and focused on my work, Mary launched into her song about what an idiot she thought Captain Samuel was. The song was humorous, yet it still sent delicious chills down my back when I heard Tessa's gorgeous singing voice. I found myself grinning as I listened to her.

I told you that you were gonna surprise a lot of people.

All my lighting and electronic work went smoothly for the most part, and I was happy and excited as the show hummed along. It was always such a thrill when a show you've worked so hard on went live. It was like seeing it for the first time. It was fun hearing the audience laugh at the parts of the show that the cast and crew had all laughed at so much earlier in rehearsal. Sometimes we forgot how entertaining a show really was until we heard the audience laugh or gasp or cry at the parts that the cast and crew had all reacted to, so much earlier in rehearsal.

I was pretty relaxed and happy until we got to the ladder scene. I held my breath as I watched Tessa rapidly climb the rope. Luke got a laugh when he looked up her skirts, then he started shaking the ladder.

The audience gasped when Tessa fell, unsure if it was part of the show. She came tumbling down into Luke's waiting arms, and all was right with my world again.

Tessa got a big laugh when she ordered Luke to put her down. I grinned.

Audra caught my eye and gave me a knowing smile. "She's doin' great, Roman."

"Yeah. Yeah, she sure is."

Though it was kind of embarrassing that everyone on the damn set was aware of my feelings for Tessa, in a weird way it was also kind of nice. I was proud of Tessa, and I wasn't ashamed of loving her.

The critics would have the final say when they released their reviews in a few days, but as far as I could tell, the first live performance was a smashing success. Tessa gave a terrific performance, as did the rest of the cast. Everybody hit all the marks, and most of the funny parts got the laughs we'd all hoped for.

"Brava," I whispered as I watched Tessa take her final bow

with the cast. Rex chuckled when he heard that. I hadn't even realized he'd sidled up to me.

"Your girl did great," Rex said, punching me just a little too hard in the shoulder.

My girl.

Even though it wasn't true, I still loved the sound of it. My chest ached with longing as I thought how wonderful it would be if she were mine. When she walked offstage, I could hug her and kiss her and tell her how proud I was of her. How she'd nailed her performance like I knew she would. Nothing was stopping me from saying those things now, without the kissing and hugging, of course. But if I were her boyfriend, I could show my affection for her openly. God, I would be so honored to be her man, and not just because she was a famous movie star. She was such a dynamic woman. People were starstruck when they first met her because of her fame, but they stayed drawn to her because she literally had an attractive personality. She had a way of making people feel good about themselves—always had a kind word to say about everyone. And even though she was one of the most famous actresses in the country, if not the world, she had a way of talking to people like they were every bit as important as she was.

The cast walked offstage after receiving a huge standing ovation. Once the curtain closed, Tessa and Rosemary grabbed each other, hugging and squealing with excitement. Next, Tessa grabbed Luke and they embraced warmly.

"You were so great tonight, Tessa. Just perfect," Luke said.

A sharp bolt of jealousy raced painfully through my body. God, I would give everything I owned in this life if I could have traded places with Luke. I desperately wanted to be the one holding her in my arms and telling her how incredible she was. More than anything, I wanted to brush her hair aside and whisper "I love you," right in her ear.

Christ, when did I become such a sap?

I'd never thought of myself as the romantic type, but somehow Tessa brought it out in me. Not that it mattered—I was stuck having to repress all my mushy-gushy feelings around her. I'd already said way too much.

"We should all go out tonight to celebrate!" Tessa exclaimed, her bright blue eyes flashing with joy. "I'm so hyped up, I won't be able to sleep anyway. Let's all go out to Squip's. Cast, crew, everybody. My treat!"

Wow. Even though Squip's was where I'd managed to thoroughly humiliate myself in front of Tessa last time, the idea of spending the evening with her thrilled me. She was so happy, and I wanted to be near her now more than ever.

"Nice!" Luke said. "Thanks, girl."

Fuck.

Of course, Luke should be there. He was her co-star. Not only did he get to put his piratey hands all over her night after night, but the leading man and leading lady often enjoyed a special bond. They'd probably sit next to each other at the bar and tell inside jokes all night about the actor life.

I briefly considered not going, but staying away from Tessa would be even more painful.

"I can fit about four or five people in my SUV when my driver comes to get me. Who wants to come with me?"

There were more than half a dozen takers before I could even open my mouth. Not that it mattered anyway. The cast could leave as soon as they got out of their costumes, but the crew had more work to do after the show. I'd get there later than the actors, so there was no way I could sit anywhere near Tessa.

"Okay, I'll text my driver, and he'll be waiting outside in just a little bit," Tessa said. "I just gotta get out of this dress."

I swallowed hard. Thinking about her in her dressing

room, taking off her clothes, got me ridiculously hot. I drew in a deep breath, knowing I needed to focus on my work. After all, the sooner I got everything shut down, the sooner I could head over to the bar and be with Tessa. Well, at least be near Tessa. My heart sank. I would probably wind up seated as far away from her as possible, since I'd be among the last to arrive, no matter how quickly I wrapped up my work.

"Oh, and I want to take just a few minutes to greet the fans waiting outside the stage door," Tessa said. "And then I'll be right out. I promise."

"Is that safe for you to do?" Luke asked before I could ask the same thing. It wasn't uncommon for Broadway stars to greet their fans out back, but we'd never had anyone as famous as Tessa here before.

"Yeah, I'll be fine. My bodyguard will be out there. He keeps a close eye on everything."

God, I hope so.

It still sounded dangerous to me, but I knew how devoted Tessa was to her fans. She couldn't bear to disappoint them, and any bodyguard, publicist, or manager who tried to talk her out of seeing her fans was fighting a losing battle. I smiled to think of how excited those fans would be to meet Therese Andrews.

* * *

As I'd expected, Squip's was packed by the time me and Audra and Rex and the other guys got there. Tessa was seated at the head of one of the long tables, as she should be. Most of the crew got stuck way in the back.

"Hey, I'm so glad you guys made it," Tessa said, greeting us when we arrived. "We saved you a bunch of seats."

"Thanks," I said, meeting her gaze and giving her a warm smile before beginning my trek to the back of the room. It was nice of her to save seats for us. Might not sound like a big deal, but the crew often got forgotten in situations like this. Tessa never treated us like second-class citizens. Neither did Luke nor Rosemary, for that matter. Yeah, we definitely had a great group this time around.

"Order anything you want," Tessa shouted over toward us, in order to be heard. Everybody in the place had turned to watch our group. The news had clearly spread that Therese Andrews was in the house. None of the other patrons came over to bother her, and I wondered if the staff were making an effort to keep people away. I spotted a huge, burly guy standing against the wall, eying up the place. Maybe that was Tessa's bodyguard.

Tessa watched us carefully, waiting until all the crew members had gotten their drinks, before addressing us all.

"Thank you all for coming out tonight," Tessa began, and a hush fell over the people gathered at our table. "As everybody here is aware, we won't know what the critics thought of our show until all the previews are done and we have our official opening night."

Slightly worried nods from around the table. It was a fact of life in the entertainment business that critics ruled our world. No matter what real people—real audience members thought, in the end it was the critics who pretty much determined the success or failure of a show. People like to claim they don't listen to critics, but they do. I'd worked on shows where the audiences had howled with laughter, but after reviews came out pronouncing the show "humorless" and "silly," the laughs stopped the very next night. It was crazy.

"Right now, none of those reviews matter," Tessa said, seemingly able to make eye contact with each one of us as she spoke from her heart. "Tonight was so wonderful, so perfect. I'm so proud of the work we did. We put on an amazing show."

Smiles and murmurs of agreement came from our cozy group huddled together.

"Everyone sang beautifully," Tessa said, taking a moment to look at each actor individually. "I managed to jump off the ladder without killing myself."

People laughed at that, and I let out a sigh of relief as I remembered how perfectly she and Luke had performed the stunt.

"The lighting," she said, looking directly at me and making my heart pound against my ribcage, "and all the set changes were smooth and perfect. Tonight was nothing short of magical."

A lump formed in my throat when I heard the catch of emotion in Tessa's voice. The entire bar was quiet except for the sound of her sweet voice. Strangers in the bar were starstruck by her, of course, hardly believing they were seeing someone famous in real life. The rest of us had stopped being starstruck by her weeks ago, but we were still spellbound by her because of who she was inside.

"I want you all to take just a moment and enjoy how you feel right now. I hope it's the same way I feel. Excited and proud and so happy to be among such an incredibly talented group of people. No matter what happens in the future with this show, with the reviews and ticket sales and all that, I want you all to remember that, if nothing else, we had this one perfect night together."

Tessa's eyes filled with tears, which made several other people tear up, too. I may or may not have been one of them. Had it been anyone else speaking, I doubt I'd have been quite as moved. As always, Tessa had a way of turning my insides into utter mush.

She lifted her glass, and we all did the same. "To the show, to pirates, and to a job very well done. To *us*!"

"To us!" we all said, clinking our glasses. I'd never felt

more proud to be part of a group in my life. I sat staring at Tessa adoringly from afar. Rosemary managed to catch my eye, and she shot me a knowing smile. It was nice to have Rosemary in my corner when it came to Tessa.

I spent the rest of the night glancing at Tessa from a distance any chance I got. I fantasized about what it would be like to be her boyfriend, getting the seat of honor right next to her. I wouldn't care if she got all the attention all night—I liked it that way. I loved to see her shine when she was around people. I fantasized about going home with her afterward, and it wasn't a sexual fantasy, either. Instead, it would just be the two of us. After being "on" all night—being her glamorous movie star self—we'd go home and she could simply be Tessa with me. We would cuddle on the couch or even fall asleep together in bed. The world was in love with Therese Andrews, but I would be the man who was in love with Tessa.

It was stupid. But I couldn't let go of that fantasy. It felt so right.

And yet, I knew I would go home alone tonight.

Somehow, it made me sadder to think of Tessa going home alone.

CHAPTER 14

*O*pening night had finally arrived. All our previews had gone quite well as far as I could tell, but I knew from experience that didn't always mean anything. I had several movie openings where I thought the film would do great, only to find the reviews were mediocre at best. Word-of-mouth was critical for any movie, television, or theatrical show, and unfortunately, it all started with the critics publishing their reviews. For Broadway, the most vital review came from the *New York Times*. A glowing review would do wonders for our show, a mediocre one would be bad, but not necessarily the kiss of death, but a bad review could mean the show could close in weeks, or even days. The prospect of the show ending like that after all our hard work was heartbreaking.

I drew in a deep breath, reminding myself that critical reviews were out of my control. All I could do was go out there and give the best performance I knew how to give. And that's what I would do.

"Okay, everyone!" I said backstage. Everyone within

earshot turned to look at me. "Real quick, everybody come here."

Cast and crew members gathered around me.

"Okay, grab somebody's hand and let's form a circle," I said. As it turned out, the hand I grabbed was Roman's. He smiled at me, and my nervousness calmed a bit.

Once the circle was complete, I said, "Everybody, take a deep breath." People did as I instructed. "I know how hard each and every one of us has worked to make this show as wonderful as possible. From the incredible off-Broadway cast who did such an amazing job that the show got transferred to Broadway, to the incredible cast we have now, and the amazing crew who keeps us all safe and keeps everything running smoothly. There's no guarantee what will happen after tonight when the reviews come out, but never forget, we're all in this together. We're one big family here ..."

My voice hitched a bit with emotion, and Roman squeezed my hand in support.

He's such a dear man.

"And all that matters is that we give this show everything we have tonight. I love you *all*," I said.

I held Roman's hand up in the air on my right and Audra's on my left. Everyone else lifted their hands in the air and cheered.

* * *

WE DID GO OUT THERE and give it everything we had. As far as I could tell, the show went just as well, if not better, than it had during previews. The laughs seemed louder, and we all fed off the delicious energy of the audience. I did my best to stay cautiously optimistic, however. After all, the entertainment world was filled with shows that were audience favorites and critical flops. As I took my bow with the cast at the end of the performance, I reminded myself I'd meant what I said. All that really mattered was we give the best performance we could, and the rest was up to fate.

After I changed out of my costume and into a shimmery, blue cocktail dress, I headed out to the limo that was waiting to take me to the Edison Ballroom in the heart of Times Square, for the opening night party. I stopped to sign some autographs and get some pictures with fans who were waiting at the stage door first. Though I didn't mind greeting the fans, it was a little stressful since everyone was waiting for my arrival at the after-party.

Not all Broadway shows had an opening party, but I'd insisted. In fact, I'd bankrolled most of it, though I made it clear I didn't want anybody to know. I just wanted the cast and crew to party and have a wonderful time to celebrate their incredible accomplishment of putting on a terrific Broadway show. I'd offered to bring Rosemary and Luke in my limo, but as it turned out, Johnny had already arranged a limo to take them. So I rode in mine alone.

I felt a little conspicuous arriving all by myself. I couldn't help the feeling that it was a big reminder to the world: *Ricky Scrivello cheated on Therese Andrews, and they broke up. That's why she's alone.*

It was just as well. I was sick to death of having my love life on public display, so even if I *had* a special someone in my life, I was not about to let the press in on it.

Flashbulbs went off like crazy as my limo driver helped me out of the car. Though movie premieres and show open-ings like this could be tiring, they were also a lot of fun. I was kind of a mix between an introvert and an extrovert—I enjoyed talking with people at parties and meeting fans, but I also enjoyed going home at the end of the night and snuggling up in my nice warm bed. Too bad I didn't have anyone to snuggle with.

The Edison Ballroom was exquisite. Gorgeous chandeliers and crystal everywhere, and the place was festively decorated with beautiful flowers. It was still surreal for me, after all these years, to be in a room like this after growing up modestly in a rowhouse in Minnesota. The fact that I'd paid for this party was still as mind-boggling as anything else.

Rosemary caught my eye and smiled excitedly. Johnny stood next to her, and it felt good to see two of my favorite friendly faces. I would meet a lot of new people tonight—critics, producers, publicists, and media members—but I had real friends here, too. Drawing in a deep breath, I tried not to think about the reviews, which would be published online any minute, if they hadn't been already. If they were good, I'd grab the microphone and read some aloud for everyone to hear. If they were bad, I wouldn't say a word, and prolong the inevitable as much as possible.

I went over and hugged Rosemary immediately. We squealed together as we embraced, and people took tons of pictures of us. Good thing she and I got along. Otherwise, stories would appear tomorrow about how much of a diva I was, or she was, or both. Johnny opened his arms and I hugged him as well.

"Great show tonight," Johnny said. "It's gonna be a huge hit."

"I hope so. God, I hope so," I said. "You look amazing!"

Johnny was one handsome guy, and he was resplendent in his tux. He spun around to give me a good look, and I laughed.

"Having this lady on my arm makes me look even better," Johnny said, pulling Rosemary into an embrace.

"I agree," I said. "Rosemary, you're a knockout in that dress."

"Thanks," she said, her green eyes glittering almost as much as her green-sequined dress.

I scanned the room and saw Luke with a pretty brunette with her arm around his waist.

That's weird. I'm almost positive Luke said Elyse was a blonde.

I wanted to make sure I introduced myself to Luke's girlfriend tonight. I'd planned to quash any insecurities she might have about him working with me, but maybe she had bigger problems to worry about. That brunette looked awfully cozy with him.

"That's not Elyse, is it?" I asked Rosemary, nodding in Luke's direction.

Rosemary turned to look. "No, no. That's Susie Peters. She was his scene partner at The Creel Foundation. She's pretty close with him."

"So I see," I said with suspicion in my voice.

Rosemary laughed. "No, really. They're just friends."

Just then, a drop-dead-gorgeous blond woman walked up to the two of them and handed them flutes of champagne. Her pretty, blue eyes were joyous as she gazed at Luke, reveling in his happiness at realizing his dream of performing on Broadway. She smiled at the brunette, too, clearly having no hard feelings about her draped all over her man. Elyse was obviously a lot more secure than I was. Then again, maybe she'd never had two different men cheat on her.

"Ah, okay. That pretty blonde is Elyse, right?"

Rosemary nodded.

"I'm gonna go say hi."

Elyse's eyes grew wide when she saw me approach. Of course she'd known Luke had been working with me for months, but it must still have been weird to see me in person. I understood. I still felt that way when I met some celebrities for the first time. She seemed more starstruck than jealous.

I looked Luke up and down. "Look at you, acting all grown up in your tux."

"I know, right?" Luke said with a grin. "I feel like a little kid playing dress-up in my dad's clothes." Luke turned to introduce me to Elyse, but I was determined to beat him to the punch.

Pointing at Elyse, I smiled and said, "Elyse Pippin. Senior Vice President of Worldwide Sales, Strategy, and Operations for WicketPro."

Elyse smiled and she nodded eagerly. I laughed and said, "Not that Luke *ever* talks about you. Nice to meet you, Elyse."

"You too!" she said with a smile, still seeming rather amazed by my presence.

"I want you to know your boyfriend is damned near impossible to work with." I'd always made it a point to let my co-star's significant others know I was totally clear that my leading man was taken. I knew how much it hurt to be cheated on, and I didn't want Elyse or any other woman losing a minute's sleep because of me.

"I believe it," Elyse said dryly, even though we both knew Luke was about as easygoing as a guy could get.

"He's just too damned funny. You know that scene where he's looking at me and he keeps trailing off and getting distracted?"

Elyse nodded.

"I can't even look at him. I can't. His expression is just too much. I lose it every time."

We shared a laugh over that.

"He must crack you up all the time," I said.

"Oh, he does," Elyse said, gazing at Luke with love and pride. Sharp pain stabbed at my heart. I wished someone would look at me like that.

Roman looks at me like that all the time.

I pushed that thought away. I had to stop confusing Roman's fandom with him having real feelings for me. Even he was confused. He thought he was in love with me, but he wasn't.

"Luke loves working with you," Elyse said, snapping me away from my thoughts of Roman. "He was so nervous on his first day when he knew you'd be there."

"Is that so?" I teased.

"Elyysyyyyse. Shut uuuup," Luke whined, making us both giggle.

"Oh, he was a mess. Excited, but really, really nervous," Elyse said, patting Luke's cheek. "But then he came home that day saying 'She's so cool! She's so nice.' You know how it is. You just never know what a celebrity will be like in real life."

"Yeah," I said.

I glanced around the room, and my gaze landed on Roman.

My heart unexpectedly lurched in my chest when I saw him.

Dear God, he looks gorgeous.

The dark fabric of Roman's tux brought out the rich darkness of his brown eyes. He was a vision of delicious manliness. Half the men here were wearing tuxedos, but none of them were anywhere near as dashing as Roman.

"Are you okay?" Elyse asked, seeming somewhat taken aback by my expression.

"Oh, y—yes. Yes, I'm fine. I'm just a little nervous about the reviews coming out tonight. Speaking of which, I really should check if the *New York Times* one is in yet. If you'll excuse me?"

"Sure," Elyse said with a smile.

"It's gonna be okay, Tessa," Luke said. He knew how terrified I was of the *New York Times* review, because we'd talked about it at length.

"Thanks," I said gratefully.

I pulled my phone out of my black beaded purse and took a quick look. My heart slammed inside my chest when I saw the headline: *"Pirated" Theater Review.*

Oh, dear God. This was it.

I saw a few reporters heading toward me the second I turned away from Luke and Elyse, but I was not about to do any interviews right now. Not until I'd had time to read the review and had a few moments to myself to deal with whatever was in it.

I rushed off to the ladies' room for a moment of privacy. Drawing in a few shallow breaths of sheer terror, I reflected on how critics, and even the general public, seemed to have no understanding of how terrifying it was to get a review of your work. It never gets any easier. Bad reviews hurt. Oh God, they hurt so badly. After reading some awful, snarky, and downright cruel comments from critics and strangers on the Internet, it was clear to me that people often forgot that celebrities were actual human beings.

Ducking my head down to avoid speaking to anyone, I quickly slipped into a bathroom stall. I closed the lid on the toilet and sat down. As much as I wanted to get this over with, I was still terrified to look.

Shaking, I clicked on the *New York Times* article on my phone. I did my usual scan of the article and see how bad it is first.

Okay. It wasn't bad. It wasn't a rave, but it wasn't terrible. The last line read: "Overall, the show is enjoyable if a bit uneven."

I let out a deep breath. The show's future was still uncertain, but it didn't get totally panned, either. When I went back out to the party, I would read some of the review to everybody. Only the good parts, of course.

The article picked on Gilbert a bit, saying that his portrayal of the old pirate was a bit wooden. I definitely would not be reading that part out loud. I kept skimming the article. "Three highly entertaining pirates," "Lots of genuine laughs," "Some snappy, memorable showtunes."

I drew in another breath as I read about Rosemary.

"To date, Rosemary Sutton is known mostly for being engaged to billionaire Johnny Creel, heir to the Creel fortune."

Dammit.

Why did they always have to throw that in her face? I wouldn't read that part aloud either, but Rosemary would see it later. And it would hurt her.

It made me sad that I couldn't even call my mother, as she would undoubtedly find a way to diminish my achievement. After all, she hadn't thought tonight was important enough to attend. Had it been a movie premiere, she would have been here. To her, theater wasn't prestigious enough for her to make the trip from Minnesota.

I couldn't let my fellow *Pirated* members sweat it out any longer. I needed to go out there and tell everyone the mostly good news.

Waving off reporters as I reentered the ballroom, I headed up to the stage area. I didn't even have to ask for people's attention, as the room quieted the moment I approached the podium.

"Hi, everybody!" I said into the mic. "It's wonderful to see everybody here tonight with their families and significant others." Except me of course. As usual, I was surrounded by people and still felt a bit alone. "First and foremost, I want to thank the incredible cast and crew of *Pirated* for giving one hell of a performance tonight."

I smiled at the crowd as everyone burst into applause.

"So, I've got the *New York Times* review here," I said, glancing down at my phone on the podium. The room went deadly quiet. "Okay, though I wouldn't call it a rave review, overall it's pretty good, so you can all relax."

Nervous laughter rippled through the room.

I read the highlights of the article, including the parts about entertaining pirates, genuine laughs, and snappy showtunes.

"Rosemary, where's Rosemary," I asked into the mic.

"Here! Here! She's right here! Look at her!" Johnny yelled, pointing at a blushing Rosemary next to him. The crowd laughed at Johnny's antics.

"According to the *New York Times*, 'Rosemary Sutton holds her own here as one of the pirate's love interests, her angelic singing voice pitch perfect,'" I said proudly, probably enjoying the applause almost as much as Rosemary did.

"'Luke Rannells,'" I began, and then stopped to point at him where he stood with Elyse and Susie. "'is so hilarious, he gives even Johnny Depp a run for his money as far as pirates go.'" I waited until the applause died down to continue. "'Rannells has a deep, sensuous voice that is well-suited to the Great White Way. He also has a commanding stage presence, which is particularly impressive, given this is his Broadway debut. Watching him perform makes me wonder if I'm looking at the next big breakout Broadway star.'"

Huge and well-deserved applause erupted for my incredible co-star. I watched with pride and not a little bit of jealousy as Elyse flung her arms around Luke and squeezed him tight. Though I was still attracted to Luke, I was more envious of what he had with Elyse than anything else.

"There's some other stuff in here of course," I said as a gentle warning to everyone in the room, who would no doubt pull up the full article and read it themselves. "Some stuff the critic said didn't work and all that, but the review says, 'Overall, the show was enjoyable if a bit uneven.' I don't know about you guys, but I'll take it. Great job, everybody!"

I started a round of applause for all of us as I walked away from the podium.

"Wait, wait, wait!" Luke yelled as he ran up onstage. He grabbed the microphone with one hand and tugged on the back of my dress with the other, pulling me back to the podium. Into the mic, he said, "Since Tessa here is way too modest to read the part about herself, I'm gonna do it!"

"Luke," I said, shaking my head. He put his arm around me and pulled me in next to him so there was no escape.

"'The big question was would Therese Andrews be able to handle the rigors of a Broadway show? The answer is a resounding YES! Everyone knew she had acting chops, and now the world will know she can sing. In the role of Mary, Andrews combines her sex appeal,'" Luke wiggled his eyebrows at me on that part. "'... and acting ability with a lovely singing voice to create a memorable character who expertly matches wits with her pirate partner, Captain Samuel, played by Luke Rannells.'" He preened a bit at the mention of his name, and then read the last part with exaggerated vigor. "'Many naysayers didn't think she could handle the role, but she a-proved a-them a-WRONG!'"

Thunderous applause ensued, and I scanned the room to see many smiling faces looking up at me. Suddenly I didn't feel quite so alone. Not everyone in this room was a stranger. Luke wasn't just being my showoff co-star—he had read the review out loud because he was my friend and wanted me to get my due. Rosemary and Johnny were out there in the crowd, too. Sure, they were celebrities, but I knew they were among the few people in the world who cared about the real me. Even so, most of these people only knew me as Therese

Andrews, movie star. For some reason, that thought saddened me.

Then I caught sight of Roman. He applauded me like everyone else, but as his eyes met mine from where I stood, elevated on the stage, his tender gaze felt like a cool, calming breeze in the swirling storm of chaos around me. It felt like he was saying, *I see you. The REAL you. And I'm so proud of you.*

As I stared at him, he smiled wider and used both hands to blow me a kiss. I felt connected to him, like I could read his thoughts—*I told you you could do it.*

I let out a deep, happy sigh. He was just so sweet.

For the rest of the night, I spoke to reporters and met as many people as I could. Most of the cast and crew members had family and friends they wanted to introduce, so I did my best to meet all their plus-ones. It was tiring but also great fun. Everybody was in a good mood, except for those moments when I caught Johnny staring daggers at Jacob. Rosemary had told Johnny all about the way Jacob had been treating her, but she forbade Johnny from doing anything about it. Always the ultimate professional, there was no way Rosemary would use her influence against anybody. Not even when they desperately deserved it. It must have been hard on Johnny, though, knowing Rosemary was hurting and not being able to do anything about it.

Throughout the launch party, my mind drifted back to Roman. I found myself scanning the room to see where he was. Often, he was talking and laughing with Audra and Rex and their spouses. Sometimes, though, I caught him watching me with that adoring expression. The one that told me he cared.

I kept thinking how natural it would feel to have Roman right by my side all night. Supporting me as I worked the room. Being proud of me.

Loving me.

More and more I found myself wanting to believe it.

Roman might have been the one obsessed with my celebrity his whole life, but it was starting to feel like I was the one with the fantasy. The fantasy that any man could ever love the real me.

And that fantasy was incredibly dangerous.

CHAPTER 15

No matter what I did, I could not stop thinking about Roman. There was no denying the ripple of excitement whenever I caught sight of him on set, or when I was on the receiving end of one of those sweet and sexy smiles. I'd had my heart broken so many times, I couldn't bear the idea of going through that again. And yet, trying to keep my distance from Roman hurt, too.

It was obvious Rosemary had been right when she'd said that Roman probably wouldn't make a move on me without my encouragement. He'd had plenty of opportunities when he'd stopped to chat with me, but it never went further than that. He probably assumed I wasn't interested, which was true at first. But that had changed since I'd gotten to know him. Suddenly, I was the one obsessing over *him*. Over and over, I thought about the way he'd treated me over the last few weeks. The kind and encouraging words he offered whenever I was feeling down about myself. The tender way he'd held me in his arms after I fell off the ladder. And my God, the way he *looked* at me. I also couldn't stop thinking about how sexy he'd looked in his tuxedo last night. Now, all I wanted was the chance to finally be alone with him.

And that scared the living hell out of me.

I loved the way he made me feel when he was near me, but what if we dated and he turned out to be a creepy fanboy like I'd feared all along? It took until the awful Roxy Rose sex experiment for me to realize that had been Derek's deal. He'd seemed to like me as a person, too, but all he'd wanted was Therese Andrews. Roman had lusted after movie-star-me practically his whole life. How could I believe things had changed for him?

"Hey, Tessa," Roman said with that damned sexy grin as he walked by me backstage.

"Hey, Roman, Roman, Roman," I responded.

My heart did that flippedy-flop in my chest, and I knew I was fighting a losing battle. As it happened, I was walking past Rosemary's dressing room, so I stopped and knocked on the door.

"Yes?" she answered.

"It's Tessa."

"Come on in."

I entered the tiny dressing room she shared with several of the other actors, and shut the door. I was already dressed and ready to perform, and it looked like Rosemary was almost done, too. I watched as she put the finishing touches on the makeup around her eyes. A lot of people would be surprised to know most Broadway actresses did their own makeup. I guess it was a cost-saving measure. I had my own makeup artist who traveled around with me, though.

Sarah stood up from her spot in front of the mirror.

"Baby, you're beautiful," I said. "You don't look a day over seventy-five."

Sarah laughed, straightening her gray wig. "You're too kind."

Rosemary turned to look at me.

"You're gorgeous too, doll," I told her.

"Thanks," she said with a laugh.

Sarah gave us a quick wave as she headed out. "See you ladies out there. Break legs!"

"You too," I said. Thankfully, that left Rosemary and me alone to talk.

"I need you to stop me from doing something stupid," I began cautiously.

"Okay ..."

I took in a deep breath and said, "I think I'm gonna ask Roman out."

"Oh, Tessa, that's wonderful!" she squealed, clasping her hands together.

"That's not exactly talking me out of it." I knew she would be on board with the whole Roman thing, which was probably why I went to her in the first place. Part of me didn't want to be talked out of it, even though I was scared to death to get involved with him. Right now, my desire to feel his arms around me, to feel his kiss, superseded any common sense I might have had. I hoped his kiss would be gentle and sweet, like his smile.

But what if it wasn't? What if he jammed his tongue down my throat, thrilled to finally be able to make out with Therese Andrews? Picturing Roman's face filled with gentle concern, I knew that wasn't likely to happen. He wasn't that kind of guy. Was he?

"Stop overthinking it," Rosemary said. She knew me so well. "Your heart is telling you to go after him, and you should listen to it. I know you're afraid he'll turn out to be just another rabid fan, but you won't know unless you try. I can't make any promises about what will happen, but God, Tessa. The way he *looks* at you sometimes."

"I know. I see it too."

"I really think he'll turn out to be different," she said.

I sighed, still feeling uneasy.

"You might really regret it if you don't go for it."

Letting out another sigh, I nodded. "I think you're right. Okay. If I don't lose my nerve, I'll talk to him after tonight's show."

* * *

I DID my best not to think about Roman as I performed, but every time I gazed into Luke's eyes onstage, it was Roman's face I saw. Every love song I sang made me think of Roman. The only thing I knew for sure was I had to get him out of my system, one way or another. Rosemary was right when she'd said I wouldn't know what could happen with Roman unless I gave it a chance. She'd also said I should listen to my heart, but my heart had steered me very, very wrong so many times.

Enough. I decided to quit overthinking it and go for it. What was the worst that could happen?

Roman could break my heart like every other man had done before him.

* * *

"ROMAN!" Rex yelled, startling me as I struggled with a bulb that had blown during the show.

"Gah! Jesus. What?" I asked.

"Tessa wants to see you in her dressing room."

I stared at him. "Why?"

"Damned if I know. I'm just the messenger. Whatever it is, hurry up about it. I'd like to get the hell out of here," Rex grumbled. He'd had a rough night with tons of problems on his end, and I didn't blame him for being in a bad mood.

There was some after-show stuff that me and Audra and him all had to be present for in order to call it a night, so I had no time to waste.

I headed toward Tessa's dressing room. Thanks to her kindness and sensitivity, things hadn't been as awkward between us as they could have been after she'd overheard me say I loved her. Even so, we'd never really been alone before. I couldn't begin to imagine why she wanted to talk to me. I hoped everything was okay.

As I turned down the hall to her dressing room, I started worrying that Rex was fucking with me. Knowing him, he might want me to burst in on her while she was getting dressed, just to make sure the rest of the run was super uncomfortable for me.

"Bastard," I muttered to myself. "I swear to God, if he's just setting me up ..."

I composed myself, doing my best to quash the jitters in my stomach, and tentatively knocked on her door.

"Tessa?" I called out, hoping I didn't sound as nervous as I felt. "It's Roman."

"Just a sec," Tessa responded, and delicious visions of her closing her robe around her naked body danced in my head.

She opened the door, dressed in jeans and a dainty white blouse.

"Hey," Tessa said with a smile.

"Hey. Ah, Rex said you wanted to see me. I wasn't sure if ..." I trailed off, not knowing what else to say.

"Yeah, yeah, come on in. Thanks for coming to see me."

I walked into the room and she closed the door behind us. I let out a breath of relief.

"Cool. I was a little afraid Rex was screwing with me."

Tessa laughed. "Oh, I don't blame you for thinking that. I probably should have asked someone else to grab you, but he was the first person I saw after the show."

"Oh," I said with a nervous laugh. "So ... what's up?"

Tessa hesitated a moment, wrapping her arms around herself as if protecting herself from something. I wanted to tell her it was okay, whatever it was. That she could tell me anything. But I kept my mouth shut and waited for her to speak.

"I feel like ... we should at least ... go out on a date. You know, to see if we're compatible or whatever."

I stared at her for a moment as my brain tried to process her words.

Did Tessa just ask me out on a date?

I wasn't sure how long I was struck dumb, but it was long enough for her to speak again.

"R—Roman?" she asked.

"Well, yes," I finally managed to spit out. "Yeah, of course I would love that. You name the time and place, and I'm there."

"Well, are you busy right now?"

"Now?" I asked like an idiot, instead of telling her I would drop everything and be all hers this very instant.

"Yeah. I figure we both work the same crazy hours right now. It's not like we're ever free on Friday and Saturday nights."

I smiled and nodded. "Good point. Sure, I'm free now. Except there's a couple of things I have to wrap up before I can leave."

"Of course. Take your time. I'll wait for you."

"Okay, cool. I won't be long. Then I'll take you anywhere you want to go."

"Actually, we should probably go straight back to my place."

I stared at her, once again trying to wrap my brain around what I was hearing.

"Oh! I didn't mean it that way," Tessa said as her hand flew to her mouth. She blushed, and it was the most adorable thing I'd ever seen in my life. "I—I just meant it can be difficult for me to go out in public. I—I mean, you know, I—"

"I get it," I reassured her. "It's a mob scene wherever you go, so it would just be easier to hang out at your place and order some food or something like that."

"Yes, yes exactly," Tessa said, seeming relieved that I knew she hadn't been propositioning me a moment ago. "First dates can be hard enough, even without the whole world watching. And believe me, they would be."

The weariness in her voice made me sad. Her love life was always splayed out in the entertainment news, and I couldn't imagine how hard that must be for her.

"I won't tell anybody we're hanging out tonight," I assured her. Though I felt like yelling from the rooftops that Tessa had agreed to go out with me, hurting her would never be worth it.

"Thank you," Tessa said, gratitude tinged with sadness in her eyes. "It's nothing personal. I'm trying really hard to keep my private life private, you know?"

"I understand."

She smiled and said, "My driver can take us whenever you're ready. I don't live too far from here."

"Cool," I said, turning to go. I paused for a moment.

Standing there, finally alone with Tessa, I knew what I was about to say was incredibly stupid, and I'd probably regret it later. But I was gonna say it anyway.

Still facing the door and away from Tessa, I said, "I meant what I said, you know." Laughing awkwardly, I turned around and forced myself to face her. "Obviously, you were *not* supposed to hear what I said back at the bar that day, but you did. I figure I can be totally humiliated about it, or I can just own it."

Swallowing hard, I looked directly into her beautiful blue eyes and said, "I do love you, Tessa."

Her expression softened and, if nothing else, I hadn't scared her off by coming on way too strong. I couldn't help wanting her to know how much I cared about her. I got the feeling that not a lot of people told her they loved her. That prick, Ricky, had betrayed her, and that must have hurt her badly. Tessa had always been vague about her family in interviews, but I doubted she was close with them. That, and Rosemary had told me Tessa was lonely sometimes. She hadn't had to tell me that, though. I knew. Just watching her, I knew.

"Well, that's very sweet of you," she said.

"But you don't believe I love you."

Tessa paused. Then, with a slightly sad smile, she said, "No."

"That's okay. I don't blame you. It's a weird situation for both of us, I know. I'm in love, and you're still in the 'getting to know you' phase. But I can't help how I feel."

"I can't, you know, promise anything," Tessa said. "But I am looking forward to getting to know you, Roman."

"Thanks. I appreciate you giving me a chance instead of running for the hills. I'd be pretty freaked out if some girl told me she was in love with me after such a short time."

"I'm not freaked out."

"Cool. And Tessa ... I just want you to know ..."

Tessa gazed at me intently as I spoke. She didn't believe me, but I got the feeling she wanted to.

"Even if nothing ever happens between us, I want you to know, *really know*, how much I love you."

With that, I quickly slipped out the door.

CHAPTER 16

I sat in the back seat of my SUV waiting for Roman, my emotions tumbling all over themselves. Biting my lip, I eagerly anticipated having this tall, dark, handsome man sitting next to me in the car. After a while, my nerves began to take over. He was taking a long time. I wasn't sure exactly what he normally did after each show, but I didn't think it was supposed to take this long. Though I usually felt relaxed around Roman, all this waiting gave me time to work myself up into a jittery mess over going on a date with him.

It was strange the way he kept saying he loved me. Although I understood his boyhood obsession with me because I'd had my own girlish crushes over the years, what I didn't understand was why he thought he loved the real me. He didn't know me all that well. And yet, he sounded so genuine when he said it, even though it couldn't possibly be true. Like lots of fans, he might have thought he knew me from TV interviews and magazine articles, but that was Therese Andrews, not me. Though I did my best to be genuine in interviews, naturally I never revealed all of me to the public. Like being on a job interview—sure, you want to be yourself, but your best self. The self that's dressed up and professional, not the self that rolls out of bed with morning breath and no makeup on. Forget loving me—what if Roman decided he didn't even like me once he got to know me?

Where in the world was he? The wait was killing me. He wouldn't stand me up, would he? I started to worry something might have happened to him.

"Mr. Pinza?" I heard Ben ask from outside the car.

"Yes, that's me," Roman responded. I listened as Ben introduced himself as my driver, then opened the car door for him.

Roman bent down enough so I could see him, but he didn't get into the car.

I gasped when I got a good look at him. He was a mess. His jeans and blue button-down shirt were streaked with black marks. His face was mostly clean, with only a small smudge of dirt near his ear where he'd obviously missed a spot.

"I'm sorry. I'm so sorry," Roman said, his dark eyes wide.

"What happened? Are you all right?"

"Yes, yes I'm fine. I—I ..."

"Come here. Sit down," I said, patting the seat next to me.

He glanced down nervously. "I don't want to get your car all dirty."

"Oh, please. I don't care. Sit down," I insisted.

He tried to brush some of the dirt off his ass, and I rather enjoyed the view. Roman had a cute butt, and his tight jeans showed it off magnificently. Gingerly, he sat down next to me, fussing with his clothes and trying to make sure he didn't leave a mess.

"Okay, Ben," I said after Roman got himself settled and buckled in. "Roman, what happened to you?"

"God, Tessa, I'm so sorry I'm such a mess. And I'm so sorry I kept you waiting! There was a problem in the basement, and I had to run some new cables and … it doesn't matter. I'm just so sorry I'm such a horrible mess."

I laughed and shook my head. "You're not a mess."

You're adorable, I was tempted to say.

I didn't care if he was dirty. I was just grateful he was okay. Taking in an eyeful of Roman, I realized he looked more than okay. He looked *hot*. I was used to dating pretty boy actors, but there was something so damned sexy about being with a man who wore blue jeans and got his hands dirty.

Roman glanced self-consciously down at his clothes. "I felt bad enough I had to go on a date with a beautiful woman wearing jeans and an old shirt, but then I had to go make it worse."

He looked so embarrassed, which only made him more endearing to me. Still, I hated for him to feel uncomfortable.

"Don't worry about it. I'm wearing jeans, too."

"Yeah, but you look …" he paused to take in my jeans and blouse, then looked up into my eyes and said, "beautiful."

There was that look again. The one I'd only ever seen in the movies, including the ones I'd been in.

He always made me feel good about myself, and more than anything, I wanted to put him at ease.

"Roman, Roman, Roman," I said, gently touching his face with his sexy five o'clock shadow. "I like this rugged, manly look." I took my time taking in his tight jeans and shirt with the first few buttons open, feeling his eyes on me as I did. Lifting my gaze back to his face, I said, "And here I didn't think you could ever look more dashing than you did in your tux on opening night, but you managed it all right. Roman Pinza, I think you look sexy as hell right now."

Roman stared at me as if processing my words. Then his face broke into a smile, and he said, "Thanks, Tessa."

I wasn't sure if he believed me or not, but I meant what

I'd said. I couldn't remember the last time I'd been this attracted to any man. Still touching his face, I wondered if his heart was beating as fast as mine. Finally, and a bit reluctantly, I dropped my hand.

"Maybe it's best that I didn't know I'd be going on a date with you tonight. I would have obsessed over getting ready and wearing the right thing." Roman glanced over at Ben in the driver's seat. "Oh, sorry," he said in a low voice. "Should I not say anything about this being a date?"

"No, no, it's fine. Everybody who works for me signs a non-disclosure agreement," I assured Roman. "Ben is trustworthy. He keeps everything I do private."

"Oh good," Roman said, looking relieved.

"Are you hungry?"

"Starved."

"Me too," I said. "What do you want to order for dinner?"

"Anything's fine by me. I'm not picky."

"Believe it or not, I haven't had pizza in a while. I could go for that."

"Perfect," he said.

I pulled out my phone and found a local pizza place and, after discussing what we wanted, we ordered online.

"So where do you live?" Roman asked.

"Sutton Place. I have a house on the water. Not too far away."

"Wow."

"Where do you live?"

"In a tiny little shack in Little Italy," he said bluntly, making me laugh. "Good thing we're going to your place, huh?"

"I'm sure your place is lovely, Roman."

He scoffed but also smiled.

After a few more minutes, we arrived at my house.

"This is it," I said as Ben pulled up in front.

Roman's eyes grew wide when he looked out the window. My place was 7000 square feet, which was huge by New York City standards.

"Holy God," he muttered.

Ben opened the car door and Roman got out first. He turned to me and held out his hand to help me step down out of the car.

Such a gentleman.

Many men I dated enjoyed the celebrity treatment so much that sometimes they seemed to forget I was there. So far, Roman was nothing like that.

"Holy God," Roman said again when we stepped into the house. I rather liked that he wasn't trying to play it cool by hiding how impressed he was.

I watched as he took in the foyer with a grand staircase leading to the second floor.

"This is the living room," I said, walking into the next room. Roman followed me, his eyes opening wider. "There's a nice view of the river from here, but it's kinda hard to see at night."

Roman nodded, eyes still wide.

I kept walking as I continued the tour. "And this is, well, it's kind of another living room, I guess." This room had a cozy fireplace and a grand piano, as well as two plush couches and several chairs.

"And this is the breakfast dining area, I guess you could call it."

Roman wandered over to the window, which took up the whole wall and half of the ceiling. It offered an incredible view of the Queensborough Bridge. "I like to sit in here in the mornings with my breakfast and coffee and, you know, read a book or just take in the view."

Roman seemed somewhat overwhelmed by his surroundings. He hadn't said a word in several minutes.

"Holy God?" I offered.

He laughed. "Yeah. Yeah, that. I mean, wow. This place is incredible. It's like a mansion."

"Wanna see the upstairs?"

"Yes, please," he said with a handsome grin.

I led him back to the grand staircase and we walked upstairs.

"How many bathrooms in this place?"

"Six full, two half."

Roman whistled. "And how many bedrooms?"

"Six. And here's my bedroom," I said, pausing by a doorway and opening the door. Roman peered curiously inside. I watched him as his eyes drifted from the windows to the walls, decorated with flowery, girly paintings, and finally to the bed. My heart pounded as I watched him look at my bed, figuring he was thinking what I was thinking.

That maybe sometime soon he would join me in that bed. I literally had to stifle a moan when I started to imagine all the pleasurable things this rugged, sexy man could do to me there.

Roman would be an incredible lover. I just know it.

Roman turned his head to meet my gaze. He'd caught me staring at him, but I didn't care. His mouth slid into a slow, sexy smile and I could only describe those rich, dark brown eyes one way.

Bedroom eyes.

The doorbell rang.

"I guess we'll have to continue the tour later," I said. It was perfect timing in a way. Like what they say in show biz—end on a high note. Always leave them wanting more. And by the look in his eye, Roman definitely wanted more.

I walked down the steps hoping Roman was checking out my ass as he trailed behind me. Once we got back to the foyer, I picked up my purse.

"Oh, I'll get it," Roman said, reaching into his back pocket for his wallet.

"Roman," I said firmly, gesturing with my hand at the opulence surrounding us. "Let me pay."

He laughed and nodded.

I was all for chivalry, but there was no sense in pretending I didn't have millions more dollars to my name than he did. Having him pay for dinner would be ridiculous.

The pizza delivery guy nervously handed me the pizza and accepted my cash, complete with a generous tip. I smiled and thanked him, and he mumbled something back. I wondered if he would go back to the pizza place and tell everyone he had a nice long conversation with Therese Andrews.

"Let's eat in the fireplace room," I said. "What do you want to drink? Soda? Beer?"

"Beer would be great."

Roman took the pizza from me and carried it into the living room. The first one. The wrong one.

"It's the next room over," I said with a giggle.

"Holy God," was his response.

I brought in a bottle of beer for him and a can of diet soda for me. I was glad I had beer on hand, since I rarely drank it.

Before settling in next to him on the couch, I turned on some background music. So far, our date had been smooth, but the music might help in case there were any uncomfortable silences.

I watched Roman devour a slice of pizza in the time it took me to open my Diet Coke. Even his appetite was sexy. I was used to going out on fancy dates with Ricky. Fancy restaurants with dainty, expensive food. Everything about Roman was so *masculine*. I loved it.

"I still cannot get over the size of your house," Roman said, shaking his head, then taking a swig of his beer.

"My place in L.A. is bigger," I said matter-of-factly.

Roman did a spit-take. A *literal* spit-take, spewing beer all over my carpet. I burst into uncontrollable laughter. As in doubling over, banging my fist on the coffee table, belly laughter.

"Oh my God, your carpet," Roman said, and his horrified expression only made me laugh harder.

"I don't care," I said, wiping tears of laughter. After eventually getting myself under control, I reassured him. "It's fine. Oh my God, I haven't laughed that hard since I don't even know when."

"Well, I'm glad you find me amusing," Roman said, still looking apologetic. "I haven't exactly been at my finest tonight."

"I think you're utterly adorable," I said with a smile. "I don't know why you're so surprised by my house. You must have known I was wealthy."

He shrugged and said, "I guess so. I don't know. I guess I never really thought about it."

Nibbling on a slice of cheese pizza, I thought about his words and how different he sounded than most of the other people in my life. Those I hung out with in Hollywood were either nearly as rich as I was, or they were enthralled with my fame and fortune. Roman was neither. He seemed content to hang out with me and eat pizza, and not ask for anything else.

I finished my slice of pizza and put my paper plate down on the coffee table.

"Is that all you're gonna have? One slice?" Roman asked. We'd gotten a large pizza, with one half plain cheese and the other half with pepperoni, sausage, bacon, and ham. Roman had already devoured all four of his meat-filled slices.

"Yep," I said.

"That can't possibly be enough food for you," he said.

"I'm good." I took a sip from my Diet Coke, which usually helped make me feel fuller.

"Come on, you gotta have at least one more slice."

I shook my head.

"Tessa, you just gave a two-hour performance on Broadway. You've gotta be starving. Just have at least one more—"

"I can't!" I snapped angrily.

Roman blinked, stung by my outburst.

"Oh Roman, I'm so sorry," I said, putting down my drink and reaching for his hand. "I didn't mean to yell at you."

Sighing, I let go of his hand and sank back into the couch. "You have to understand … It's like this ongoing battle for me. Constant peer pressure to eat more. 'Have a dessert. Come on, just have one glass of wine! Don't be a party pooper!' And yet, if I gain one pound, the gossip rags are all over me. Not to mention my mother will tell me I'm fat."

"Your mother calls you fat?" Roman asked, looking horrified.

"Yup. God forbid a stiff breeze blows and the paparazzi gets a shot of my shirt puffing out. She'll call me and tell me to ease up on the French fries. Which I haven't had in over a year. Do you know what I hate?" I asked, suddenly unable to stop ranting at poor Roman.

"Tell me," he said, leaning forward as if he really wanted to know.

"I hate it in romantic comedies where the guy and girl are out on a date, and the girl orders a steak and a baked potato or something, and the guy is like, 'Good for you. I like a girl who's not afraid to eat,' and she's all, "Oh, I don't care what people say. I eat what I want,' and she's sitting there skinny as a rail. This girl's got a rockin' perfect body and acting like she's some kind of feminist hero because she eats whatever she wants. Which she does because she knows she has a fast metabolism and she can eat anything she wants and not get fat. And the guy doesn't care because she looks like a super-model, so what does he care what she eats? If she was a size 18, then that conversation would mean something. But it doesn't. It's just another unrealistic expectation for women. Don't bring the party down by ordering a salad and a water, but don't you dare get fat."

Poor, unsuspecting Roman had accidentally touched on one of my hot-button issues. I was afraid he might be annoyed with me for getting so upset.

After a moment's contemplation, he said, "That's a really good point. I never thought about it that way." He paused again, looking rather sad. He glanced at the pizza and then back at me. "But you're still hungry, right?"

I nodded. "I'm kinda low-key hungry all the time. You get used to it, I guess."

Roman picked up one of the cheese slices, tore it in half and then held it up to me. "Compromise?" His gentle brown eyes were filled with concern.

"How can I possibly say no to that face?" I picked up my paper plate and allowed him to give me the half slice. He smiled, content, as I ate it.

"Thanks, Roman. I really appreciate it," I said, and I didn't only mean the pizza. It was cathartic talking to him because I felt like he understood me. "You can have the rest if you want," I said, gesturing at the leftovers.

"I'm good," Roman said. He started gathering up the plates, dirty napkins, and pizza.

"Oh, you don't have to do that."

He chuckled. "Yes, yes I do. You might as well know this about me now. I am super anal about cleanliness. I'm totally annoying, so I apologize in advance."

I laughed. "That's okay. There are far worse quirks to have." I got up and helped him with the trash and leftovers, and he followed me to the kitchen so we could put every-thing away.

Roman's eyes explored my gigantic kitchen, and I waited for another "Holy God" from him, but he didn't say it.

As I wrapped the pizza in foil, I said, "I'm not a total slob, but I'm no neat freak either. I'm pretty lazy about stuff like that."

"Your house looks immaculate to me."

"High praise, indeed, from someone like you. But I have a housekeeper who comes in every day. It's like living in a hotel. I don't even make my own bed. Like I said, I'm lazy."

"You work a lot, Tessa. I wouldn't call you lazy."

I smiled at him, then led him back to the fireplace room so we could relax on the couch.

Once he was seated next to me, he said, "I won't stay too much longer. You need your rest."

Though I was tired, I didn't really want the evening to end. Even so, I was grateful for his words. Roman had made it clear he had no intention of pressuring me into having sex on the first date.

"You've gotta be tired, too, after being on your feet all day."

"Yeah, kinda."

"Do you like working at the theater?"

"I love it," Roman said, and I saw the flash of excitement in his eyes. "I especially love being the head electrician because I get to be in charge of everything."

"You like being the boss," I said with a smile.

"Yeah, I do, but it's less about being the boss over people, and more about having control over what's going on. I'm a neat freak, and also a bit of a control freak, I have to admit. A Broadway theater has so many moving parts, you know? And there's a lot that can go wrong."

"I believe it. Everything you guys do on set looks so complicated."

"You want to hear about something that really went wrong?" Roman asked, and I nodded. "It didn't happen in my theater, it was over at The Marquis, but I swear stuff like this keeps me up at night. Some theaters have this thing called a deluge curtain. It's a pipe that runs along the top of the stage, and it's designed to contain a fire in case one breaks out. With so many people crammed into a theater, things could turn tragic in a heartbeat if a fire broke out."

I smiled, enjoying the sound of Roman's deep, sexy voice. I loved hearing Roman talk passionately about the theater.

"So, when you trigger the deluge curtain, 200,000 gallons of water come crashing down onto the stage. And one day one of the stagehands accidentally hit the sensor." I gasped, and Roman laughed. "I know. It was crazy. So water came bursting out of everywhere, soaking the orchestra pit and sending instruments floating all over the place. The stage was drenched. It was a miracle they only missed three performances."

"Oh, dear God. I can't imagine."

"Right? So I'm paranoid about something like that happening on my watch."

"I don't blame you," I said.

Roman and I talked like that for more than an hour. The time absolutely flew by. We traded stories about show business and laughed a lot together. Though I told stories about working with famous actors and about what it was like to work in the movies, I was the one who brought those things up. Roman listened intently and asked questions, but he wasn't the one to jump in and ask things like what it was like to work with a famous actor, or what it was like to do a sex scene.

In other words, Roman didn't act like a fanboy. Not in the

slightest. And he was one of very few people to treat me like a person and not like a movie star.

"You ever see the musical *Waitress*?" Roman asked.

"No. I've heard it's really good, but I've never seen it."

"I filled in doing some electrical work when the head electrician at another theater was out for a family emergency. There's a song in the show that really reminds me of you. You should listen to it."

"I will. What's it called?"

"It's called 'She Used to Be Mine.' It's a pretty song. Kinda sad. But … it's you. It's just … you."

I nodded thoughtfully, feeling quite curious about the song and why it reminded him of me.

Roman glanced at his phone. "Damn. It's really late. I'm gonna go, and let you get some sleep."

"I hate for you to go, but I guess I do need some rest. I'll text Ben to have him come get you."

Our conversation fell into a lull, but it wasn't uncomfortable. I felt a sense of calm being there with Roman. Soft, romantic music still played in the background.

Roman smiled at me. "Do you want to dance?"

"Really?"

"Sure, why not?" Roman got up from the couch and reached for my hand. He pulled me close into his arms and we started dancing. His touch was gentle yet strong, and I marveled at how comfortable I was being held by him. As if we fit perfectly together.

Roman was quite a bit taller than me, so instead of resting my head on his shoulder, I snuggled against his broad chest. He held me tighter and even though I couldn't see his face, I was pretty sure he smiled.

"Tonight was so perfect, Roman, Roman, Roman," I murmured into his chest. I couldn't get over how perfect it really had been. Even though Roman had been lusting after

Threse Andrews for most of his life, I saw no trace of fanboy in him tonight. He didn't care that we'd stayed hidden in my house. He was on a date with a movie star and no one would ever know, but he didn't seem to give a damn. Feeling his body relax against mine, I knew he was perfectly content being alone with me. And that meant more to me than he would ever know.

I lifted my head and gazed into Roman's eyes, eagerly anticipating the moment I'd been waiting for all night.

He tenderly brushed my hair back, taking his time, making me want his kiss even more. He gazed deeply into my eyes in a way that made me know he was seeing the real me and not the fake, glitzy movie-star-me. Then he cupped my face with his hands, bent down, and pressed his lips to mine.

Roman's kiss was tender and sensual. Everything I'd hoped it would be. I ran my fingers through his rich, dark hair as the kiss deepened and grew more passionate. Roman had perfect rhythm on the dance floor, and the way he kissed me showed me he knew instinctively how to touch me.

Oh God, the things he could do to me with his touch, his rhythm, in the bedroom.

A moan escaped my lips. Roman's mouth traveled from my lips to my neck.

"Tessa," he murmured as he trailed sexy kisses down my throat. I loved that he had never once called me Therese. Always Tessa.

My phone buzzed, and I sighed with frustration. "That probably means Ben is here."

"Just in the nick of time, before you did something you might regret," Roman said with a chuckle.

"Hard to imagine I would regret it," I said with a smile. "Even so, it's a bit soon."

168

"I hear ya." Roman caressed my face with his fingers. "I'll see ya at work tomorrow. Get some rest, okay?"

Such simple words, but they made me feel all choked up inside. People constantly made demands of me, but they rarely worried about my needs unless there was something in it for them. It seemed Roman was always looking after me, telling me to take it easy and rest. That it was really okay to eat another half slice of pizza.

"I will," I said, trying not to tear up. "You too."

He nodded and dipped his head down for another tender kiss. Then he brushed his lips past my cheek and close to my ear, and whispered, "I love you."

So help me God, in that moment, I actually believed him.

CHAPTER 17

I woke up the next morning with a smile when I remembered my perfect date with Roman. It was like waking from a dream that makes you feel warm and happy all over, only to discover it wasn't a dream after all. It was real.

It was *real.*

Naturally, I was back to second-guessing myself when it came to believing that Roman was actually in love with me. In a way, it didn't really matter. Roman seemed to genuinely care for me, and that was more than enough. It was too soon for me, but I could see myself falling in love with him. Being with him felt right, and he made me happy. I couldn't remember the last time any man made me feel so good just to be with him.

Roman also happened to be gorgeous. Though I'd always loved a man in a suit, I preferred Roman's tight jeans look. He'd apologized for being dirty, but it had actually been a huge turn-on for me. I'd meant it when I told him I loved his manly ruggedness.

I made my usual breakfast of scrambled egg whites, fruit,

and hot tea. Though I much preferred coffee, tea was better for my voice. I sat in my usual breakfast nook overlooking the Queensborough Bridge and smiled when I remembered Roman's awestruck reaction to my house. Seeing my home through his eyes gave me a renewed appreciation.

As I ate, I scrolled through my phone to find some information on the musical *Waitress* that Roman had told me about. Based on the movie of the same name, it was about a poor waitress who accidentally gets pregnant by her abusive husband and then has an affair with her gynecologist.

I frowned. Roman had insisted that a song from the show was just like me, but so far, I wasn't getting the connection. I wasn't the type who would ever cheat. I was the type who got cheated *on*. And Roman knew that. Why on earth would he recommend a song from this show? I read on about how the main character, Jenna, the waitress, has dreams of winning a pie-making contest with a large reward. At the end of the show, she takes over the diner where she works and finds success at making her famous pies.

Still unsure of what to think, I put my breakfast dishes in the sink. I poured myself another cup of tea and went into the fireplace room where Roman and I had our date. Nervously, I cued up "She Used to Be Mine" and thought about what Roman had said about it.

It's you. It's just ... you.

My stomach felt jittery as the music began to play. For better or worse, this song was about to tell me exactly what Roman thought of me.

As I listened to the words, it quickly became clear "She Used to Be Mine" was Jenna singing about herself. After hearing the first verse, my hand flew to my mouth. My eyes filled with tears. The song was lovely and haunting, beautiful and sad. Jenna sings about how she is imperfect, and yet she's kind. The lyrics spoke of how hard she is on herself. That's she's broken, but she refuses to ask for help. She's messy and scared, yet she has learned how to toughen up when she's been beaten down. That she is all sorts of conflicting things mixed up together in a beautiful pie.

I listened to the song three times in a row, and by the third time, I had broken down into wracking sobs.

It was *me.*

I hugged myself and cried and cried, but in a good way, finally letting go of some of the pressure I'd put on myself, and the pressure I let others put on me. Directors, producers, managers, agents, gossip columnists, and my mother, to name a few.

I thought about all the times Roman had looked at me when I'd had the overwhelming sensation that he was seeing through the movie star façade, and into the real me. Sharing this song with me had done more to convince me that he cared for the real Tessa than any of the wonderful and kind things he'd said so far.

The song had cut to the heart of all my insecurities, my feelings of never being good enough. The fact that Roman thought this song was just like me meant he knew about those insecurities, my messiness, and my imperfections.

And he loved me anyway.

IT WAS a wonder I could get any work done at all today. I'd been in a happy daze ever since my date with Tessa last night, and I was still unable to wrap my head around the fact that it had actually happened. When I'd woken up yesterday morning, I was a man hopelessly in love with a woman who I thought was forever out of my reach, and I'd ended the day holding her in my arms and kissing her.

I'd fantasized for months about just being alone with her,

away from all the cast and crew and all her fans, and when it finally happened, it was even better than I'd hoped. Last night had confirmed the weird feeling I'd had that we really belonged together, at least for me. The time had flown by. It was by far the best date I'd ever been on, and we hadn't even gone out anywhere, nor did we end up in bed together. It didn't matter. Just being with her was everything I dreamed it would be. And, unless I was totally misreading Tessa's vibe, she had felt the same way.

Right before the show, Tessa rushed up to me, her dress swishing as she briskly walked over. My God, she looked beautiful. She always did, but dressed in her fancy costume with her hair and makeup all done, she reminded me of a Disney princess,. And she was hurrying over to see *me*.

"Hey," she said, her impossibly blue eyes shining.

"Hey."

"I listened to that song you told me about." Tessa swallowed, and her eyes filled with tears. "You were right. It *was* me. How did you know?"

I smiled at her. "I know you better than you think I do."

"Apparently so," Tessa said, wiping a tear from her eye. I hoped I hadn't upset her by telling her about the song, though I thought she was more touched than anything else.

"You are too hard on yourself most of the time, you know," I said.

"Maybe so."

We gazed into each other's eyes for a moment. Dating a famous movie star came with a set of rules I was still learning, and one of them was that Tessa wasn't about to go out in public to display our brand-new relationship to the world any time soon. I understood completely. People were used to me gazing at her adoringly, but she wasn't hiding her own affectionate look.

"It's very hard not to kiss you right now," I said in a low

voice so no one else could hear. I also hoped I sounded sexy to her.

"It's hard not to let you," she whispered back.

Relief swept through my body. Her tender gaze and soft-spoken affection assured me that last night was not a dream, and that I hadn't been imagining the connection between us. She'd felt it too.

As much as I wanted to stand and stare into her eyes all night, I couldn't do it without arousing suspicion. Besides, we did have a show to put on.

"Have a great show, Tessa."

"You too, Roman," she said. She smiled and turned away. But then she turned back and said, "Do you want to come back to my place tonight?"

I opened my mouth to say "Hell yes," but she spoke again before I could respond.

"I just meant for, you know, another date," she added. I could honestly say that my mind hadn't gone immediately to sex when she'd said it. I was just happy to spend more time with her.

"I know what you meant, Tessa. And hell yes, I want to have another date with you," I said with a laugh.

"Okay." She smiled. "I'll see you after the show."

I nodded, and she rushed off to get ready for her grand stage entrance.

Rex walked up to me as soon as Tessa was out of sight. "Everything okay?"

"Yeah, fine," I said.

"Was she crying?" Rex asked.

"Oh, well yeah. A little."

Rex shot me a quizzical look as if to say "Why the hell was she crying, and why don't you seem more upset about it?"

I laughed. "It's okay, really. I told her to listen to a sad song I knew she'd relate to, and she did. That's all."

"Oh," Rex said, seeming satisfied with my explanation. It was the truth, after all.

Rex wandered off, and I got back to work. The selfish part of me wished Tessa wouldn't keep it a secret that we'd been out on a date and were going on another one. But she'd been hurt publicly before, and I knew she had no desire to go through that again. Besides, as much as I longed to dive headlong into a serious relationship with the woman I loved, I couldn't afford to get too far ahead of myself. I was in love, but Tessa wasn't. Not yet, anyway. She possibly never would be.

I tried not to think about it. Drawing in a deep breath I reminded myself to take this one day at a time.

* * *

OVER THE NEXT FEW WEEKS, Tessa and I had a bunch more dates. All of them were at her house, and then one day she insisted on going to my place. It had to happen eventually, but I was kind of dreading it.

"We don't have to stay too long," she told me, kissing my lips and making it impossible to say no to her. "But I want to at least see where you live."

"Okay, if you insist, but I'm telling you, it's silly for us to hang out in my teeny-tiny apartment when we have your mansion."

"Fine. I just wanna see!" Tessa chirped.

She asked Ben to drive us to my shithole place in Little Italy. It wasn't really a shithole—I was proud of it in a weird way. I'm Italian, so I liked being in Little Italy, and my tiny place really wasn't bad. But Jesus, compared to hers? She probably had boxes delivered to her house that were bigger than where I lived.

When Ben stopped in front of my apartment building on

Mulberry Street, I took Tessa's hand and helped her out of the SUV. Since it was late March, the weather had finally turned a bit warmer, and we were wearing only light jackets. It was a cloudy day, but Tessa wore sunglasses anyway.

Once again, the selfish part of me would have killed to have my neighbors see me with Therese Andrews. I knew that wasn't fair, though. I was careful to never treat her like a movie star like everyone else did, and I'd stopped thinking of her as famous a long time ago. To me, she was sweet Tessa Gumm.

I let out a shaky sigh as we walked up to my building. Though I knew being poor was nothing to be ashamed of, it felt emasculating to have Tessa see my embarrassingly small living space. My God, her house in L.A. must look like the Taj Mahal.

We walked into my apartment building and were immediately assaulted by the smell of a bunch of different meals being cooked at the same time. Normally, I was immune to it, but I was experiencing everything through Tessa's point of view. If the smell bothered her, she didn't show it. I unlocked the front door, reluctantly ushering Tessa inside. She took off her sunglasses and scanned my tiny living room, dining area, and kitchen that were pretty much all in one space.

And she laughed.

I felt my face get hot with both shame and anger. I couldn't believe Tessa would actually laugh at me, especially when she knew how self-conscious I was about showing her my apartment.

"Just as I suspected," Tessa said, patting my warm cheek. "It's as neat as a pin. It's definitely your place, Roman, Roman, Roman."

I laughed, feeling stupid for thinking Tessa was making fun of me for living in a humble apartment. Instead, she was making fun of me for being a neat freak. Somehow that didn't bother me. She wasn't wrong.

Tessa peered into the kitchen area, and then looked around at the rest of the place.

"What you see is about it," I said. "Over there's the bathroom. And that's my bedroom."

"Can I see?" she asked.

"Of course."

Tessa walked over to my bedroom and I opened the door. I watched her eyes explore my personal space, and it reminded me of the first time I'd seen her bedroom.

Unfortunately, it was also the last time. We'd never gone anywhere near her bedroom since the first day, when she gave me a tour of her house.

"It's nice," Tessa said as she surveyed my bedroom, which was plain compared to hers. I had a gray bedspread with matching sheets and pillows, a television, and a nightstand. Pretty no-nonsense. "It's manly, like you."

I chuckled. Tessa's bedroom was really girly. It suited her. After lingering at my bedroom door long enough to make me wonder what she was thinking, Tessa walked back into the living room and flopped down on the couch.

I sat down next to her, and she smiled at me. She seemed as comfortable as if she'd been here a bunch of times already. It was cool.

"I love your place, Roman. It's cozy. And I don't mean cozy as in code for small. It's really very nice and welcoming, yet sturdy and manly. It's so *you*."

"Thanks," I said, beginning to wonder why I'd been so resistant to show her where I lived in the first place. I'd never treated her like a movie star, and she'd never acted like one. I should have known it would be okay to bring her here.

Tessa pulled me in for a kiss, and before long we were making out hot and heavy. But I knew better than to expect more than passionate kissing. Though my raging hard cock had high hopes, I knew it was not to be. So far, all our dates had ended with passionate make-out sessions that had left me frustrated and forced me to finish the job with my hand when I got home. Tessa seemed to enjoy touching me, kissing me, and letting me hold her in my arms, but that was as far as she was willing to go. Honestly, I was a little afraid to ask how long she wanted to wait.

Tessa pulled away from me and sighed.

"You okay?"

"Yeah," she said wearily. "I know you're probably wondering why we haven't, you know, been intimate yet."

"Well, it has crossed my mind," I ventured carefully, grateful she'd broached the subject.

Tessa sat back on the couch, looking uncertain.

"Whatever it is, you know you can tell me," I assured her. My body tensed as I geared up for her rejection. I wanted to know, but at the same time, I didn't.

She nodded, still looking worried. "I guess I'm ... afraid."

"Afraid of me?" I asked, horrified.

"Well, no. Not exactly." Tessa drew in a deep breath. "It's just that you've been such a huge fan of Therese Andrews for such a long time. I'm sure you've fantasized about being with her."

"You could say that. I learned how to jerk off because of a poster of you."

"Roman!" Tessa exclaimed, her cheeks turning adorably red.

"Sorry," I said, chuckling. "I don't mean to be blunt. I just feel like I can talk to you about anything."

"Well, yeah. You *can* talk to me about anything, but..."

"Except jerking off?" I teased.

She blushed deeper. "Can you at least stop saying it?"

Still laughing, I stroked her warm cheek with the back of

my hand. "Look, I get why it's weird for you. But you must be aware lots of guys … do that thing I'm not allowed to say, when thinking about you."

"Yeah, I know," Tessa said, wincing. "It's kind of flattering in a creepy sort of way. But that's just it. It *is* kind of creepy, and I don't want to go to bed with a guy who just wants to fulfill a fantasy of having sex with Therese Andrews."

Hearing the quiver in her voice suddenly made this subject a lot less funny. I nodded, understanding she was genuinely afraid of having sex with me. It broke my heart, but I was glad she'd told me.

I started to say something, but she held up a hand to cut me off.

"Roman," she said, taking my hand in hers. "You have never, ever treated me like that. You've never made me feel like I'm just a celebrity you want to have sex with. But you have to understand … Even before all that stuff with Ricky cheating, that made me never want to trust another man with my body again, I dated another guy. And he was a fan, like you were."

I nodded, squeezing her hand as she spilled her guts to me. Rosemary had warned me that Tessa had dated a fan before me, and that it had ended badly.

"For the most part, he didn't act like a fanboy, either. I guess there were some warning signs. Something in the way he looked at me sometimes. Like he wasn't really seeing the real me. Deep down, maybe I was aware he was still a little starstruck by dating me, but I didn't want to believe it. We'd had sex a few times and it was fine."

I felt a sharp, stabbing pain in my chest when Tessa talked about having sex with another guy. I was aware she'd dated lots of guys before me, of course. It just hurt to hear about it. Once again, pettiness rose up in me, and I found myself wondering how long she'd made him wait before taking him to bed.

"Then, one time he thought it would be fun if I dressed up as Roxy Rose. He was always telling me how sexy I was in that movie, and he said it would be hot if I dressed up like her when we had sex."

I swallowed hard. I wanted to be supportive, but Tessa filling my head with specific details about her sex life with another man was killing me.

"I thought it would be okay. Role playing in the bedroom can be fun, you know?"

"Uh-huh," I said, my stomach tight. It wasn't only sexual jealousy. Tessa was the woman I loved, and it hurt to imagine her being intimate with another man.

Tessa wrapped her arms around herself and shivered. "The way he looked at me. The way he touched me. It made me feel cheap and used. Violated, even. It wasn't his fault, I guess. I mean, I consented to doing it, but I shouldn't have."

"Well, maybe he shouldn't have asked you to do it," I snapped angrily. Tessa jumped, startled by my outburst.

"Sorry. Didn't mean to yell. But he should've had more respect for you. If he knew you at all, he would have known how sensitive you are about being liked only for your fame."

Tessa unwrapped her arms from her chest. "Maybe he didn't know. We never talked about stuff like that the way you and I do all the time." She smiled gratefully at me, and my jealousy and anger subsided a little bit. Maybe other men had been privileged enough to have sex with her, but nobody knew Tessa the way I did. And nobody could ever love her more than I did.

"I never would have done it if I'd known it would affect me like that. Afterward, I realized Derek was just a fanboy after all. I lay in bed and just cried and cried."

"I'm so sorry that happened to you," I said, the ache in my

heart no longer from jealousy, but from pain over her suffering. I was an idiot for trying to make Tessa's traumatic experience into a pity party for me.

"Thanks, Roman," she said quietly. "I broke up with him after that." She paused and studied my face with a haunted look in her blue eyes. "I think that's what terrifies me the most. That we'll have sex and it'll feel wrong like it did with him. And then we'd have to break up. And I—I can't even think about that."

Her voice quavered again. I was about to reach for her, but she wrapped her arms around herself again.

"After we broke up, I found out he'd been cheating on me."

I couldn't begin to imagine how badly that must have hurt. No wonder Tessa had such a hard time believing my love for her was real. The men in her life had treated her like she was disposable. Rage boiled up in me, and I wanted to punch the ever-living shit out of every guy who'd ever harmed her.

I drew in a deep breath to steady myself. Tessa needed my understanding right now. Not my anger.

"Even Therese Andrews and Roxy Rose weren't enough for Ricky and Derek. And you," she said softly, her eyes filling with fresh tears. "You've been fantasizing about having sex with Therese Andrews since you were a teenager. You're bound to be disappointed. I can't compete with a perfect fantasy. Even if we do have sex, it'll never be enough."

I didn't speak at first. Tessa watched me, looking worried. I turned over what she'd said in my mind.

"I'm so glad you told me all of this," I said at last. "These are things I never thought about, but they make total sense to me. Of course you're afraid, after everything you've been through. I understand exactly what you're saying."

Tessa let out a deep, relieved sigh.

"Did you think I'd be mad or something?"

"No," she said, wiping tears from her eyes. "I didn't think you'd be mad. But I didn't expect you to understand, yet you do. Somehow, you always understand me."

I opened my arms. "Come here."

Instead of sliding toward me on the couch, she stood up. For a terrible second, I thought she was about to walk away from me, but she wanted to sit in my lap. She sat crosswise on me, and I wrapped my arms around her.

"God, you're so tiny."

Tessa giggled. It was a beautiful sound.

I held her in my arms for a long time, stroking her back and her hair, without saying anything. Knowing Tessa, that was exactly what she needed right now. After a while her breathing became so calm and steady, I thought she might have fallen asleep.

She let out a soft, contented sigh.

"Tessa," I said. "There's no timetable for us to have sex, so please stop stressing out over it. And when the time comes, it will be wonderful. Of course it will be enough for me, because what we have right here and right now, is already more than enough."

Tessa put her arms around my neck and snuggled up closer to me. "Roman, Roman, Roman," she murmured in my ear. "You're so wonderful." She seemed to feel better after confiding in me, and I loved how relaxed her body felt against mine.

Considering everything she'd been through, I realized it still might be a long time before she was ready to go to bed with me. She clearly needed more time to trust me, and I really did understand. I felt terrible that she'd been carrying around this pain and fear all this time.

Ben came to pick her up later that evening. Before she left, I gave her a long goodnight kiss.

"Promise me you're not gonna stress over this anymore, okay?"

"I promise," she said with a smile.

I kissed her again. "I love you so much, Tessa. I'm not going anywhere. You take all the time you need."

I looked at her sternly, holding her face with my hands. "You are more than enough."

"Thank you," she whispered.

After walking her to the car, I headed back inside my apartment. I sighed, still feeling incredibly sexually frustrated. But Tessa was worth waiting for. As long as I had Tessa in my life, everything would be okay. I'd wait years if I had to.

A few hours later, Tessa texted me.

Bring an overnight bag to work tomorrow. You won't be going home.

CHAPTER 18

"*A*re you sure?" Roman asked for the millionth time. We'd just finished eating dinner and cleaning up after, of course, and now we were kissing on my couch. Though that was usually where our dates ended, I'd made it clear tonight would be different.

"If I didn't know better, I'd think you were trying to get out of this," I teased. He'd texted me a bunch of times during the day asking if I was sure I was okay with this, and we'd talked at length about it during dinner. His concern only made me more confident I was making the right decision to have sex with him. Honestly, I was still afraid, but I was ready at the same time.

For our entire relationship, I always feared he would treat me like Therese Andrews, but he never did. And, although he never called me Therese, I was afraid he would during sex.

I did my best to shake off those thoughts and focus on Roman.

"Come on," I said, taking his hand. "Let's go upstairs before you change your mind."

He chuckled at that, letting me lead him up the staircase to my bedroom.

Straight away, I pulled him down on the bed and started kissing him. Suddenly, I felt like a teenager, and not in a good way. I couldn't remember the last time I'd been nervous about having sex. I hated feeling that way, especially with Roman. I cared deeply about him, and I didn't want to be uneasy. I wanted to live in the moment, but it was almost as if I'd forgotten how.

Lucky for me, Roman hadn't. Now that he knew I really wanted this, he took charge. He pressed me against the bed, kissing me passionately. His kiss was perfect—forceful and dominant, yet somehow still tender. I expected him to rip off my clothes, but he didn't. Roman took his time.

He started slowly kissing down my neck, which he knew I loved from our frequent make-out sessions. Slowly, sensually, he made his way toward my breasts and began unbuttoning my blouse one button at a time. Roman was such a neatnik, he'd never rip off my clothes. How like him to carefully undress me.

Finally freeing me from my blouse, he reached behind and expertly unclasped my bra. He pulled it off and began kissing my breasts, one at a time. I moaned, arching my back.

"Oh Roman, that feels so good."

His tongue teased my nipples, making me cry out with pleasure. As always, Roman knew exactly how to touch me and that I needed him to take his time with me, especially for our first time together. God only knew where he got his restraint, considering how long I'd made him wait. Yet, he seemed in no rush to get his long-denied gratification.

I started unbuttoning his shirt. As I pulled it off, I admired his muscular chest, with dark hair that matched the rich, dark wavy hair on his head. God, how I loved his sexy

Italian look. I wasn't sure if he worked out or if his muscular physique was a result of his job, but I was impressed, whatever the reason. I liked to think he got that way from doing the physical stuff like carrying heavy equipment at work. Picturing Roman in those tight jeans, getting all dirty while doing his job was an incredible turn-on.

Roman paused for a moment, glancing down at his chest. Self-consciously, he said, "Sorry. I'm kinda hairy. I know you're probably used to smooth chests with huge muscles."

I gazed at him in wonder. I'd been worried I wouldn't measure up to his expectations, but it never dawned on me that he might feel the same way. After all, he'd seen me do love scenes with some of the hottest men in Hollywood.

"Roman," I said, running my hands over his delightfully hairy chest. "You know how much I love your rugged look. You're different from those Hollywood pretty boys in the most wonderful way." I paused as I bit my lip. "You have *no* idea how much it turns me on to see you in action at the theater. I love to watch you work with your hands, and I have fantasies about being able to watch you work shirtless in tight jeans."

"Really?" he asked, looking astonished.

"Oh yeah."

"Wow."

"Yeah," I said, raising an eyebrow. "I never knew that kind of thing would get me hot, but it does."

I pulled him in for another kiss, and he massaged my breasts while his tongue explored my mouth. His touch was more forceful now, like my words had perhaps given him more confidence.

"As much as I love your sexy jeans, I want them off," I said after he broke off our kiss. I tugged on his pants, and he took a moment to pull them off, taking his underwear with them.

I felt his eyes on me as he watched me look at his cock for the first time.

I drew in a deep breath and let out an impressed *mmmm* sound. "I love where this little trail of hair leads," I said, tracing the dark hair on his chest that led to his delicious groin area.

Roman tugged off my jeans, and soon I was naked too. He admired my body, running his eyes lovingly over my legs, stomach, up to my breasts, and then my face. He smiled at me, filling me with happiness. He didn't look like a man who had finally seen his celebrity crush naked after years of curiosity. Roman gazed at me like I was the woman he loved.

He slid down the bed and began kissing the bottom of my foot. I gasped, delighting in the feel of him opening my legs a bit. I was already soaking wet, enjoying the delicious anticipation of what was to come. Still taking his time, he kissed the bottom of the other foot, and then began slowly kissing his way up my legs.

And then between them.

He kissed the mound between my legs, teasing me with his tongue all around my clit. A sudden bolt of intense, sharp pleasure rocketed through me when his tongue finally reached my most sensitive spot.

I arched my back and let out a cry of pleasure. If he kept that up, I would come in a matter of seconds. I was that turned on. Roman teased me with his tongue just long enough to bring me to the brink then he stopped, leaving me panting and desperate for more.

Roman kissed all over my body, making his way back up to my mouth. He stopped for a moment so he could gaze into my eyes.

"You're so beautiful, Tessa," he said tenderly.

Roman positioned himself between my legs and paused

there for a moment, and just when I felt I couldn't wait another second, he slid himself inside me.

I let out a cry and Roman moaned deep in his throat, but he never broke eye contact with me. God it was sexy, seeing the unmistakable look of deepest pleasure cross his manly face.

He leaned down and kissed me tenderly as he moved inside me. Everything about his lovemaking was slow and sensual. It was everything I didn't even know I wanted, and it was nothing like what I was used to. Roman focused on me and my needs. He took notice of every little noise I made, every small cry or moan of enjoyment, and took care to repeat whatever he was doing to intensify the sensation for me.

"Ahh, ahhh," I cried out, arching my back as Roman found a particularly pleasurable rhythm with his slow, steady thrusts. We moved together in perfect sync and I was within seconds of reaching orgasm.

"Will you turn around for me," Roman murmured in my ear.

A ripple of disappointment went through me. Not only had I been close to release, but facing him was so tender and intimate. It felt so right. All the same, he had made this entire sexual experience all about my needs so far, so it was only fair to do what he asked. What would be pleasurable for him.

"Of course," I whispered. I bit back a cry of frustration when he pulled out of me so we could change positions. God, I really had been *close* ...

I turned over, positioning myself on all fours. I suddenly felt awkward, even though I'd had sex in this position many times. Somehow it felt wrong to do it this way for our first time.

Until Roman entered me again. I gasped with renewed pleasure, but that was only the beginning. He reached around, his arm across my breasts, he pulled me close to him and lifted me up. Arching my back, I was able to put my head on his right shoulder. Our faces cheek to cheek, we began to move together, once again in perfect rhythm. He couldn't penetrate me as deeply in this position, but I didn't care. No one had ever held me this way during sex.

"Tessa," he murmured in my ear as he slid in and out of me. His movement was every bit as tender and intimate as it had been when he was on top of me, maybe even more so. With his gentle, perfect motion, it felt like he was physically loving me with his body. My eyes filled with tears of emotion at the sheer beauty of it. It felt as if Roman's tender love-making was healing me from the pain of all the times men had used me for my body.

"Oh Roman," I said, tenderly rubbing his face with mine as we moved together. Physically, the pleasure wasn't as intense in this position, it was pure emotional bliss. After moving together like this for a while, my pleasure began to grow again.

"Ahhh, Roman," I cried. Soon, I couldn't take it anymore. As much as I adored Roman's tenderness as he held me this way, my need for sexual release was growing desperate. I pulled out of his grasp and dropped down on all fours.

"Roman, I need to feel all of you," I cried, nearly begging. The position that had felt wrong just moments ago was suddenly perfect.

I let out a sharp cry as Roman gave me what I needed. He planted his hands on the mattress and rammed into me with all his might.

"Yes, God *yes*, Roman!" I called out as the bed slammed into the wall with his thrusts. "Oh, God, I'm gonna come …"

"Oh no, you're not," Roman said, abruptly pulling out of me, once again denying me my release.

"Roman!" I cried out with frustration bordering on anger

at this point. I was all for slow lovemaking for our first time, but he was *torturing* me now. I flipped over onto my back. "Roman, I need—"

"I know what you need," Roman growled. He straddled me, his impressively sized cock standing ramrod straight between his legs. "And I'm gonna give it to you."

I drew in a breath of desperate anticipation.

His face softened a bit into that look I craved from him. That unmistakable look of pure love. "But I need to be facing you first."

"Yes," I whispered as I gazed into those rich, dark eyes. As hard as it had been to wait for relief, this was what I wanted too.

I opened my legs for him, and Roman slammed into me. I threw my head back and cried out as a deep, intense jolt of pleasure went through me. Roman was clearly done with the gentle part of our lovemaking. I knew he would deliver on his promise. He pounded into me over, and over, and over again and it wasn't long before I felt my orgasm begin to claim me. Arching my back, I gripped the headboard, my legs flung open as wide as they could go.

A delicious tingling sensation of utter bliss blossomed between my legs and soon erupted into a level of ecstasy I had never known was possible.

"Oh God, oh God, oh God," I cried out, repeating it every time a fresh ripple of pleasure went through my body. I quickly lost count of how many times I'd said it. And, just when I thought my orgasm was about to subside, a renewed wave of bliss washed over me. "Oh God!" I screamed again.

Multiple orgasms. I'm having multiple orgasms.

I hadn't even known that was a real thing until this moment. I found out in the best possible way that it was *quite* real.

When my climaxes finally subsided, I panted heavily.

Gazing up at Roman, I saw a look of unmistakable pride mixed with intense need. I would never know how he had managed to last as long as he had. I just knew I was grateful.

He continued his forceful thrusts, and I watched as his eyes fluttered closed. He grunted deep in his throat as he finally gratified his own needs.

"*Tessa,*" Roman growled in my ear just before he exploded inside of me.

He would never know how much that simple word meant to me. During his most intimate, out-of-control moment he said *my name*. Not Therese, not Roxy. *Tessa.*

Tears of emotion and relief welled up in my eyes. I had never felt happier, more relaxed, not to mention sexually satisfied, in my entire life.

"Oh Roman," I said, holding him tightly in my arms while he was still inside me. We stayed that way for a few minutes.

"Tessa," he said, kissing my cheek. "You are so much more than enough."

He kissed me softly before pulling out of me, then he lay down beside me.

"Oh Roman, Roman, Roman," I said in the most sensual voice I had the strength to muster. "You were incredible. So that's what it feels like to have multiple orgasms."

Roman's eyes opened wide. "Did you really?"

I nodded. "Oh yeah. No one's ever done that to me before."

He lay on his side facing me, tracing his fingers down the length of my body for a while. Then, out of nowhere, he said, "I can't do this."

"What?" I asked, scared about what he was going to say. He seemed so serious.

"I have to pick up our clothes from the floor."

I burst out laughing from both amusement and relief.

"I know it's stupid, but I seriously won't be able to go to

sleep unless I clean up," Roman said apologetically as he got up from the bed.

"It's okay. You can toss my clothes in the hamper, and you can fold yours neatly and put them on the dresser, or whatever you need to do. I promise I won't judge you. Much."

I watched with great interest as Roman, still naked, bent over and started gathering our clothes.

"Mmmmmm, this makes me want to fire my housekeeper and pay you to clean up naked instead," I said, making him chuckle.

Once he was happy with the appearance of my bedroom again, he turned to me and said, "I just gotta wash up and brush my teeth, and then I'll come back to bed, okay?"

"Okay," I said, and he disappeared into the bathroom that was attached to the bedroom. I sat up in bed, enjoying the delightful tingle between my legs. Roman had pounded me so hard, and I loved feeling the physical reminder in my body. Not only was the sex wonderful, but I looked forward to cuddling up with Roman all night. It had been a long time since I'd had a man in my bed. It would be cozy and wonderful.

I was still worried about one thing, though. I hugged my knees to my chest, lost in thought when Roman came out of the bathroom.

"What's the matter?" he asked, eying me with concern.

"It's gonna sound stupid."

"Tell me anyway," he said in a breezy voice that calmed me. We always said we could tell each other anything.

I smiled at him a bit sadly. "You've never seen me without my makeup on."

"That's true. It's about time, don'tcha think?" he said with a sexy grin. "It's okay, Tessy. It's gonna be fine."

"Tessy. I like that."

"Does anybody else call you that?"

I shook my head, and Roman smiled. "Cool."

Groaning a bit, I got up from the bed and headed into the bathroom. After I brushed my teeth, I used cold cream to take off my foundation, eyeliner, mascara, and lipstick. My skin was pretty good, but not perfect. The makeup covered a few red blotches, and my dark eye makeup made my blue eyes look much brighter than they actually were. Roman had seen me in heavy stage makeup for the show, and he had seen me in lighter makeup during rehearsal when I'd just worn the basics. He'd never seen my face without anything. It was funny that I was more scared to have him see my naked face than my naked body.

Sighing, I reluctantly opened the bathroom door. Roman sat on the bed wearing pajama bottoms, waiting for me. His face broke into a huge grin when he saw me.

"You're so beautiful, Tessy. You really have no idea." He opened his arms for me, and I sat down next to him, letting him pull me close to him. He was probably just being nice, but it didn't matter. It still made me feel better.

"You could be covered from head to toe except for your eyes, and I would still know it was you. I'd know those pretty eyes anywhere." He gazed directly at my face. It made me nervous, but I refused to look away. I figured it was best to let him get a good look and get it over with.

He stroked my cheek, not saying anything for a while. I was used to his silences by now. It meant he was contemplating, taking his time, so he would find the right thing to say. Which he always did.

"It's a privilege to see you like this. An honor. Not many people get to see you this way." Roman kissed my lips.

Yes. He always knew just the right thing to say.

"What's your side of the bed? I don't want to screw up your routine," I said.

Roman laughed and pointed to the left side. I climbed

over to the right, and he lay down next to me. I switched off the lamp and we held each other silently.

We didn't need to say anything. Just being together was enough.

More than enough.

CHAPTER 19

*J*liked to think I was good in bed, but *damn.* I'd *never* made a woman scream like that before. Then again, I'd never made a woman wait to come as long as I'd made Tessa wait. Thank God she'd given me a heads up via text we would be having sex that night. Gave me time to prepare. I jerked off twice before I left for work that afternoon. I'd wanted to make sure I could last as long as possible for her, and it'd worked like a charm.

As much as I kept telling myself I'd finally achieved my lifelong dream of having sex with Therese Andrews a couple of days ago, I knew it wasn't true. Tessa was so different from that fantasy. Not that it was a bad thing. Not at all. Tessa was the woman of my dreams, and it was still hard to believe she let me have sex with her. *Tessa.* The woman who lit up every room she walked into and commanded attention even when she wasn't trying. The woman who had a knack for making everybody feel good about themselves. The woman with incredible talent, who conquered stage and screen. That woman had had sex with *me.* I had never been so happy and proud in my life.

Too bad I couldn't tell anyone.

Tessa had been through hell and back when it came to the media, so I understood why she wanted to keep things between us a secret. For now, at least.

I only got to see her once very quickly before she had to go onstage. She shot me the briefest of glances, but her expression said it all. Her gaze was steamy, affectionate, and mischievous at the same time. It was kind of fun keeping our sexy secret.

"Quit staring, Roman, Roman, Roman," Les teased me. "You got work to do."

Yeah. That was the sucky part about keeping our relationship quiet. Everybody at the theater still thought I was a pathetic fanboy with a silly, unrequited crush. It was hard not to yell, *Shows what you know. We had sex the other night, and I made her fucking come, like, a million times.*

Well, even if I *could* tell people about our relationship, I would never say anything like that. Not about Tessa. But still. It was hard not to be able to say anything.

After the show, Rex came up to me and said, "Hey. Tessa wants to see you in her dressing room." It was a genuine struggle to keep the grin off my face. Rex squinted at me and added, "What's that about?"

Being called to her dressing room twice was highly suspicious. At this point in a show's run, there was no real reason the lead actress would need to see the head electrician, since all the lighting cues had been locked down long ago. At least, there was no *professional* reason Tessa should need to see me.

"How should I know?" I asked, forcing myself to maintain my poker face.

Rex still eyed me curiously. I would never betray Tessa's trust by telling anyone about our relationship, but I wouldn't exactly be upset if somebody accidentally found out we were involved.

"Well hurry up," Rex grumbled. I nodded, allowing myself to break into a huge grin the second he walked away.

I rushed up to Tessa's dressing room and knocked on the door.

"It's Roman."

Tessa opened the door, still dressed in her lovely gown from the show. She was always beautiful, but in full costume and makeup as Mary, she was a knockout. She smiled at me and gave me a moment to look her up and down.

"God, you look amazing," I told her.

"Thanks."

"Everything okay?" I asked.

"Yeah, yeah. Come on in," Tessa said, closing the door behind me. Then she pulled me close and kissed me. It took me by delicious surprise. We kissed passionately, our hands all over each other.

"I just had to see you, Roman," Tessa said breathlessly between kisses.

"Hmmm," was my intelligent response as I continued to devour her lips with mine.

I pressed the hardness between my legs against the softness between hers, making her cry, "Oh!"

"Oh Roman," she said sensually in my ear. "I can't stop thinking about you and everything you did to me the other night."

A groan of desire escaped my lips. I knew I'd never forget the way Tessa had looked while she was having multiple orgasms. The way she'd thrown her head back, arched her back, and kept screaming *oh God, oh God* ... Christ, I could come now just thinking about it.

"Well, there's more where that came from. All you gotta do is ask."

Tessa stopped kissing me long enough to meet my gaze. Her eyes were wild with desire. "I'm asking, Roman. *Now.*"

"Now?" I asked incredulously.

"Yes," she said, practically panting with need. "Do you have time?"

"Are you kidding? I'll *make* time."

Tessa nodded. Never taking her eyes off mine, she reached behind her and locked the door.

Oh my God, this is really happening. Tessa wants to have sex in her dressing room.

I cupped her face and kissed her passionately, half-crazed with my own painful need. Hard to believe it had only been two days since we'd had sex. I was about to push her to the floor, but she had other ideas. Tessa began frantically tugging and pulling up her fancy costume dress.

She wanted me to take her up against the wall.

While she fussed with her dress, I started unbuckling my belt. Tessa bit her lip with anticipation as she watched me pull my jeans and underwear down. The way she stared hungrily at my cock was unbelievably erotic.

She finally got her dress pulled up enough for me to reach her. I grabbed her right leg and opened her up wide, then rammed into her as hard as I could.

Tessa dug her fingernails into my shoulders, and I watched her fight the urge to scream. She'd made lots of noise in bed the other night, and I was fascinated watching her struggle to be quiet during sex.

"Ah, ah, ah," she cried out softly, trying to keep her voice a whisper as I thrust myself in and out of her with all my might.

I still could not wrap my head around the fact that this was really happening. As Mary onstage, Tessa had been sweet and chaste. The audience had no idea that their beautiful leading lady was currently getting banged against her dressing room door by a crew member.

I felt a little guilty thinking about Tessa like that, but

damn. This was like something out of a porno. And it was so goddamn hot.

"Fuck me, Roman," Tessa moaned. "Oh God, fuck me hard, baby."

My eyes bugged out of their sockets. I'd *never* heard Tessa talk like that. I didn't think I'd ever heard her curse, let alone say the f-word.

I suddenly felt a lot less guilty, since she was clearly as turned on as I was. The other night had been making love. This was pure, animal sex. And I loved every second of it.

It was so hot, though, that I couldn't hold out much longer. I reached down to massage her clit to help her come faster.

"Ah!" Tessa screamed, then dropped her voice back down to a whisper. "Sorry. It's so … hard … to be … quiet," she said through panting breaths.

"That's okay, Tessy. Means I'm doing it right."

"God yes, you're doing it right," she whispered.

"Are you almost there, baby?" I asked, because I sure as hell was. I was ready to explode. I looked at her face to find she couldn't answer. She was already having an orgasm.

Tessa's eyes rolled back and her body shook. Gripping my shoulders, she whispered, "Oh God, oh God …"

Watching her come was all the inspiration I needed for my own release. I gripped her shoulders, probably a bit too hard, and grunted as I came and came hard. It was, without a doubt, the most satisfying orgasm I'd ever had after the most exciting sex of my life.

Exhausted, I pulled her close, and she wrapped her arms around my neck the same way she had the first time we had sex. We stayed like that for a moment, with me still inside her.

I kissed her gently as I pulled out of her. After I pulled up my pants, I pulled her skirt down for her. I winced when I saw the red marks I'd left on her shoulders.

Kissing her right shoulder and then her left, I said, "I'm sorry. I must have grabbed you too hard."

Tessa smiled, and I reveled in the expression of sheer sexual satisfaction on her face. "It's okay. It was done in a moment of passion."

"Speaking of passion," I said. "I can't believe you said 'Fuck me, Roman.'"

Tessa giggled and blushed slightly. She pulled me in for a kiss and said, "Thank you for obeying my orders. It's funny. I've never said anything like that during sex. I've never done anything like this before. I guess you just bring out the wild woman in me."

"Cool," I said, grinning at her.

"That and …" She hesitated.

"And?"

"And I feel safe with you," she said with a smile.

"You are safe with me, Tessy," I said, gazing into her eyes and feeling slightly choked up. After what she'd been through, this was a big deal for her.

My phone started buzzing like crazy. I pulled it out of my pocket to see a bunch of angry messages from Rex. It was probably buzzing the whole time, but I was too busy to notice.

"Damn. Tessy, I'm so, so sorry but I have to go," I said, looking at her sadly. "There's some stuff they're not allowed to do without me present. Union rules."

Tessa nodded. "It's okay. I understand. I have to change clothes and go see the fans outside anyway."

"You do that every night after the show, don't you?"

She nodded, looking tired.

"You must be exhausted after the show," I said, caressing her face. My phone buzzed again.

"Not too tired for you, though." She kissed me.

My phone buzzed again. I had no choice but to go.

"It's okay," she said with a laugh. "Get out of here."

"I'm sorry for leaving so soon after ..."

"It's all right, Roman. I'm the one who seduced you, remember?"

I chuckled. "Yeah, you did. I'll see you soon, okay?"

Tessa nodded. She kissed me, then swatted me on the ass. "Get out of here before Rex and Audra kill you."

I hurried out the door and back down to the stage area.

"Roman!" Rex growled angrily. He stalked toward me. "Where the hell have you—" He stopped, looked me up and down and then said, "You had sex with Tessa in her dressing room."

"Wh—what? N—no!" I stammered unconvincingly.

"Dude," Rex said, his expression rapidly changing from fury to amusement. "You never have a hair out of place." He smoothed down my hair. "Your belt is buckled wrong, and you have lipstick on your neck. I may not know what sex with a woman feels like, but I sure as hell know what it looks like."

I stared at him, trying desperately to come up with a reasonable explanation. My silence was all the confirmation he needed.

Rex's eyes went wide. "Oh ... my ... God."

Fumbling with my belt, I said, "Okay, okay you got me." I'd never been a good liar, and I knew when I was beaten. Rex laughed heartily as he rubbed Tessa's lipstick off my neck. "I can't believe it. After a lifetime of lust, you actually sealed the deal with Therese Andrews."

"Her name is Tessa!" I snapped. "Rex, you can't tell anyone about this. I mean it."

Though I'd thought it would be great to have people know about Tessa and me, this was not the way for people to find out. If they knew what we'd done tonight, I would be a hero and Tessa would be branded a slut. It was cruel and unfair, but that was the way the world worked.

"Please," I begged him. "She's had her personal life dragged through the gossip columns her whole life. She's not ready to go public about us yet. You can't tell *anyone*."

Rex's expression softened. "I know how much you love her. And she's a great girl, Roman. I'd never do anything to hurt her. I won't tell. I swear."

I let out a deep sigh of relief. Rex could be a dick sometimes, but he was a loyal friend when it came down to it.

"Is it serious between you two?" he asked.

That was a good question.

"It is for me. Can't speak for her. We're still, you know, working things out I guess."

"Cool. That's cool, Roman. Really. I hope it works out."

"Thanks."

"Now do your fucking job so I can get the hell out of here."

$\mathcal{I}$'d been dating Roman for several weeks now, and I was deliriously happy. He made me feel like no one ever had. Up until now, I'd never felt good enough for anyone—not my mother, not Derek, not Ricky, nor any other man I'd been with. Roman had said it all when he told me "You are more than enough." And he hadn't simply said it. He showed me in every way possible. The way he looked at me, the way he kissed me and held me in his arms, and the way he made love to me. And he had the patience of a saint. Our relationship was still under wraps, and he never complained.

I had found the perfect man, for me, in Roman. He'd come along at a time in my life when I no longer believed there was such a thing as the perfect guy, and yet here he was. I was addicted to the way he made me feel about myself when I was with him, and I found him utterly irresistible.

Which explained why we had sex in my dressing room that time. I still blushed whenever I thought about it. I didn't know what had come over me. I hadn't planned to have sex with him when I called him up to my dressing room. All I wanted was to see him, kiss him, and hold him in my arms.

But when I saw him in those tight jeans, I just couldn't resist him. Especially since I had discovered what an incredible lover he was.

There had been a high risk of fanboyism during that particular escapade, since I was in full dress and makeup. Very Therese Andrews, movie star-like. Once again, I'd been nervous he might call me Therese, but he didn't. He never did. It was always Tessa or Tessy. I loved when he called me Tessy.

I also loved *him*.

I knew I should tell him. Roman had been open about his feelings for me, even when it was awkward and uncomfortable in the beginning. But I wasn't ready to be that vulnerable with him yet. I truly believed this time would be different, yet I was still scared. Though I didn't think Roman would ever cheat or that he'd turn out to be a fanboy in hiding, I didn't think I would ever recover from it if he did. Especially if we went public with our relationship. The hounding by reporters about my breakup with Ricky had been hard enough; I couldn't take the heartbreak if I had to answer questions about breaking up with Roman. Both my heart and my stomach ached just thinking about that. I pushed the thought out of my mind.

Things were going great with the show, but I was exhausted. Nothing in my career had prepared me for the grueling pace of doing two Broadway shows a day. Fortunately, the two shows were only on Wednesdays and Sundays. At least after Sunday's last show, we had Mondays off. Wednesdays were the real killers.

This week had been particularly tough because I'd had to do three television interviews—two for a documentary on acting I'd done last year that was finally being released, and one this morning for *Pirated*. Being Wednesday, I'd done the matinee already and I was dead on my feet. And I still had tonight's show to do.

Roman caught up with me backstage after the matinee.

"Come here, you," he said, pulling me aside. He kept his voice low, but several people turned to look at us. Rumors were likely flying by now about us since we were frequently seen talking quietly together. That was okay, I guess. As long as nobody snapped pictures and tried to sell them to a tabloid or something.

"What?" I asked. His expression was rather serious.

"Tessy, you're exhausted. You need to go home immediately after the show and take it easy."

"But I have to meet with—"

"Baby, I know you like to greet the fans after the show, but I really need you to take care of yourself. You need all the rest you can get."

"I know. I just hate to disappoint my fans. Some of them travel really far to come see the show, and it only takes a few minutes to say hi."

"Sometimes it takes a few minutes," Roman said, his eyes filled with worry. "And other times you're out there for an hour or more. You need to catch up on your sleep. Sweetie, that's how you got hurt in rehearsal that day. You were over-tired and your concentration slipped."

I gazed into those tender brown eyes. He was so dear to be concerned about me. I hesitated, still not ready to promise I wouldn't greet my fans after the show.

"If this was a real job, you could just call in sick. Take a mental health day. I know better than to dare suggest you let your understudy go on."

I scoffed. "Never." People paid a lot of money to see a Broadway show, and there was no worse feeling for them than to hear the dreaded announcement that the star they came to see would not appear. I would only let that happen if

I completely lost my voice. Or I was dead. Barring those worst-case scenarios, I'd always go on.

"I know, Tessy. But please. Just this once. Skip the meet-and-greet and go home right after the show. Do it for me," Roman pleaded. That man was impossible to resist.

"Okay, just this once. I'll go right home."

The look of immense relief on his face made it worthwhile. In truth, I felt a bit relieved myself. I already wasn't sure where I'd get the energy to do tonight's show, so falling into bed straight afterward really was the sane thing to do.

* * *

SOMEHOW, I made it through the show without screwing up or killing myself. I took extra care during the ladder scene, making sure to stay focused. I was ready to drop from exhaustion after the show and more than ready to go home and sleep.

It wasn't until after I'd changed out of my costume and into my street clothes that I realized I hadn't told Ben about my change in plans.

There was a knock on my dressing room door.

"It's me," Roman said.

"Hey," I said when I opened the door.

He took an exaggerated step back, holding his hands up. "I know it's hard for you to control yourself around me, but no sex tonight. You gotta go home."

Laughing, I swatted him on his tight butt. Tempting as it was, I couldn't have sex with him now if I tried. I was ready to pass out.

"I know, I know. Problem is I forgot to tell Ben to go around front. He'll be waiting out back where the fans are."

Roman thought for a moment. "You all ready to go now?"

I nodded.

"Okay, come with me. I'll take you out there."

"But Roman, we can't—"

"Don't worry. Nobody will know we're together," he said with an unmistakable hint of weariness, even irritation, in his voice. So, it *did* bother him that we were keeping our relationship a secret. I wanted to say something to comfort him, but I couldn't find the right words. I was too tired to think right now.

"Come on, sweetie," Roman said, his irritation already replaced with concern. "Let's get you home."

He walked out of the dressing room, and I followed him to the backstage door that led outside. I drew in a deep breath. Roman meant well, but he had no idea how difficult it was for me to disappoint the fans that had been waiting for me for who knew how long in the cold. Even though it was early April, the temperature had dropped again, and it was freezing out.

Roman opened the backstage door and walked out first. He took my hand and led me through the crowd.

"Therese! I—I mean Ms. Andrews," called one of my male teenage fans. My heart squeezed in my chest.

"Hey there," I called back, grateful that I could at least meet his eye.

Roman kept pulling me through the crowd. "Excuse me, coming through. Make room, please."

He was polite but firm.

"Sorry, guys. She has to get going," he said as we weaved through the crowd.

"Damn. Her bodyguard won't let her talk to us," someone said.

That got a chuckle out of Roman. He seemed to like the idea of being my bodyguard.

It was hard for me to look into the faces of the eager

crowd, knowing I couldn't stop to talk to them, but I couldn't bear the thought of ignoring them completely.

"Thanks for coming out tonight, guys. Thanks so much. You guys are the best!" I smiled and waved and made eye contact with as many people as I could. My throat closed up when I caught sight of a girl of about ten years old, clutching a glossy photo of me and a pen. I managed to smile and wave directly at her, but that was all I could do before Roman pulled me over to the SUV.

Roman opened the door and practically pushed me in. He was about to close the door before any fans could get closer, but I stopped him.

"Wait, come in here with me for a second," I said.

Roman climbed into the car, shutting and locking the door immediately.

"You okay?" he asked.

"Yes," I said wearily. I still felt guilty about abandoning the fans, but I knew it had been the right thing to do. I had reached my limit over the last few days, and I desperately needed a break. "Thanks, Roman. I really appreciate it."

"You're welcome, Tessy," he said with a smile.

"I have something for you," I said, rummaging through my purse. I handed him a key to my house.

"Wow." Roman took it from me and examined it like it was a diamond or something.

"You already know the security code to the house, but now, you know, you can come by any time you want. You can come over tonight if you want."

"I will," he said, gazing at me tenderly. "But you better be asleep when I get there. I mean it."

"Believe me, I will be."

"Good." Roman glanced toward the tinted window of the car. We could still hear the fans outside chattering. They probably wouldn't leave until the Lexus drove away.

"You shouldn't need me to fight this battle for you, you know."

"What do you mean?"

"I mean you should respect yourself enough to know your limits. You're always doing tons of publicity, and I know you never want to disappoint your fans. You do that stuff because you have such a good heart. But you have to learn to speak up for yourself and your own needs. You have to take care of yourself, because you're worth taking care of."

I stared at him in wonder. "Nobody ever says stuff like that to me."

"I know," Roman said sadly. "Because everybody else is more worried about what they can get from you. More working hours on set, another interview, more autographs, and whatnot. But *I'm* saying it to you. I'm saying you are worth taking care of, and now you need to start saying it to yourself."

"Thanks, Roman," I said, tearing up.

He glanced out the window and then back at me. I thought he wanted to kiss me but he wasn't sure if the tinted windows were enough to block people from seeing inside the car.

"Go home, Tessy. Rest. I'll see you soon."

I nodded, and Roman got out of the car.

Ben had to wake me up after the short drive home. Once inside, I washed up and brushed my teeth as quickly as possible so I could get to bed.

The next thing I knew, Roman was sliding in beside me. I had no idea what time it was. Barely conscious, I managed to move over to his side. He was wearing pajama bottoms and no shirt, so I rested my head on his bare chest.

"I love your hairy chest, Roman," I mumbled.

He chuckled, tenderly stroking my hair. "That's it, Tessy. Rest, honey. Just rest."

We both slept in late, but Roman got up before me. I heard him downstairs moving in the kitchen when I woke up. I was still a bit tired, but I felt a lot better after getting a good night's sleep. I showered, then headed down to the kitchen.

I stood in the doorway a moment, admiring how Roman looked in his tight jeans while making breakfast. He had made himself bacon and eggs.

"Good morning, Sleeping Beauty," he said without turning around.

"Good morning, sexy," I said.

He opened the fridge and took out an orange and my carton of egg whites. It was thoughtful how he remembered exactly what I ate for breakfast. I was starving, though, and needed something a bit heartier for once. Roman's pep talk last night reminded me it was okay to take care of myself, and that meant eating the extra calories I needed.

"Thanks," I said, looking at the food he'd put on the counter for me. "But I think I might actually eat real eggs today."

"Yeah?" Roman asked, looking pleased with my statement. "All riiiight," he said with enthusiasm. He started scraping the eggs he'd made for himself onto a plate in front of me.

"Wait, don't—"

"It'll take me two minutes to make more. Shut up and eat," he ordered, making me laugh.

"Thanks. You're the best."

"I know, right?" he said with a grin. "You want tea or coffee?"

"Tea."

"Well, you want coffee, but you're settling for tea," he said as he put the kettle on the stove.

"Exactly. Doing two shows in one day really kills my voice, so I gotta go with tea and water for now."

"Gotcha," he said, grabbing a bottle of water from the fridge for me.

"Thanks for taking care of me. I really appreciate it. I'm sorry I'm such a mess," I told him. He'd worked two shows yesterday, too, and he wasn't falling apart.

"You're not a mess, honey. You're tired."

"Aren't you tired? You work just as hard as I do."

Roman laughed at that. "No. No, I do not." He looked over at me and said, "You have to be Therese Andrews every time you go out. And that, all by itself, is exhausting. And your schedule is crazy."

"I still appreciate everything you do for me. I know it's boring to just come home and sleep next to me."

"It's not boring. I love sleeping next to you," he said with a smile.

"I might be Therese Andrews when I go out, but I know I can be boring sometimes in real life."

"Tessy," he said firmly. "You are never boring. Baby, you once told me to fuck you against your dressing room door."

That got a small smile out of me.

Roman finished cooking his breakfast and sat down at the kitchen counter with me. He eyed me thoughtfully for a few seconds, and then said, "I never told you how amazing and exciting that was. I still can't believe it actually happened. And you made it happen. It was your idea. It was like something out of—"

Roman stopped himself before he could finish his thought.

"A movie. You were gonna say it was like something out of a movie," I said, pointing my fork at him in teasing accusation.

"Yeah. A certain *kind* of movie," he said, eyes wide.

I giggled and felt my face get hot.

"Yeah Tessy, it was like something out of a movie, but it

211

really happened. Because of you. You weren't being Therese Andrews, and you were still hot as hell. It was exciting because you are an exciting woman. I know you don't believe it, but it's true."

I watched him as he dug into his eggs and bacon. God, how I adored him.

"You're so good to me. I know I can be high maintenance sometimes."

Roman frowned and open his mouth to argue.

"I mean, I know I'm not celebrity-diva high maintenance, but I need constant reassurance and that's got to be annoying sometimes. Deep inside every performer there's usually a very insecure person who needs lots of attention and encouragement."

"I know," Roman said matter-of-factly. "I work with performers all the time. And some of those performers lash out at other people because of their insecurity. Believe it or not, I even have sympathy for Velma because of that. It's fear that makes her yell at other people. *You* don't yell at people when you're feeling insecure. Instead, you keep it all inside, constantly worrying you're not good enough."

"You know me so well, Roman," I said.

"Yes. I do," he said with a smile. "And I'm proud of you. And I don't mind reassuring you. I kinda like being the man behind the woman," he said, and then laughed. "So to speak. I mean, I like that you go out and shine bright onstage for everyone else, but then you come home to me. Or, you know, I come home to you."

He grinned, glancing around at my huge house.

"It makes you feel bad that we hide our relationship, doesn't it?" I finally asked him.

Roman took that long pause he always did when he was thinking carefully about what to say.

"Yeah," he said at last. "I'm proud of you, Tessy. And I

would be really proud to be out in public with you." He paused again, and then added, "Also, it's kind of embarrassing for me."

"What do you mean?"

"Well, everybody at work thinks I'm still some pathetic guy suffering from puppy love for you. They bust my balls for it all the time. I don't know. I guess it shouldn't matter what anybody else thinks, but it still sucks. They give me shit for pining after you all the time, and here they have no idea that we're like, together. Or whatever we are."

"Roman, I'm so sorry," I said. He took such good care of me and never asked for anything in return. He deserved so much better.

"I know, sweetie. I'm not saying this to make you feel bad. I'm just telling you how I feel since you asked. It's okay. There's no timetable for this, I guess. We'll just have to take it one day at a time."

"Do you ever wish you could go out in public and be seen with Therese Andrews?"

There was a really long pause this time. Then the kettle whistled.

"Saved by the bell," Roman said, jumping up to pour my tea.

"Roman," I said sternly when he brought over my tea.

"I feel like I'm walking around a landmine with that question," he said.

"I don't want you to feel that way. Please tell me what you're thinking."

Roman sighed heavily. After another long pause, he met my gaze and said, "Tessy, I love you for *you*. But would I love to be seen in public with the most beautiful movie star on the planet? Would I love to be the envy of every man in the world? Would I love to have all my family and friends and neighbors aware of the fact that I am dating a movie star?

Yes. Yes, I believe I would enjoy that quite a bit. I mean, that's not why I'm with you. Of course it's not. But would I love that? Hell fucking yeah, I would."

I laughed. He looked relieved.

"You're not mad?"

"Of course I'm not mad. I want you to be honest with me, and everything you said sounds perfectly reasonable. There's times where I wish all the paparazzi and even the fans would just leave me alone, but there are also times when I'm feeling down on myself and I go out in public just to be seen and recognized. It can be really fun and a real rush. It makes perfect sense why you would want that. Why you would want the world to know."

"The world and Heather Applegate."

"What? Who?" I asked.

"Heather Applegate. From high school. I asked her to the prom, she said yes, and the day before the prom, after I'd hired the limo and bought a suit and a corsage and all that, she dumped me. Got a better offer from a more popular guy. I know it's petty and vindictive, but I would love for Heather to know that *my* date is Therese Andrews."

"Oh Roman, that's horrible. I mean, what she did to you, not wanting to get back at her with me. That's horrible!"

My heart ached in my chest as Roman recounted that painful memory. Picturing a heartbroken teenaged Roman made me want to get back at Heather too.

"I want to go public about us, Roman. I really, really do. I just ... I'm not ready," I said, feeling on the verge of tears. Hiding Roman was hurting him and that was unbearable, but I was still petrified. I grabbed his hand and squeezed it. "I know you're different than those other guys, Roman. I know that. But even so ... I never thought they would cheat on me, either. Everyone in the whole world knows Ricky cheated on me. And though I never confirmed it to the press or anything, the rumors that Derek cheated were true and everybody pretty much knows it. I told you how having them cheat confirmed my worst insecurities about myself. That I'm not good enough. And as if that wasn't painful enough, I still have reporters in my face asking about all of it. Lights and cameras and microphones in my face, people asking about the worst thing I ever—"

"Hey, hey," Roman said softly. "It's okay, baby. It's okay. I didn't mean to upset you."

"I know. It's all right. We should be able to talk about this, and I should be able to handle it without falling apart. I don't want you to be afraid to tell me what you're thinking."

Roman nodded, still looking concerned.

"Ugh, and it's not just the media I'll have to deal with. My mother will give me crap about dating an electrician."

"Really?"

"Oh yeah. She only wants me dating other famous people. She told me I should take Ricky back after he cheated."

"Jesus Christ," he muttered angrily.

"And I'm not about to let her disparage you, which means we'll get into a huge fight."

"I don't want you to fight with your mom, sweetie."

I moaned, putting my head in my hands. Roman tenderly rubbed my shoulders to soothe me. After a moment, I lifted my head.

"I hate hurting you, Roman."

"I know. But it's okay, Tessy. It really is."

Poor Roman. Forced to reassure me yet again, and when he was the one being wronged.

"I'm sorry things are so uncomfortable for you at work," I said with a sigh. "I never really thought about it, but I totally get what you're saying. If it makes you feel any better, Rosemary knows all about us."

"Really?" I asked.

I nodded. "Yeah, she's been in your corner from the get-go. She told me you may have started out as a fan, but she believed your feelings for me were real and that I might be missing out on something great if I didn't give you a chance."

He grinned. "I'll have to thank her for that."

"She's a great friend, and I knew I could trust her, so she knows we're together. Know what else I told her?" Roman shook his head. "I told her you were, by far, the best lover I've ever had."

He looked stunned. "You did not tell her that."

"Oh, yes I did," I said with a smile. "Because it happens to be the truth."

I watched Roman turn this over in his head for a moment, and I could see the pride in his expression. "Did you tell her …"

"What?" I asked.

"Did you tell her, you know, that you had multiple …"

I laughed. "Yes! Yes. I did tell her that."

"Wow. Cool."

"I also told her we had sex in my dressing room."

"You did? Awesome," Roman said, his eyes lighting up. I think it helped him to know at least one member of *Pirated* was aware that he wasn't just a fan with a crush.

I giggled. "She told me she and Johnny once had sex in the middle of a theater stage."

"Damn," Roman said, looking impressed. "Well, I should tell you … Rex knows about us, too. I didn't tell him anything. I swear. But he caught me coming out of your dressing room with my belt unbuckled and your lipstick on my neck."

I gasped, horrified.

"It's okay. I swore him to secrecy. I know he can be a dick sometimes, but when it comes down to it, he's got my back."

I nodded, calming down a bit. I was actually grateful Rex

knew, since he used to tease Roman about me all the time. Now he couldn't do it anymore.

"So at least there's two people at work who know you're not just a fanboy," I said, and he nodded. "Tell you what. Why don't we all go to Squip's together with everybody soon. I'll make sure you sit right next to me to make it clear to everybody that we're really close friends. That way, maybe it won't feel so one-sided to you all the time."

He thought for a while and then nodded. "I like that idea. Kinda like a baby step toward going public."

"Exactly. That way people will at least know I care about you. Because I do, Roman. I care so much about you."

"Good," he said, looking immensely relieved, and I realized I hadn't done a great job of making sure he knew how much he meant to me.

"Of course I care, Roman," I said squeezing his hands in mine.

I love you, Roman. I'm just too scared to say it.

CHAPTER 21

*A*s always, the cast was able to get to Squip's before us crew members. They were all seated and half-buzzed by the time I got there.

"Roman, Roman, Roman!" Tessa called to me as soon as I walked in. "Saved you a seat."

She smiled at me as she patted the seat next to her at our usual table in the back.

"Thanks, Tessy!" I said cheerfully. I loved that I was the only one who called her that. She shot me a wry look as if to say, watch it, buddy—we're still supposed to be just friends here.

Even so, she put her arm around me and gave me a squeeze once I sat down next to her. That got a few raised eyebrows from around the table, which I enjoyed quite a bit.

That's right, suckers. Tessa happens to be quite fond of me, too.

I already felt better about the whole thing. Baby steps. Yeah. I was cool with that.

"I ordered your usual already," she said.

A thoughtful touch from Tessa. Showed people she knew me well enough to know my beer of choice.

"So, we were all talking about the wedding of the century coming up," Tessa said with a smile.

Rosemary laughed. "Oh, I don't know about all that. We're not royalty. Although, sometimes the Creels act like we are. They're going a bit overboard on the wedding."

"Wow. When the bride says things are overboard, it must really be nuts," I said. Rosemary smiled warmly at me. Damn, it felt good to know at least Rosemary was aware Tessa and I were together. And that we'd had sex. Lots of sex. Lots of amazing, exciting sex where Tessa had lots of orgasms and called me the best lover she'd ever had. I wanted to pump my fist in the air with pride, but I managed to keep my mouth shut.

Rosemary talked about some of the details of her upcoming wedding to Johnny, but it was hard to concentrate on what she was saying. Because Tessa had reached underneath the table and had started rubbing my crotch, enough to get me uncomfortably hard. My cock strained against the tight jeans she loved so much.

Her poker face was incredible. She watched Rosemary carefully, clearly listening to every word. Then Tessa glanced briefly at me and gave me a friendly smile.

It was both maddening and hilarious at the same time. She literally had me by the balls.

I pulled my cell phone out of my pocket and sent her a quick text.

Keep torturing me, girl, and I'll return the favor in bed. I'll make you wait. You know I will.

Tessa glanced at the message on her phone and then dropped her hand from between my legs. I had to bite my cheek to keep from laughing. She took my hand in hers for a second and squeezed it. It was a simple gesture, but it meant a lot to me.

Rosemary rarely talked about herself since she was

usually too busy worrying about everybody else. She and Tessa were a lot alike in that regard. Rosemary spoke about how strange it was to have a wedding on a Monday night, but they'd had to change their earlier plans so she wouldn't have to miss any performances of *Pirated*. The honeymoon was postponed indefinitely because of the show, but they'd get to go eventually.

"The main thing I'm stressing about is all the publicity," Rosemary said.

"Ugh. I hear ya. Hard to keep it from turning into a circus," Tessa commiserated.

"I'm so torn, because I really don't like all the attention, but Johnny loves it. And so does his entire family, who are footing the bill for the whole wedding. Johnny and I have even had some—well not exactly fights, but let's say discussions on the matter. His view is the more cameras there, the better, and I just want to get married."

"That kinda sucks," I said. "There's got to be some kind of middle ground between having your whole wedding covered by the media and having a complete media blackout."

"Exactly," Rosemary said. "That's kind of what we're trying to work out. Don't get me wrong. I love the idea of standing up in front of the whole world and making it clear how much I love Johnny. It's just ... for the rest of my life I'll be known as Mrs. Johnny Creel. No matter what professional accomplishments I might have, the headline will always be 'Wife of Johnny Creel.'"

"'Wife of Johnny Creel, Rosemary Sutton, wins Tony Award for Best Leading Actress in a Broadway Musical,'" I said.

Rosemary laughed. "Exactly. And they'd probably use my wedding photo instead of my headshot. I want this wedding to be wonderful, and I want Johnny to be happy. And the

Creels are giving me anything I want. Ugh, listen to me whine. Poor little rich girl. I just want …"

She trailed off and remained quiet for a moment.

"I just want to marry him, you know? I mean, I am excited about wearing a beautiful gown and getting married in a gorgeous church. Not gonna lie. I do want to be treated like a princess." She paused again, tearing up slightly. "Princess. That's what he calls me. Always has. Even when we were both broke, he treated me like a princess. I love him and he loves me, and we want to get married. I guess at the end of the day, that's all that matters."

Tessa reached over and took Rosemary's hand. "I'm sure you guys can come up with some great compromises by the time the wedding day comes. Stuff like … Well, maybe the TV cameras can get you guys walking into the church. You know, when you're coming out of the limo or whatever. And then keep the media out for the important stuff. The actual ceremony, and when you do your vows."

"Yeah, that's a good idea," Rosemary said, squeezing Tessa's hand before letting go of it. "Thanks."

"The biggest challenge for your wedding," Luke said sternly, "is how the hell are you gonna get through your vows without crying?"

Everyone at the table laughed good-naturedly.

"Oh my God," Rosemary said with a laugh. "I'll be a mess. A total mess. Thank God for waterproof mascara."

Rosemary took a sip from her wine. She glanced at the front door of the bar and suddenly winced hard. It was as if some invisible person had just slapped her across the face.

We all turned to see Jacob walk in. He headed straight to our table. My muscles tensed, and I was ready to play body-guard for Rosemary, as I'd done for Tessa.

I felt Tessa go tense beside me, too, as Jacob stood at the head of our table.

"I don't want to bother you guys. I'm not gonna stay long or anything. I just wanted to say I owe everybody here an apology," Jacob said with genuine remorse in his eyes. He looked over at Rosemary. "Especially you, Rosemary."

He swallowed, looking uncomfortable.

"Here, Jacob," Tessa said gently. "Why don't you sit with us. Can you guys make room?"

Tessa gestured toward the seat next to Rosemary, which was occupied by Luke. He got up and grabbed another chair from an empty table, and everyone else shifted down. I was still on high alert as I watched Jacob sit next to Rosemary. If he said one mean thing to her, I'd ask him to step outside and we'd settle this once and for all.

Our server showed up when she saw someone new join our table. Tessa quietly ordered a beer for Jacob, and he smiled gratefully at her.

"Rosemary, I'm so sorry for the way I've been carrying on this whole time. It had nothing to do with you," Jacob said. "I mean, I told myself it did. I told myself I had a right to be mad, and that everything was your fault, but … You see, the woman who had the role of Elizabeth during the whole off-Broadway run is—"

"Your wife," Rosemary said softly. "I know."

"Yeah," Jacob said. "God, this was like … This was supposed to be our big break together, you know? It was so perfect. We'd both worked so hard for so many years, and then we get cast opposite each other in this show. Casting directors had no idea we were husband and wife when they cast us separately. It was crazy. They were like, you guys have great chemistry!"

That made people laugh a little, and the mood lightened a bit.

"And then the show gets transferred to Broadway."

Rosemary nodded. She was already crying. She felt things so deeply, and Jacob probably hadn't realized how torn apart she'd felt about taking the role from someone else. Tessa handed Rosemary a tissue from her purse.

"It was amazing to make my Broadway debut, but it hurt like hell that Emily wasn't with me. That she hadn't made it. She was hurting, and I couldn't fix it."

More tears fell from Rosemary's eyes. The server brought Jacob's beer and hurried off. It was obvious we were in the middle of something.

"And this whole time I blamed you that Emily wasn't with me onstage." Jacob drew in a deep breath and let it out. "But you're better in the role than she was."

Rosemary stared at Jacob in shock. We all did. I couldn't imagine how tough that was to admit out loud.

"Emily's a terrific dramatic actress. That's her forte, and it's really what she wants to do anyway. Do dramatic plays on Broadway. Rosemary, your singing voice is stronger than hers, and you have this terrific comic timing. All that blocking stuff you changed during rehearsals? It's great. It kills."

Several of us nodded. Jacob wasn't kidding. That scene got huge laughs every night, especially when Rosemary's character paces and suddenly stops, and Jacob nearly runs into her. Often, his shoes made a loud squeaking noise on the stage when he stopped short, and it was just really, really funny.

"I wanted to believe you got the part because you're marrying Johnny Creel, but it's not true. Well, it may be partly true."

Rosemary nodded, which made my chest hurt. I knew how sensitive she was on that topic.

"But the truth is, it was the right move no matter how it

happened. The show is better because of you. I'm so sorry for being such a dick to you. I guess I just get a little crazy when it comes to Emily."

"I understand," Rosemary said with a smile.

"I finally told her how I'd been acting around you and, well, she was totally horrified. She told me, in no uncertain terms, I had to apologize. But really, that's not the only reason I'm here. I mean, she made me realize what an ass I've been, and I'm here because I am really, really sorry. I hope you can accept my apology."

"Of course I can," Rosemary said graciously, with relief in her eyes. Rosemary Sutton was not one to hold grudges. All she wanted was for everyone to be happy and to get along.

"God, Rosemary," Jacob said with a grimace. "That look on your face when I walked in. It was like you were terrified of me. I don't want to be the kind of person who makes people feel like that. I promise you, I'm really not that guy. Most of the time anyway."

"That's what Luke's been saying all along," Rosemary said, glancing over at Luke. He nodded, seeming relieved that Jacob had finally gotten his shit together. Luke was friends with both Jacob and Rosemary, and I was sure he'd hated being caught in the middle.

Rosemary put down her tissue and reached over to give Jacob a big hug. I saw his tense shoulders relax.

After Rosemary released Jacob from her embrace, he gazed at her fondly and said, "Girl, you deserve a Tony Award for pretending to be in love with me every night. That's been some stellar acting."

"Thanks," she said with a laugh. He wasn't wrong. Rosemary was an incredible actress, and the way she looked at Jacob onstage, people might actually think they were an item. The audience would never have known what was really going on.

"Do you guys realize the Tony nominations are gonna be announced in just a few days?" Tessa said, her eyes lighting up with excitement. "I can't help but hope *Pirated* gets some recognition. But at the same time, I'm afraid to hope, you know?"

I scanned the faces and saw nearly everyone nodding. A Tony nomination would be an incredibly high honor.

"More than anything, I would love it if the show itself was nominated," Tessa said, her pretty, blue eyes shining. "Individual awards are awesome, but if we could all be recognized together, it would be so wonderful."

As always, Tessa held the rapt attention of everyone there. She spoke from her heart, and people hung on her every word.

"I've worked on lots of movies and projects, but this one has felt different right from the beginning. I've made so many wonderful friends," Tessa said, gazing at Rosemary and Luke. "With every project I've worked on, I've been hopeful we would all stay in touch after the show wraps, but that almost never happens. I can't help but hope this time will be different, you know? That the friendships will last this time, long after we go our separate ways someday. You guys are all so dear to me."

Tessa took her time looking at everyone individually. She probably didn't realize the effect she had, but every person here felt cherished and valued because of her. When she met Rex's gaze, he smiled and gave her a quick wink. Tessa's smile widened. I had told Rex that Tessa was aware he knew about us, and it was a nice shared moment between the two of them.

"Sometimes you meet people on set you know you'll carry in your heart long after the show ends," she said.

With that, she squeezed my hand under the table again.

I found myself wishing she would express her feelings for me, whatever they were. But I told myself this was enough.

For now.

CHAPTER 22

$\mathcal{T}$he Tony nominations had just been announced, and I gathered everyone together for a quick meeting before we gave our evening performance of *Pirated*. I was already in my costume dress, and we were all only moments away from performing. It was a terrible time to make an announcement, good or bad, because it could wreck their concentration before a show. But I had no choice.

I had to tell them. They were going to find out anyway, and I figured the news was better coming from me than hearing it from a stranger in the entertainment media.

"Thanks for getting together so quickly," I said to the entire cast and crew as we crammed into a tiny room at the back of the Al Hirschfeld Theater. My hands were shaking. I couldn't look at Roman as I spoke. I'd never get through this if I had to look at his face when I broke the news.

"I don't know how to say this, so I'll say it straight out." I drew in a deep breath. "We've received our closing notice."

Gasps sucked up all the air in the room. I stood there and watched two hundred hearts break right before my eyes.

"I'm so sorry," I said, still feeling too stunned to cry. "We close in just a few weeks."

Rosemary covered her mouth and began to tear up, and Jacob put a comforting arm around her. It was sweet, yet so sad.

"I want you all to know I am so proud of each and every one of you, and of everything we've accomplished with this show. Let us all take a moment to remember that every person in this room made it to Broadway, and that in and of itself is a huge deal. We've also put on one hell of a show for the last few months. I know how hard it will be to go out there knowing the show will end soon, but we're gonna go out there tonight and give it our all, like we do every single night. We're gonna sing and dance and make people laugh and feel good, because that's what we do. That's our gift to the world. I love you guys. All of you."

I blew everyone a kiss and walked away before I broke down in tears in public. I managed to grab Roman's arm without looking him in the eye.

"Come with me," I whispered.

People were too shocked to pay any attention to what Roman and I were doing, so it was easy to slip away and into my dressing room.

Once I had Roman safely inside with me, I locked the door and spun around to face him. He seemed upset, but he looked more worried about me than anything else.

"Oh Roman, I'm so sorry I couldn't tell you privately first! My agent called and gave me a heads up just a few minutes ago, and the closing notice is already up on the board. I just couldn't let everyone find out that way."

"I understand," Roman said, tenderly stroking my face.

"Oh, all those people are gonna be out of work," I moaned. "*You're* gonna be out of work until the next show moves in." I wasn't worried about money when it came to

Roman, because I would provide anything he needed. But there were so many crew members who had families to feed. "All those crew members ..."

"Tessa—"

"And will this mean Luke has to go back to working in maintenance?"

"Tessa, I—"

"And what about—"

"Tessy!" Roman said sharply, finally forcing me to listen to him. He tenderly stroked my hair and said, "This is your loss, too. It's okay to mourn it."

I nodded, finally letting the tears spill. Roman wrapped his arms around me, and we held each other close.

"Oh Roman, I wanted this to work out so much," I said.

"I know, baby. I know," he said soothingly. "You did the best you could. We all did, baby."

I nodded, pulling away and wiping my tears. "I have to go on now."

"I know. I know it's gonna be hard, but you're gonna be great tonight. But please ... be careful on the ladder tonight. I know you're distracted, but—"

"I will. I promise."

"Go have a great show, Tessy. Then I'll come over tonight, and we'll cry and eat ice cream or something."

I laughed and hugged him once more for luck.

This wasn't the first time a project I'd worked on had ended in heartbreak, but it was the first time I could go through it with someone who really understood me.

essa waited for me to wrap up after the show, and we went back to her place together. She was upset but seemed to be doing okay, all things considered. It was always tough when a show closed, and she was right that it's harder when you get close to the cast and crew. I'd been through it a bunch of times before, and I had gotten kind of used to it. I figured this was gonna be much harder on her than it was for me. Though it was true I'd be out of work for a short while, it wouldn't be long before another show moved into the Al Hirschfeld Theater and I'd be back in business again.

God, it would be hard to go to work without Tessa being there. We were both so busy at work that we didn't see each other a lot at the theater, but I loved watching her perform and hearing her sing every night. I would really miss that.

We ordered pizza and ate together. I could tell how upset Tessa was—she ate two slices. I'd never seen her do that.

"You okay?" I asked after we'd finished eating and cleaning up. I planned to take care of her as best I could. I figured she'd probably just want to cuddle up in bed and go to sleep.

"Yeah. I'm kinda depressed, but I'll get over it. Nothing I haven't been through before. I've had movies tank at the box office that I thought would do well, that sort of thing. It hurts. It never stops hurting. You'd think it would get easier, but it doesn't."

I nodded. I was sure it was more painful and felt more personal for actors when a show closed. After all, a show never closed because of bad lighting.

"But I'll be okay, Roman. Really." She eyed me curiously.

"What?"

She walked over to me and put her arms around me. "I have an idea of something we could do to take my mind off the show," she purred in my ear.

So maybe she didn't want to go right to sleep after all. I was cool with that.

"Okay. Hear me out first. Don't say no," she said cautiously.

"When have I ever said no to you?"

"You might this time. But I need you to listen first."

"Okay," I said a bit warily. "You have my attention."

Tessa ran her fingers through my hair. "It occurred to me you never really did get a chance to have sex with Therese Andrews. So tonight, I want to be a movie star for you so you can finally fulfill your boyhood fantasy."

"What?" I asked, hardly believing what I was hearing. "No. Tessy, just no. No way. Absolutely not."

"Roman—"

"Baby, you tried role playing once before and it was a nightmare for you. I would never do that to you. I would never ask you to do that."

"You're not asking. I'm offering."

"There is no way I'm gonna—"

She put a finger on my lips. "Will you please listen to me?"
I sighed and nodded.

Tessa smiled. "The first time we made love it was beautiful and wonderful and perfect. I know what you were doing that night."

"What do you mean?"

"You made that whole night all about me. The way you touched me, held me, kissed me. And pleasured me. You were completely focused on my needs. No one had ever done that for me before. You treated me like a person. A woman, and not a celebrity. You were so patient and took your time with me. The whole time I've been with you, you have never treated me like Therese Andrews. But tonight is your chance. You've had a fantasy for most of your life about having sex with Therese Andrews, and I want to make it happen. I'll dress up like a movie star, and we can do it just like your fantasy."

God help me, I was tempted. Suddenly, all my teenage fantasies came flooding back. I'd done my best to repress them since we got together because I didn't want her to think, not even for a second, that I was with her because of her celebrity. I found myself remembering my old familiar fantasy of having my way with movie star, Therese Andrews.

Never taking her eyes off mine, Tessa reached between my legs and felt my rigid cock.

"You want to do this, Roman. I know you do."

"Yes," I admitted. "I am tempted to do this. But I can't. I'd rather die than hurt you, Tessy. And you might get hurt. You thought you would be okay doing the Roxy Rose thing, but you weren't. It was traumatic for you. I won't do that to you."

"No. You won't do that to me. You won't have that effect on me because you're not Derek. I've thought a lot about this. I know it seems spur of the moment, but it's not. I've thought this through. I want to do this for you. It's kind of my way of showing you how much I ..."

I held my breath waiting for her to say the words I ached to hear.

"Trust you," she said finally.

Trying not to show my disappointment, I stroked her hair as I contemplated her proposal.

"I can dress up and do everything you always dreamed of. You can call me Therese with no guilt whatsoever. You can push me down on the bed and spread my legs and do everything to me, to Therese, you always fantasized about."

My resolve was weakening by the moment. This could be the most erotic experience of my entire life. Or Tessa could wind up hating me afterward.

"If we do this ..." I began cautiously.

She smiled widely. I got the impression she was excited about it, too. That made me feel a tiny bit better.

"You have to know you can put an end to it at any time. No matter how far we get, you can stop. If you feel uncomfortable, or if you change your mind." Nervously, I ran my hand through my hair. "We need a safe word or phrase or something."

"How about 'Roman, I changed my mind. I don't want to do this anymore,'" she said.

"Okay. As long as you promise me, you *swear*, you won't do anything that makes you feel bad. You promise you'll stop—"

She put her hand on her heart and said, "I solemnly swear I will stop if I feel uncomfortable with anything we're doing."

I was already insanely turned on at the idea of having sex with Therese Andrews. The woman I'd drooled over and lusted for my whole life.

"Now," she said, tracing her fingers across my cheek. "I want you to tell me everything about your fantasy."

I suddenly felt uncomfortable. It hadn't occurred to me that I'd have to tell her the details of my imagination if she was going to try to act it out.

"I want you to tell me everything. Tell me exactly what you thought about. How you pictured it."

I winced a bit, still feeling uneasy. Tessa took my hand in hers, gazed into my eyes, and said, "You're safe with me."

My tension eased a bit. She'd never laugh at me, so it was okay to tell her everything.

"So, how does it happen? Like, how do we meet?" she prompted. "Do we know each other? Like, are you another actor on the set, or ..."

"No," I said, shaking my head. "I'm just a fan of yours. Of Therese."

"Okay. And how do we meet?"

"At a party or movie premiere or something like that. We just, you know, meet and strike up a conversation."

Tessa nodded thoughtfully. "What am I wearing?"

"You're all done up in your makeup and hair and stuff. Wearing some kind of fancy dress. Like a short dress, I guess. And stilettos."

She nodded again, with the same thoughtful expression on her face as she had when the director gave her performance notes. As if she was really taking this seriously. Like she was building a character in her head, so she could make it real for me.

"All right, we meet and then what?"

"Well," I thought for a moment. My face got hot thinking of all the stuff I would have to say out loud to her. It wasn't bad, really. Just very, very personal.

"It's okay, Roman. Tell me."

"Well, it's kinda like you're not dating anybody, and you haven't dated for a while. So, you know, it's been a while since you've been with anybody. So you're kind of, you know …"

"Horny," she finished for me.

I laughed uncomfortably. "Yeah."

"Okay, it's been a while since I've had sex, and I need to hook up with somebody like you, who can satisfy my needs." Tessa spoke kindly. She must have known how hard it was to confess all of this, but she was eager to know what to do to please me. She'd been right when she said I went out of my way to make our first time together all about her, and it was sweet of her to return the favor.

"Yeah, exactly."

"Oh Roman, this is gonna be so much fun," Tessa said in a sly, sexy voice. So far, she genuinely seemed into it. "So, we go to the bedroom. How do we do it? Like, what positions did you imagine?"

"Honestly? It's really the most basic one. Me on top of you. That was how I envisioned it as a young teenager, when that was all I really knew about sex. As I got older and learned more, and actually did more, somehow my fantasy of you never really changed."

Tessa nodded thoughtfully again. "Tell me any specifics. Like what I say or do."

I paused for a while, and she gave me space to gather my thoughts. And my courage.

"Well, you say my name a lot."

"Uh-huh. And what else?"

For some reason, it was hard to say the next part. And yet, I really wanted her to do it. It was like my favorite part.

"Just before you, you know, *finish*, you keep begging me not to stop."

Tessa nodded once again, looking intrigued. "Anything else?"

"No, I think that's it. Oh, wait. You're naked while we do it except you're wearing stilettos."

"Hmmm. That's hot. I like it," Tessa said, her eyes flashing with interest. "Is there anything else you can think of? Anything at all?"

"No."

Tessa eyed me carefully.

"No, really. That's really it. Honestly. I mean, I've experimented with different fantasies of you over the years, but I always went back to that one. It's my favorite."

She thought for a moment. "Which poster was it?"

"What?"

"Which poster did you have when you first learned to ... explore your body."

"Oh," I said with a laugh. "The one from *For Forever.*"

"I remember that poster. God, I was so young!"

"Yeah, but I was around the same age then. So, it's not creepy."

"I know, sweetheart," she said with a smile. "Okay, my darling. Wait here while I go get ready."

"Tessy. If you change your mind, you *have* to tell me. I won't be upset. I'll be way more upset if you go through with it and it freaks you out."

"I'll tell you if I'm not okay. I promise."

I started pacing as I waited for her to come back downstairs. The more time it took, the more I started overthinking. I was both excited and terrified that this would turn out to be a huge mistake.

"Hey," came a sultry voice from behind me. Crazy, that one word sounded different coming from her lips. She was in character already.

I literally staggered back a few steps when I saw her.

She wore a short, shimmery black dress complete with

the tallest, hottest stilettos I'd ever seen. In full makeup, her hair was done in waves. *She was Therese Andrews.*

It felt like I was meeting her for the first time, reminding me of how terrified and tongue-tied I'd been the first time I saw her on set.

I stood there awkwardly, unsure how to begin. In my fantasy, I was in charge of the situation. Masculine. Dominant. Right now, I felt like the awkward teenager I'd once been. She was the actress, not me.

Tessa glanced around the room, then took my hand. "Come with me. We should be able to sneak away from the party now."

I felt a bit silly as she led me by the hand up the stairs. We didn't go to the master bedroom. Instead, she took me to one of the spare bedrooms I hadn't even seen yet.

"I don't usually do stuff like this," she purred. "You know, take fans back to my hotel room."

Tessa looked into my eyes with an intensity that was so goddamn hot, I stopped feeling silly and started to feel aroused.

Then she laughed self-consciously. She looked awkward suddenly. "I'm sorry ..."

She changed her mind. She can't do it.

I was crushed. I hadn't realized how badly I'd wanted this. Determined not to let her know I was disappointed, I was about to tell her it was okay, but I didn't get the chance.

"I'm so sorry," she said biting her lip. "What was your name again?"

I chuckled. That twinkle in her eye told me it was an intentional nod to when we first met.

"It's okay. It's Roman."

"Rrrooooman," she said, running the name sensually across her lips. "How could I forget that? I love it. It's strong and masculine. It suits you. I'm on the pill. So if you're clean, we don't have to use anything."

"I'm clean. I swear."

She nodded. "Like I said, I don't usually do stuff like this, but … It's been kind of a while for me." Therese … I told myself it was okay to think of her at Therese Andrews, just this once … dropped her gaze demurely and seemed bashful, embarrassed. Oh, she was good. "I might be a famous movie star, but I still have *needs*, you know what I mean?"

Therese looked at me expectantly. It was time for me to take over and start doing the things I'd been fantasizing about since I was fifteen.

"I understand. I'll take care of you." I brushed the hair out of her face and stared intently into her eyes. She gasped and looked at me with anticipation. I leaned in and kissed her, and she eagerly, hungrily kissed me back. "Tell me what you want me to do to you."

She moaned, and then said softly into my ear. "Make me come, Roman. I don't care how you do it, just make me *come*."

She was pleading with me already, and I loved it. Every sound she made, every simple glance exuded desperate need. As if it had been years since she'd had sex, and I was the only one who could satisfy her.

God, it was fun dating an actress. I had never considered the possibilities of all the things we could do in bed together.

"I'll make you come, baby. Don't you worry," I said huskily. My self-consciousness about confessing my fantasy and the awkwardness of getting into it faded as we went on. Experimenting like this required a huge amount of trust, for both of us—that I wouldn't make her feel used, and that she wouldn't laugh or make me feel uncomfortable about my deepest fantasies.

I pushed her against the wall and kissed her roughly. She made all kinds of delightful moaning sounds, and when I started kissing down her neck, she said, "Roman. Touch me, Roman. *Please.*"

I rubbed my hands over the outside of her dress and across her breasts. She gasped and moaned again. "Oh God, it's been so long since I've had a man's hands on me."

I reached behind her and slowly unzipped her dress. Even the sound of the zipper was sexy. "I want this dress off," I ordered.

"Yes," she whispered, and I pulled it off her in one quick motion. I took a step back to admire her in her matching black bra and panty set, and she bit her lip shyly.

"I need to see you, too," she said. She tentatively began unbuttoning my shirt, but soon began to work much faster, as if her desire had gotten the best of her. She seemed torn between trying to play it cool and trying to get what she needed—sexual relief—as fast as possible. She pulled my shirt off and drew in a deep breath as she gazed hungrily at me.

Therese bit her lip again and ran her hands all over my chest. She dropped her gaze and then, hesitating only a second or two, began feverishly unbuckling my belt. I watched as she pulled down my pants and underwear and stood staring at my cock.

"Oh God," she moaned again, the physical need evident in her voice. "I just knew you'd be big, Roman."

She reached down and stroked my cock for a moment. "Oh God, I want you so badly."

I unclasped her bra and whipped it off her, then I pulled her close to me, crushing her mouth against mine and pressing my cock between her legs. Therese let out a strangled cry of desperation, which was all she could do with my mouth on hers. My tongue explored her mouth and she responded eagerly with her own.

"Oh Roman. Roman, *please.* Don't make me wait. I need you. I need you inside me. *Now.*"

Her bright blue eyes pleaded with me for release. I grabbed her panties and yanked them down so we were both completely naked. Then I reached under her knees and swept her off her feet. She threw her arms around me as I carried her to the bed. Forcefully, I dropped her down onto the bed.

"Spread your legs for me," I commanded, finally feeling utterly powerful and in control.

"Yes," she cried as she eagerly obeyed. She drew in a breath and held it, waiting for me to plunge into her.

"Tell me what you want," I growled. "Tell me what you need." I couldn't help myself. In my sexual fantasies, the movie star had begged and pleaded with me to give her what she needed.

"You, Roman. I need you. I need you inside me now. Please. I can't wait anymore. I *can't,*" Therese said, opening her legs wider. She was so convincing, it felt cruel to tease her anymore. I'd never seen a woman so horny and desperate, and I loved every second of it.

I forced myself to count to five, just so I could watch her squirm a little more, and then I rammed into her as hard as I could. Therese screamed and threw her head back.

"Yes, oh God, yes!" She dug her nails into my back and screamed my name several times. Maybe it was a little over-the-top, but I didn't care. It fed my male ego like nothing ever had, and it was hot as hell. I stared into her eyes as I pounded her as hard as I could.

"God, Therese you feel so good," I said, watching her carefully as I uttered her stage name.

She gazed up at me, lust in her eyes. She didn't miss a beat.

"Give it to me, Roman," she panted as I thrusted in and out of her. "Give it to me. Every ... fucking ... inch ..."

The pleasure was so intense, I knew I couldn't last. Though a lot of Tessa's desire was acting, not all of it was. She was soaking wet between her legs and her nipples were rock hard. Not even a terrific actress like her could fake that.

"Tessy," I whispered. "I gotta take care of you first. If we keep going like this, I'm never gonna make it."

"Okay," she whispered, not spoiling the fantasy by saying too much out of character.

I pulled out of her and slid down between her legs. I began stroking her clit with my tongue, and she put her hands on my head.

"Roman, oh God, Roman," she moaned. I could tell she was back to being Tessa, just by the way she spoke.

"Oh God, oh God," she cried. I stroked her until she stopped saying oh God, knowing she was done.

I crawled back up to face her and she smiled, a sleepy, satisfied look in her eyes.

It didn't last. Within seconds, she was back to playing Therese Andrews for me.

"Give it to me, Roman. *Hard*," she pleaded, and I plunged back inside her. She cried out as loudly as the first time I entered her, a slightly unsettling reminder that this was an act, but after a few seconds, I got lost in the fantasy again. "Yes, yes, yes," she cried, digging her nails into my back like she was holding on for dear life.

She tilted her head slightly to the left and opened her mouth, with her tongue touching the roof of her mouth.

She was doing the pose from the For Forever *poster. The one I'd spent most of my teen years whacking off to.*

I groaned as a renewed sensation of intense pleasure tingled its way through my rigid cock.

I started panting heavily, which I usually did when I was getting close to orgasm. She ramped up her performance, digging her stiletto-clad heels into my back.

"Oh Roman. Oh please, please, don't stop! Don't stop, don't stop," she cried out over and over again. "Oh God, baby, I'm gonna come. I'm gonna ... Don't stop, Roman, please don't stop ..." She cried out don't stop until she was practically screaming it. Her desperation was the most erotic sound I'd ever heard.

In what was surely no accident, Therese arched her back and timed her final scream of release to coincide with my orgasm. Grunting out loud, I came more forcefully than I'd ever thought possible.

Spent, I collapsed on top of her. I didn't want to crush her tiny frame, but I was so exhausted ... and satisfied ... that I could hardly move.

"Oh Roman," she purred. "You were *incredible.* I knew you could give me what I needed. I just knew it."

She panted heavily, and I wasn't sure if it was from exhaustion, sexual relief, or the fact that she had a two-hundred-pound man slumped on top of her. In case it was the latter, I rolled off her.

After taking a few seconds to catch my breath, I glanced over at her.

"Are you okay?" I asked.

This was the moment of truth.

Tessa had seemed pretty into it the whole time, but she was one hell of an actress. She might have hated every second of it, for all I knew.

"Yes," she said, and she certainly looked okay. Better than okay. Her pretty, blue eyes were shining with happiness.

Relief washed over me. *Thank God.* I would have never forgiven myself if she'd felt used or uncomfortable. No amount of pleasurable sex was worth that.

"I love you, Roman," she said, eyes still bright and happy.

"Wait ... is that Therese talking, or ..."

Tessa sat up in bed and put her hand over her heart, and said, "I, Tessa Carol Gumm, love you, Roman Pinza."

I stared at her. I'd just had the most amazing sex of my life, and now the woman I loved was telling me she loved me too? Who knew the day *Pirated* got cancelled would be the best day of my life?

"You … you do?"

"Yes, Roman. I love you. I love you so much. I should have told you long ago. I was just …"

"Scared," I finished for her.

She nodded, and she seemed relieved I understood her feelings.

"I knew how I felt before, but this …" Tessa said, glancing down at the bed where we'd just had wild sex. "Tonight confirmed it more than anything else."

"Really?" I asked, astonished.

"Yes," she said, tearing up a little. "This whole experience couldn't have been more different than the last time I tried it. This time, it felt like …" She paused for a moment, gathering her thoughts. "Even though we were pretending to be two perfect strangers hooking up, deep down it still felt like two people pleasuring each other because we love each other."

Tessa lay back down beside me and gazed into my eyes. She seemed calm and at peace.

I thought about what she'd said and realized how right she was. Her pretending to be Therese Andrews to fulfill my sexual fantasy was an incredible expression of her love for me.

"It's amazing to me I could do something like that," she said, her eyes filled with wonder, "and still feel so safe and so loved the whole time."

"I do love you, Tessy. So, so much. Thank you for doing this for me."

Tessa smiled and purred, "It was my pleasure. Believe me."

"Did you really come twice?" I asked.

She hesitated for a moment and then shook her head.

"But I did take care of you, right?"

"Yes," she said. "You made me come when you went down on me. And it was *wonderful*."

I thought for a moment.

"Have you ever faked it before?" I asked, suddenly concerned about how good of a performer she really was.

Tessa burst out laughing, which didn't exactly fill me with confidence.

Lying on her side and gazing fondly at me, she said, "I'm laughing because I knew you were gonna ask me that. Yes, I have faked it lots of times. But not with you."

I shot her a skeptical look.

"No, I mean it! Look, I told you before lots of guys I've been with were more concerned with screwing a celebrity than worrying about my needs."

I nodded sadly.

"Sex is an imperfect thing. You've always satisfied me, Roman. I've never had to fake it with you. But I'll make you a promise. If there's ever a time I, you know, don't get there for some reason, I won't pretend I did. Okay?"

"Yeah. Okay. I don't want you to ever be unsatisfied."

Tessa smiled at me.

"You really are one hell of an actress," I said.

I thought a bit more about the whole Tessa vs. Therese thing. I guess I was quiet for a while, because she asked me, "What are you thinking about?"

"I was thinking I understand why you want to keep Therese Andrews and Tessa Gumm separate, but I think you go too far with it sometimes."

"What do you mean?"

"You're so talented, Tessy. God, I love to hear you sing onstage. After all these months, it still gives me chills."

"Wow," she said softly.

"And it's like you act like Therese Andrews is this totally other person, but she's still you. The actress that lights up stage and screen, and who becomes every new character so completely. The lady who shines in TV interviews and was hilarious on *Saturday Night Live*. That's all you, baby. I mean, the Tessy part of your personality is my favorite. The one I love most. But Therese is awesome too. Not the fame and the money. That stuff doesn't matter. But the talent. That incredible talent of yours. And the way you treat your fans. And the way you have of talking to people and making them feel important and valued. That's so amazing. You have such a gift, sweetheart. I love that about you. So very much."

Tessa started to cry, and I wasn't exactly sure whether she was happy, or if I'd upset her. I wiped her tears and gave her time and space to talk when she was ready.

"Why is it that I'm enough for you but I was never enough for anyone else in my life?"

"Well, you know all that stuff I said about how cool it would be to have my friends and family and neighbors know I was dating Therese Andrews and make other men jealous?"

She nodded, still wiping tears.

"That's *all* some people want. And they don't fucking care who they hurt in the process. They're shallow assholes, baby. And that's a reflection of them, not you."

Tessa pulled me close, and I held her for a while.

"I love you so much, Roman," she said.

"I love you too, sweet Tessy."

"What are we gonna do when the show closes?"

"What do you mean?"

"I might have to go to L.A. to work on a movie, and your work is here. Or I might have to work somewhere else on location. Or—"

"I'll tell you what we're gonna do," I said, holding her

tighter. "We're gonna be together. One way or another, we're gonna be together. I'll fly to see you all the time, or you can come see me. It doesn't matter where our careers take us or what we're doing. We will be together. I mean, as long as that's what you want."

"Yes," Tessa said. "That's what I want more than anything in the world." After a moment, she asked, "Was sex with Therese Andrews everything you thought it would be?"

I smiled. "Everything and a lot more. I never dreamed it would actually happen, and never in my wildest fantasies did I think I would be in love with Therese Andrews if it ever did happen. But I am. I'm in love with Therese the movie star, and Tessy the sweet girl from Minnesota. I got the whole package right here."

Tessa let out a happy sigh, and we held each other.

"Tessy?" I said after a while.

"I know, I know. Go pick up the clothes."

I chuckled, and she gently smacked my bare ass as I got out of bed to tidy up.

CHAPTER 24

*T*he last few weeks had been a whirlwind of emotion, and today had been the most difficult day of all. I was a mess all day. Tonight's performance of *Pirated* was our last, but Roman had been my rock, as always. His calm and even temper was the perfect balance to my emotional and insecure nature, and I couldn't have gotten through it without him nearby.

The final show went well. All the hugs and kisses between the lovers onstage were charged with genuine emotion, and I could have sworn I saw Jacob tear up when he read love poems to Rosemary's character, knowing it was the last time. We were all a mess, but we leaned on each other.

We had a little surprise planned for the crew right after the show. I was glad we were doing it, but I knew our tribute would take even more emotional stamina than the show itself.

When we took our final bow after the performance, I thought I was an emotional wreck, but Rosemary was full out sobbing. She felt things so deeply, that girl. I loved her so much. I knew she had lots of other female friends in her life besides me, but she was really my only close woman friend.

I'd met her friends over the last few weeks for brides-maids fittings, and I'd even met secretly with them as we planned a surprise for her wedding day. I'd gotten to know Susie and Elyse better, and I met Rosemary's friend, Crista, whose husband worked with Elyse. I also got to know Rose-mary's good friend, Ryan, who'd come to New York from Washington D.C. for the wedding. They were all so wonder-ful, and they loved Rosemary as much as I did.

The six lead actors of *Pirated*—Rosemary, Jacob, Luke, Gilbert, Sarah, and I had wanted to express our love and gratitude to all of the unsung heroes of the production. The behind-the-scenes people like Roman, Rex, Audra, and everyone else who had helped us shine so brightly every night.

As we'd planned, I stepped to the front of the stage after we finished taking our final bow. Many of the audience members had started heading out, but most of them returned to their seats when they saw I had something to say.

"I want to thank you all for joining us here tonight for our final performance of *Pirated*." It was incredibly difficult to say those words out loud, but I gathered my strength and charged forward, determined to give the show and its crew a proper sendoff. "Show business is full of beginnings and endings, but you always carry the people you work with in your heart. Every night, we have hundreds of audience members come to see us put on a show. It is mainly us that you see," I said gesturing to the actors gathered onstage. "But there are so many people who contribute to the success of the show. People who might feel invisible sometimes, but we want to take a moment to thank them, and to tell them, we see you. I would like to invite all the crew members, understudies, and cleaning and maintenance staff of the theater to please join us onstage."

The audience began applauding as the stage quickly filled with all the incredible people who made this show as wonderful as it was.

When everyone was gathered onstage, and after the applause died down a bit, I said, "To all of you amazing men and woman who work so hard behind the scenes, this is for you."

Music began to play, and my eyes welled up with tears. I gazed at Roman, who stood a few feet away from me. He smiled, and I felt at peace. Calmed just by seeing him, I knew I could get through this.

Together, the cast of *Pirated* sang the song "For Good," from the show *Wicked* about friendship and parting ways, and how lives can be changed for the better for having known one another. We kept most of the lyrics intact, making only minor changes to fit our situation. The version we sang was purely a song of love, friendship, and gratitude.

I performed the first part, my emotions whirling inside, as I sang about people coming into our lives for a reason, about having been changed for the better, and having been changed for good. I looked at all the crew members as I sang, but my eyes lingered on Roman.

Luke sang the next verse, and then it was Rosemary's turn. We had given her a difficult, emotional verse, and I'd been worried she wouldn't be able to do it. She nailed it, though. I felt a searing ache in my heart when she sang the part about how we may never meet again in this lifetime. That was my greatest fear about the show ending—that Rosemary and Luke and I would grow apart once we didn't see each other every day anymore. They were so dear to me. They, along with Roman, had been more like family than my own blood family had ever been.

Rosemary's sweet, angelic voice soared when she sang the line about these special people remaining with her like a handprint on her heart. Her voice caught a little, but she made it through.

I saw Johnny, sitting in the front row, wiping a tear from his eye. Rosemary was hurting, and it was killing him. I was grateful she had such a good man to lean on. Soon, they would be joined together as husband and wife, and I couldn't have been happier for them.

Sarah, Gilbert, and Jacob took their turns singing, and then we all joined in to sing at the end. In perfect, practiced precision, the three male leads stepped to stage left and the three female leads went to the right. Together, we all gestured toward the cast and crew, telling them through song that we had been forever changed, for the better, because we knew them.

By the end, many of the crew members were crying, as were many members of the audience who had stayed behind to watch our tribute.

Roman locked eyes with me and put his hand over his heart to show he was touched by our gesture.

Truer words had never been sung before.

I had, unquestionably, been changed for good.

CHAPTER 25

*I*t took two bridesmaids to get Rosemary and her wedding dress into the stretch limousine. Elyse and I giggled madly as we practically had to shove her inside the car with her long wedding train. It was clear Johnny had spared no expense when it came to her stunning lacy dress with a sweetheart neckline. Thank goodness the limo was big enough to fit all four of her bridesmaids plus her huge dress. The Mercedes Sprinter looked like a private jet inside. I was no stranger to traveling by limo, but even I'd never seen a car this big.

Rosemary collapsed with a giggle into one of the large captain's chairs. "Thank God I'll be able to ditch the train and a few layers of this gown at the reception. I'll barely be able to make it down the aisle in this thing."

"You look so beautiful, Rosemary," I said. She was absolutely breathtaking in her Sarah Burton wedding gown, but it was more than just the dress that made her so lovely. Rosemary was positively glowing with happiness. The closing of the show had been hard on all of us, but her wedding would give many of us in the cast and crew a chance to reunite, to celebrate a happy occasion.

"This limo is incredible," Susie said, her pretty, blue eyes dancing with joy. She was one of Rosemary's dearest friends and her boyfriend, David, was Johnny's best friend. Once I'd gotten a good look at that guy, I understood why it didn't bother Elyse that Susie and Luke were so close. David was a stunningly handsome man who could rock a suit like nobody I'd ever seen. He was a fashion designer with his own line of men's luxury clothing.

"It really is," Crista said, gazing at the huge car in wonder. Crista was a lovely Hispanic woman with the prettiest, smoothest skin I'd ever seen. She was studying theater at NYU, and I could tell she considered Rosemary a mentor to her when it came to theater.

"Tell Tessa about the transportation you had at your wedding," Rosemary said.

"Oh my gosh," Crista said, putting her hand over her heart. She had gotten married just a few weeks ago. "It's funny. Keith and I got engaged long after Johnny and Rosemary did, but we got married soon after he proposed. All I really wanted was a low-key ceremony and reception, you know? Family and a few close friends. Nothing too crazy."

I nodded, enjoying watching Crista's face light up when she talked about her wedding. Both Rosemary and Elyse had spoken highly of her new husband, Keith.

"Most of the wedding was like that, but Keith arranged to have this super fancy horse and carriage pick me up and take me to the church," Crista said with a happy laugh. "And then it took us both to the wedding reception after the ceremony. It was so thoughtful of him. I had recently played Cinderella in the musical at The Creel Foundation, and *Cinderella* has always been my favorite musical."

"Oh, that is so sweet," I said with a smile. I glanced over at Rosemary. "You nervous?"

"A little," she said.

"Not too late to back out, you know," Elyse said dryly.

"No, no," Rosemary said with a laugh. "I'm not nervous about marrying Johnny. It's just that it's gonna be such a circus."

"Well, you are marrying a clown," Elyse joked.

"You guys work things out as far as the media goes?" I asked.

"Yeah. Yeah, we did, and I feel pretty good about it," Rosemary said. "I think it's gonna be okay. Like you suggested, I said it was okay for the media to record us stepping out of the limo and walking up to the church, but absolutely no cameras or reporters inside."

"And Johnny's cool with that?"

"Oh yeah. He actually thought it was a great idea. We talked it out, and I told him I was kinda worried he might get caught up in the media frenzy and forget all about me. I give him a lot of credit. He was self-aware enough to realize that really could happen, and I was right to be a little worried. He suggested that, throughout the day, we take a few minutes to be alone. You know, step away from the madness and just be together. Your wedding day goes by so fast, you wanna take time to really experience it, you know?"

"It does go by fast. You wouldn't believe it," Crista said.

"Yeah, so right after we get married and before we get pictures taken at the altar and stuff, we're just gonna step into a room and just, you know, be together for a moment. As husband and wife."

Rosemary dabbed at her wet eyes with a tissue, and we all laughed.

"I just hope you can get through your vows without sobbing," I said.

"Oh, I know. And then we kind of compromised on the rest of the day as far as the media goes. Like, I'm okay with them taping our first dance, but I told Johnny I wanted the cameras off during the best man's toast." Rosemary looked over at Susie. "I want David to be able to speak from the heart and not feel the pressure of having cameras on him. I mean, not all of us are performers, and it's not fair to put people on the spot like that."

"True," I said. "But then again, most of the people attending today would probably love to be in the news. See and be seen, that's what people want at a major social event like this."

"Don't I know it," Rosemary said with a slightly weary smile. She'd more or less gotten used to the fame of being with Johnny, but I knew it could be tiring at times. She was the type of genuine performer I loved working with. The kind who was passionate about being onstage, but not necessarily concerned about being a star. I was more famous than Johnny, by a wide margin. I'd been concerned my presence at the wedding would be a distraction, and that the cameras would be more focused on me than the bride. I'd discussed my concerns with Rosemary, and I'd even told her I would bow out of serving as a bridesmaid, but she would have none of it. She assured me she didn't care one bit about my stealing her thunder. Instead, she kind of welcomed it. Rosemary told me all she really wanted was to wear a pretty dress and feel beautiful and marry the love of her life. She wasn't interested in being the center of attention every second of the day, even though she was the bride. Besides, she told me my presence would raise the profile of the wedding considerably, and Johnny loved that.

The truth was, the cameras would show up because it was Johnny Creel's wedding. They would stay because of me.

Rosemary squealed when the limo arrived at the church.

"Oh, I can't wait to see Johnny at the altar. Ugh, I can't help but wish we could skip right to that part. Okay, girls. The cameras are waiting out there." For the first time, I saw genuine fear in her eyes. I understood. It could be really scary to feel like the whole world was watching. "It's not gonna be easy to get out of this limo gracefully. Please, please make sure I don't fall flat on my face out there."

"We got this, honey," Elyse said firmly. "Don't you worry, okay?"

I could tell she was concerned for her friend, as were Susie and Crista. All four of us were determined not to let her down.

"Want me to get out first?" I offered.

"Yes," Rosemary said, eyes shining with relief. Having Therese Andrews step out of the car first would take a lot of pressure off her.

"You got it. I'll get out, come around, and then we'll all help you out."

She nodded.

I got out of the limo and, of course, the cameras were on. People shouted questions, but I ignored them. Susie got out, too, and walked around to Rosemary's door. Susie and I carefully pulled Rosemary out, and I think Elyse and Crista gave her a good push from inside the car.

Rosemary wobbled a little but straightened up in no time. Susie and I grabbed the train, and Crista and Elyse held the bride's hands. Slowly, carefully, and gracefully, we helped Rosemary get up the church steps and safely inside.

The church was beautiful with flowers absolutely every-where, bursting from every pew and cascading down the altar. I had the feeling it was a bit of overkill for Rosemary, but there was no stopping the Creels when it came to showing off their wealth. Rosemary was entirely focused on Johnny, and she was determined not to let anything bother

her on her wedding day. She said as long as she was married to her best friend by the end of the day, everything would be perfect, as far as she was concerned.

As the maid of honor, Susie walked down the aisle first, then Elyse, Crista, and then me.

I managed to catch Roman's eye as I walked down past him. He looked me up and down, admiring my dark green, off-the-shoulder floor-length bridesmaid gown. He mouthed "Wow." And oh, how dashing he looked in his tuxedo. I wished with all my heart I could have him on my arm all night. How proud I would be. I hoped with all my heart he knew that my hiding him had nothing to do with him, and everything to do with my own petty insecurities.

Rosemary's parents both walked her down the aisle. They seemed a tad overwhelmed by the grandeur of the wedding, no doubt quite unaccustomed to such wealth. I could see the joy in their eyes, though. Her father teared up as he gave his only daughter away, which naturally made Rosemary cry, too. The ceremony was beautiful, and Rosemary held it together pretty well for the most part. She choked up a bit during the vows, and Johnny tenderly wiped her tears. It was sweet and lovely. The officiant pronounced them husband and wife, and the two shared their first kiss as a married couple.

But Rosemary didn't know that Johnny had a special surprise planned for her. Rosemary glanced toward the church organ, waiting for the organist to play the processional music so they could walk back down the aisle. The music started, but it wasn't the song she expected. The music for "Come What May" from *Moulin Rouge* began to play.

Rosemary turned her head to look questioningly at Johnny. He smiled warmly at her and took both of her hands in his. And he began to sing.

We'd all heard Johnny sing in the two videos that had

gone viral, but this was the first time we'd heard him sing an entire song. I'd forgotten how beautiful his voice was. The lyrics were so lovely and perfect for a wedding day. The song was all about powerful love that would last forever, come what may. Johnny's deep, rich voice soared through the church as everyone listened raptly to every touching word.

Rosemary was positively overcome as she held Johnny's hands and listened to him serenade her.

I drew in a deep breath, hoping with all my heart that the final part of the song would go off without a hitch. On the last verse of the song, the entire congregation stood and sang backup for Johnny.

Rosemary gasped as she looked out at the hundreds of people who were now on their feet singing the words "Come what may," in perfect unison. She dropped Johnny's hands so she could cover her mouth in shock. I'd never seen her so overwhelmed with emotion, and that was really saying something when it came to Rosemary.

Johnny had pulled it off *perfectly*. It hadn't been easy to keep this a secret with hundreds of people in it. He'd sent out a special request to every single person invited to the wedding, asking them to listen to the recording of the song and be prepared to sing the final verse as a tribute to his new bride. And by God, his surprise had worked wonderfully.

Everything went completely silent when the song ended. The only sound was Rosemary's soft sob as she wrapped her arms around Johnny. They held each other close, and it was the most beautiful moment of pure love I'd ever witnessed.

When she eventually let go of him, she managed to whisper to Johnny, "Thank you."

Then, she turned to the congregation and said, only slightly louder as she was still choked up, "Thank you all so much."

After taking a moment to catch her breath, she said in a

louder voice, "Let's hear it for Johnny!" She began to clap, and we all joined in with loud applause and whistles.

Once it died down, I heard Rosemary say quietly to Johnny, "You could have done this at the reception when the cameras were around."

Johnny smiled tenderly at her and said, "No way. This wasn't for the cameras. This was only for you. In fact, I made it clear I didn't want anyone recording this on their cell phones or anything like that. I didn't want you remembering the way it looked on video. I just want you to remember how it made you feel."

Tears dripped from her eyes, and she said, "I'll never, ever forget the way this made me feel, Johnny."

Rosemary's new husband tenderly wiped her eyes and then took her hand in his. The processional music began, and they walked back down the aisle hand in hand.

* * *

AT THE RECEPTION, Johnny and Rosemary had their own table. That had been another one of my suggestions. Have them sit alone so they could at least talk privately during dinner. The cameras were there in the reception room but turned off at the moment. Even Johnny agreed it would be rude to record people eating.

I was the only single woman at a table with Elyse and Luke, Crista and Keith, and Susie and David. Although I was all right with that, it really bothered me that Roman had to go stag to the wedding, and it was my fault. He sat with Rex and Audra and their husbands, as well as some other members of the *Pirated* crew and their significant others. I guess even if the cameras weren't here tonight, I still couldn't have danced with Roman. It would have been too risky. But with the media here it was utterly impossible.

And that was the other big issue with this wedding. The cameras would watch every move I made, which meant I couldn't go near Roman or any other man for that matter, for the entire day. I told Roman the only man I could safely dance with today would be Johnny. As a bridesmaid, dancing with the groom in full view of his new wife wouldn't arouse any suspicion. However, if I danced with any other man, the media would go into a frenzy. The gossip rags would report that the guy was my new boyfriend, and then I'd be on the baby bump watch. There was no escaping that craziness.

I knew Roman was hurt that he wouldn't be my date at the Creel wedding, but we talked about it at length, and we agreed it would be too much, too soon. I wanted to wait until after the wedding, and then I suggested we take it slow. Start going out on dates in public. Holding hands, that sort of thing. And then I could make an official statement through my publicist or something. Though we didn't set a specific timetable, I assured him it would be soon.

It would be nice to finally make our relationship public. Right now, I was utterly miserable without Roman by my side.

Though we'd discussed and agreed to remain apart for the day, I knew he was hurt. And I hated that I was the one who was hurting him.

The cameras were fired up after dinner as Johnny and Rosemary prepared for their first dance. I sighed happily as I watched Johnny sweep Rosemary across the floor. Her dress was lighter now, but it was still a gorgeous gown. She wore a delicate veil that cascaded down the back of her deeply rich and lovely red hair. I'd never seen her look so beautiful.

For the second dance, the bridal party was asked to join in. The other three bridesmaids danced with their significant others who were also in the wedding. I danced with Ryan. I felt guilty about dancing with another man while I left Roman on the sidelines, but I couldn't ignore Rosemary's wishes that the bridal party participate in this dance. Though the media would try their best to make a case that Ryan and I were an item, they would quickly find out that not only was Ryan married, he was gay. It was safe to dance with him.

Rosemary rested her head on Johnny's shoulder as they danced. Susie and David gazed into each other's eyes as they slow danced together. Luke and Elyse laughed as they held each other. I'd never seen a couple laugh and have more fun than those two. I saw Keith tenderly kiss his new wife. Ryan glanced over at his husband, who was smiling as he watched us dance. Then Ryan looked at me and smiled.

"Don't look now, but that hot guy at table four is checking you out," Ryan said with a sly grin. He knew Roman and I were an item.

I glanced over at Roman, who gave me a sweet but sad smile. My heart squeezed in my chest.

"I know it sucks to have to hide," Ryan said kindly. "I've been there."

Though Jack and Ryan were openly, happily married, I guess there had been a time when Ryan had had to hide who he was.

"Yeah. It's hard," I said. "It's nice dancing with you, though."

"Thanks. You too," he said.

After the dance ended, Rosemary gave the signal to turn off the cameras. David approached the microphone to give his speech, and Rosemary and Johnny returned to their table.

"Wait, wait, wait!" Johnny said suddenly. Everyone turned to look at him. He got up, grabbed a tissue box, and put it on the table in front of Rosemary. "I know my wife."

Laughter and several *awwww*s came up from the crowd. It was the first time Johnny had called Rosemary his wife in public. And he wasn't wrong—she would definitely cry during the speech.

David scanned the room for a moment looking calm and cool, not to mention incredibly handsome in his tux. "There was a time," he began, "not so very long ago when Johnny was rich and carefree, and women everywhere wanted him."

There was a bit of a gasp at that. After all, it wasn't a great idea to talk about other women at a man's wedding.

"Known as *The* Johnny Creel, Johnny was known for throwing cash around and making friends everywhere he went. Then, one day, all that changed. As we all know, there was a brief period where all the assets of the Creel fortune were frozen. And, as we all know, Walter Creel was completely exonerated from any wrongdoing." David gestured respectfully at Walter Creel, the rich and famous attorney who had bankrolled the entire posh wedding. "But the point is, at the time, the Creel fortune was gone. Nobody knew what would happen, nor if the Creels would ever be rich again."

People listened intently, wondering exactly where David was going with this.

"That was a tough period in Johnny's life. He found out who his friends were," David said, then paused for a moment. "There weren't many people left when he was broke. During that time, when everybody else walked out of Johnny's life, Rosemary walked back in."

Johnny smiled and put his arm around Rosemary.

"When Johnny was down and out, Rosemary reached out and lifted him up. Because that's what she does. She's a loving, giving woman who's loyal to the end and is never willing to let anyone suffer alone."

There were murmurs of agreement, and Rosemary put her hand over her heart.

"And during this time, she got to know the real Johnny.

The good guy, with a good heart, who found out what he was made of when he no longer had the family fortune to lean on. And it was during this time that Johnny and Rosemary fell in love. Because they knew they didn't need money. All they needed was each other."

Rosemary reached for a tissue from the box Johnny had given her and dabbed her eyes. Gentle laughter came up from the crowd.

"As you all know, we have an incredible pool of talented people in this room, who recently put on one hell of a show called *Pirated*." David paused to allow people to applaud loudly. It was nice, and it made Rosemary smile. "And even though the show was amazing, it didn't last as long as we'd all hoped. And that was hard. Rosemary is a terrific and passionate performer, and it caused a lot of sorrow and heartache for her when the show closed. But that's the thing about heartache. It is always lessened when it is shared. Those of us who know Johnny and Rosemary best have seen Johnny share in Rosemary's heartache over the last few weeks. Just as Rosemary had done for him, he reached down and lifted her up. He encouraged her, cheered her. Made her laugh and dried her tears."

Rosemary laughed as she continued wiping her eyes.

"Because that, ladies and gentleman," David said gesturing at Johnny and Rosemary, "is what true love looks like. True love triumphs through the darkness. We often joke about celebrity marriages and how long they last, but I think everyone fortunate enough to be gathered here today knows we have undoubtedly witnessed something special. The joining of two people who truly will love each other through richer, through poorer, through sickness and in health, good times and bad, for as long as they both shall live."

A choked sob escaped from Rosemary and Johnny held her close.

Lifting a glass, David said, "To Johnny and Rosemary."

We all lifted a glass and toasted the new Mr. And Mrs. Creel.

Wiping my own eyes, I watched as Rosemary rushed to David to hug him and thank for him for his moving speech. Johnny tenderly placed his hand on Rosemary's back as they spoke to their dear friend.

A whirl of emotions and visions of the evening suddenly assaulted my senses. All night I'd watched happy couples like Susie and David, Elyse and Luke, Keith and Crista, and Ryan and Jack. Dancing together and sharing their love openly. I thought about David's beautiful tribute to the way Johnny and Rosemary loved and supported each other. I thought about how Roman had shared the heartache of losing the show with me. How he, too, had dried my tears and made me laugh.

Right then I knew with absolute certainty that Roman and I had the kind of forever love David had just described.

So, what in the hell was I doing sitting here all by myself? How could I abandon my forever love, Roman, and let him sit alone?

I loved Roman Pinza with all of my heart. I knew that.

And the time had come for the rest of the world to know it, too.

CHAPTER 26

"*R*oman, Roman, Roman!" I heard Tessa's booming voice behind me. She was using her stage voice, which meant she was deliberately trying to command attention.

I turned around in my seat and she smiled down at me. I briefly wondered if she was drunk, but the only time I'd seen her drink all night was during the toast just now. And I had been watching her all night as Les, Mitchell, and most of the others at my table had gleefully pointed out.

Tessa smiled at me and asked, "May I have this dance?"

I glanced nervously toward the cameras lining the reception wall.

"Are you sure?" I asked her.

"Yes, I'm sure," Tessa said, gazing down at me with tender affection. Still using her stage voice, she said, "True love does not hide. True love is not ashamed." My eyes grew wide as I listened to her boldly quote her climactic speech from *Pirated*. "It announces itself, loudly and boldly. Love is to be celebrated and shared, not hidden."

Everyone around us had gone quiet. None of us, least of all me, could believe what we were hearing.

Tessa extended her hand to me and said, "I love you, Roman. And I want the whole world to know."

I stared at her, looking unbelievably glamorous in her bridesmaid gown. This woman, this incredible woman who the entire world adored, from the people who dreamed of her from afar, to the people who were privileged enough to know her personally, loved *me*. Sometimes I still couldn't believe it was true, and now she was telling the world about her feelings for me. Almost every head in the place had turned to see Tessa. People had been gawking at her all night.

Tessa suddenly looked uncomfortable, embarrassed even. At first, I thought she'd already regretted her actions. It finally dawned on me that, in my shock, I'd literally left her hanging. Her hand was still extended to me while I sat there like a dope.

"Y—yes! Yes, Tessy, of course I'll dance with you." I grabbed her hand and pulled a giggling Tessa to the dance floor.

Knowing all eyes were on us, I spun her around dramatically on the dance floor before pulling her close. Her smile was so beautiful, and I'd never seen her look so happy. You'd have thought it was her wedding day. It was kind of like a wedding for us in a way. Like Rosemary and Johnny, we were professing our love for each other publicly.

Continuing the scene from *Pirated* Tessa had started, I whispered in her ear, "I love her, I love her, I love her."

She rested her head on my chest as we danced. Then she lifted her head and gazed at me expectantly, and I knew that was my cue to kiss her. This would be the moment—the one that left absolutely no doubt that she and I were a couple. I happily obliged and dipped my head to kiss her, loving the *ooh*s and *ahh*s I heard from all around us. I was kissing my sweet Tessy-girl, but to the rest of the world, it looked like I was making out with Therese Andrews.

And I was okay with that.

In the end, how we felt about each other was all that really mattered, but it still felt so good to be acknowledged. Finally, all the cast and crew of *Pirated* would know I wasn't crazy and pathetic, and my love wasn't unrequited after all.

I was going to ask Tessa, why now? Why the sudden change of heart? But I realized I already knew. Tessa was right. Love should be celebrated. After all, that was why we were all gathered here today.

"Dip me," she said.

"What?"

"Dip me and kiss me."

"Yes, ma'am." I dipped her down low and planted a big kiss on her. Louder *oohs* and *ahhs* this time. Oh, yeah. Tessa was going all-in on this.

She grinned mischievously when I pulled her back up. "*That* was for Heather Applegate."

"Nice!" I said, feeling a renewed sense of euphoria.

The moment the song ended, the reporters headed right toward us.

"Don't worry," Tessa said. "I'll handle this. Unless you want to say something?"

I shook my head vehemently. "No way. I wouldn't know what to say. I'll mess it all up and say something stupid."

"It's okay. I got this."

The reporters all started talking at once, and Tessa held up her hand to silence them. Then she pointed to one of them.

"Therese, do you want to introduce us to your friend?" the guy asked.

"Yes, I do," Tessa responded, sounding poised and confident. "This," she said, gesturing proudly at me, "is Roman Pinza. And he's the love of my life."

The reporter's eyes grew wide. I doubted he expected to get such a great scoop tonight.

"We met on the set of *Pirated*, and we've been inseparable ever since. He's the head electrician at the Al Hirschfeld Theater, and he keeps me grounded," she said with a wink.

The reporters talked all at once and, once again, Tessa silenced them with her hand. "And that's all I'm gonna say right now. Tonight is all about Johnny and Rosemary."

When they kept talking, Tessa firmly pointed in the direction of the newlyweds, making it clear she meant business. She would say no more tonight.

I grinned at her after the reporters finally gave up.

"Grounded, huh? You've been waiting to use that one for a while now, haven't you?"

She giggled and said, "Yeah, I have."

I glanced back over at the table where I'd been sitting all night. It cracked me up to see the stunned expressions on the faces of my fellow crew members. Audra and Rex looked happy for me, and the rest of the guys looked shocked and as jealous as hell.

Cool.

Tessa followed my gaze and smiled warmly at me. I knew how bad she felt about hiding me, and I could tell she was happy and relieved we no longer had to keep our love a secret from anyone.

"Thank you, baby. Thank you for doing this. It means a lot to me."

"You mean a lot to me, my love," she told me. "Thank you for being patient with me."

"You're more than worth the wait, Tessy. And I've been waiting most of my life to be with you."

She smiled happily and kissed me.

Elyse, Susie, and Crista started walking over to us.

"I'll be right back. As you know, there's a little something I gotta do."

"I know you do. Break a leg, baby."

* * *

I WALKED to the center of the dance floor and loudly asked for everyone's attention. It was mostly unnecessary, since people had been watching my every move all night.

Rosemary squealed excitedly when she saw her friends forming a line on the dance floor. We knew the fact that we'd prepared a song for her wedding wouldn't be a huge surprise for her. After all, her friends had prepared a song for her to help when Johnny had proposed to her. Elyse, Susie, and Luke had all taken part in that one. That was before Rosemary had met Crista and Keith, but both would join us today.

I saw Johnny nudge Rosemary and then gesture questioningly toward the cameras. Rosemary smiled and nodded her consent to let the cameras roll during our performance. Our little song was bound to be another viral hit, but I was glad Johnny had checked with Rosemary first about involving the media.

"We've prepared a special song as a tribute to the happy couple," I announced, and people began applauding.

I heard David draw in a shaky breath.

"You're gonna be fine, baby," Susie reassured him.

This would be easy and fun for Susie, Crista, Luke, Ryan, and I because we were all performers. Elyse might not be a professional singer, but she was pretty fearless. However, this was pretty far out of the comfort zone for Keith, and especially for David, but they'd agreed to be involved because of their friendship with Johnny and Rosemary. We assured them that we, as professional singers, would carry them.

The music from "Do You Hear the People Sing" from *Les Miserables* began, and we all began to sing lyrics written by Luke especially for the occasion.

"Do you hear your friends all sing? Sing at the Wedding of the Creels ..." we sang in unison. Then the men took a step forward, singing, "Here we're all decked out in our tuxes."

Next, the women stepped forward. "And we girls are in our heels."

With that, Elyse, Susie, Crista, and I kicked our legs out, showing off our fancy high-heeled shoes.

Rosemary clapped her hands and laughed heartily. I could feel the goodwill of the crowd as they laughed generously. They were with us, genuinely enjoying our special tribute.

"What can we all say?" both the men and women sang together. "This is the day you've waited for. Your life together is 'bout to start on this sweet day."

Johnny and Rosemary swayed together to the music as they listened raptly to our song. Roman smiled proudly as he watched us, and I felt a surge of renewed joy when I caught his eye.

"We gladly join you on this day, proud to stand with our dear friends," we sang on. "We all love you both, it is your joy we love to see. For richer or poorer but hopefully richer you'll be!"

That line got the huge, healthy laugh we'd hoped for. We had to sing the next part much louder in order to be heard.

"Do you hear your friends all sing? Sing at the wedding of the Creels. Johnny, Rosemary we all love you, and we loved the free wine and beer!"

More healthy laughter. It was so contagious that even we performers had to hold it together for the last part.

"We wish you a happy wedding day, and many more

happy days to come. We love the two of you as much as a pirate loves rum!"

We got a huge standing ovation when we finished, full of laughter and love and applause. Rosemary and Johnny looked so happy, and it felt so good to share in their joy.

Holding hands with my current cast members and dear friends, I gazed over at Johnny and Rosemary, and finally at Roman, who looked as filled with joy and happiness as I was.

I had truly found the place where I belonged. It didn't matter where in the world I traveled, my home would always be with Roman and my real, true friends.

For the first time I felt like enough.

More than enough.

Still holding hands with my fellow performers, we took one final bow.

THE CURTAIN FALLS

BELOVED READER,

I want to let you know that if you sign up for my email list, you will receive a FREE steamy sports novella that is EXCLUSIVE to my email list subscribers! It's the prequel to the baseball romance series, The Boys of Baltimore.

HEARTFELT THANKS to you for coming with me on this five-book journey. As a huge fan of musicals, I had a wonderful time writing The Wall Street to Broadway Series. For those of you who are also theater fans – perhaps you picked up on the large number of theater references included in the books – everything from names of people and locations, songs, and of course the shows themselves. *Pirated* isn't a real musical, but I wrote about a funny, romantic musical that I would want to see! Though I'm not a theater performer myself, I included a lot of my own emotional experiences in these books. Those moments of triumphant joy to those days filled with despair and rejection when you wonder if you'll ever be good enough. Those experiences are common to artists of all kinds.

IT'S ALWAYS hard to say goodbye to characters in a book series, but thanks to you guys, Rosemary, Johnny, and all of the rest of them will still live on.

THANK YOU, thank you, thank you for reading.

WAIT! BEFORE YOU GO!

Don't forget to join the email list if you want a FREE, steamy sports romance novella!

Sign up today, and I will send you a **FREE** novella entitled Starting From Zero. The novella is available <u>exclusively</u> to Author Linda Fausnet email list subscribers, and it is the prequel to my steamy sports romance series, The Boys of Baltimore Series.

Join the email list so you will always know when I've got a new book out.

I promise not to cram your inbox with too many emails – pinky swear!

You can also keep in touch by:

Following me on Amazon
Following me on Bookbub
Following me on Instagram
Joining my Author Reader's Group on Facebook.

Why Leave a Book Review? I'll give you 3 good reasons.

You can do it in <u>less than a minute</u>! Just choose a star rating from 1 to 5 stars and add a sentence or two on how you felt about the book.

1. Most readers choose the books they read based on the reviews, but <u>only a few readers</u> are kind enough to leave a review.
2. Most readers are not aware of this, but authors live and die by reviews. We really do.
3. It only takes a minute to leave a review, but the impact lasts for the lifetime of the book.

Thank you so very much.

ATTENTION ROMANCE NOVEL FANS!

I hope you'll join my romance novel fan club, Romance Novel Addicts Anonymous, on Facebook, Instagram, Twitter, and Pinterest. Join the email list, and you'll receive WHAT'S YOUR PLEASURE? RNAA'S OFFICIAL GUIDE TO FINDING YOUR NEXT GREAT ROMANCE READ.

www.ingramcontent.com/pod-product-compliance
Lightning Source LLC
Chambersburg PA
CBHW050717180626
46814CB00002B/487